DANCE LEGACY SERIES

The Legend

of

L'Esprit

— A NOVEL —

DORIS GREENBERG and PANDRÉ SHANDLEY

www.ten16press.com - Waukesha, WI

Dedications

For Ray, my husband, with whom every day is an adventure.
Thank you from the bottom of my heart
for believing in my dream.
For Jon, Christopher, Shannon, Marcie,
A.J., Lauren, Caroline, Jack, and Emily.
Because of you I am blessed beyond measure.
You are my heaven on earth.

DAG

For my ever-supportive husband, Michael,
your love and laughter
saves me ~ with you my soul dances free.
To my greatest blessings from above, Ryan and Kahlin,
You are the light in my world, my reason for being.

PAS

A heavenly star
sparkles
because a
dancer's spirit
performs
in front of it
for all the world
to see . . .

Porté (pawr-TAY) Carried. This ballet movement travels a dancer's step in the air from one spot to another.

Chapter One

Riverfield, Wisconsin

*B*uried beneath the covers, *I* shiver when a floorboard creaks in the dark. The whistling wind howls, and branches like an evil witch's long, black fingernails scratch at the window. Barney's deep rumbling growl churns my stomach, and I struggle to keep my wild imagination in check. When I dare to peek, only innocent moonlight dances across my bedroom wall, casting the eerie, black shadows that harmlessly stalk us. I squint as they slowly morph into menacing shapes. Maybe Barney watches them, too. Stroking his thick furry coat—more for my reassurance than his—I wonder why after fifteen years of mostly sweet dreams, these awful visions suddenly invade my sleep.

Dad's endless snore drones from the end of the hallway while I review choreography in my mind; a trick that's always worked before on the occasional restless night. The neon green glow of my digital clock taunts 3:33 a.m. Tossing and turning with each passing minute, I wrestle with my bed-hogging dog. Eventually, I give in to the heaviness of my eyelids, strangely

1

lulled by the scent of lilacs that gently wafts into my room. Like a dancer's porté, my dream carries me to the one place I am most desperate to avoid.

...I drift into a brightly lit room where an unfamiliar teenage girl dances weightlessly with a hazy feminine figure. Mesmerized by the duet, I long to join them, but unseen and uninvited, I cannot. The girl reflects joyously in a sparkling mirror that flows like a silvery waterfall, yet her partner's image remains wispy and blurred. A piano's lingering melody accompanies the pair as they perform an unearthly pas de deux. When the ghostly ballerina releases her grasp of the young dancer, it turns to notice me. With an outstretched arm and a slow roll of her skeletal fingers, she beckons.

Trembling, I step forward. Her face instantly distorts and solidifies into rock. In one gravity-defying leap, the apparition performs the perfect, seamless grand jeté and disappears. The abandoned girl moves to follow but instead sinks into the darkness of a bottomless pit, her bloodcurdling screams echo cruelly in my head. In the grayness of fog, my world spins. I see the young dancer again. This time, she lies deathly ill on a sterile hospital bed surrounded by grieving mourners; the painful scene is crushingly sad.

I want to cry with the onlookers, but the encircling haze pulls me against my will along a peculiar corridor of an old turn of the century building. A chandelier dancing with the soft glow of a thousand crystals briefly illuminates a magnificent foyer. Through the dreary mist, a winding staircase and trickling fountain fade in and out of view.

Two ornately framed portraits of women glide mysteriously in the ominous cloud. In one, the face at first beautiful and serene, horrifically melts like dripping wax before it erupts into a searing ball of flames. In the other, a woman stands rigidly.

Her eyes reflect an underlying wickedness as she reaches beyond the canvas for a heart-shaped locket that hypnotically floats towards me. She snatches the necklace and clutches it to her chest, scowling as though I were a thief in the night. Within seconds, her face ages grotesquely like a decaying corpse. I cringe at the morbid scene and breathe in sharply. Out of thin air, the dancing ghost reappears. She resembles a weathered statue with cold marbled eyes that lack comfort. If only I could wake up right now, but I've been here before and know the worst is yet to come.

A screeching iron gate imprisons me, and I beg for this ride to end. From above and below, scalding flames attack. A disturbing voice whispers, "Li . . . bee." I kick and claw, frantic to escape. Without warning, I drop in a sickening *Tower of Terror* plunge. The disembodied voice whose very breath now brushes the back of my neck again whispers my name. From beyond the shadows, the chilling voice declares, "She deserves to die."

Ballon (ba-LAWN) Bounce. A light, elastic jump in which the dancer bounds upward, pauses momentarily in the air, then descends before rebounding like the smooth bounce of a ball.

Chapter Two

*M**y flailing arms bat away** the unknown hands that grab and shake me.

"Libby, Libby! Wake up! You're having another nightmare."

Dad rips the bedcovers from my head. My eyes fly open, darting wildly until they land on my mother's concerned face. She presses me tightly against her. "Will, her heart is racing. She's drenched in sweat again." When dad opens my window, I suck in the cool air in huge gulps, thankful to be alive. *Can a person die of fright? God, I hope not.*

"Honey, it's over now, you're okay!" Mom says while looking directly into my eyes. Barney slathers me with warm golden retriever kisses, and Dad's promises steady the pounding in my chest. Their faces crumble when I describe the dream in vivid detail. I deliberately leave out the part about someone deserving to die. Some things are just too upsetting to share, especially with my overprotective parents.

After they hug me a dozen times more, Mom fully opens the bedroom blinds. Morning light floods my nearly empty room but does not dispel the weight of the dream. I worry that the nightmare's emotional residue will stay with me for hours if not days.

"Libby, I'm sorry," Dad says. "I know you're having problems sleeping. This move to Chicago has seriously rattled you. The *Tribune's* offer to syndicate my column came out of the blue. We realize it's tough. None of us have had time to adjust, but we will."

"I hate this, Dad! I feel like my whole world is being turned upside down. I don't want to move right now! I know you can't pass up this chance, but every night my dreams get worse. Nothing makes sense anymore. Why does this keep happening?"

"Change is always difficult, but everything's gonna be okay," Mom soothes. "You'll see. These nightmares will stop soon. Won't they, Will?"

"Your mom's right, Libz. Give it time."

"I'm trying. I promise I am! I just never thought I'd have to leave Riverfield until I was older, much older! I told you before that I'm not ready!" My nerves a jangled mess, I bury my face in my pillow and cry.

"A big change like this is never easy," my mom says, "but we can either focus on the ending as impossibly sad and scary like your dream, or we can look forward to the excitement of a new beginning."

She might mean well, but I wish she'd stop lecturing me as she wipes the long, dark tousled hair from my tear-filled eyes. "We understand; this is the only home you've ever known."

"Really? I don't think you guys understand anything! Haven't you been listening? I'm *not* going!"

"Calm down, Libby! We've had this argument too many times before, and we can't turn back now," Dad says.

I want to tell them to leave without me, but deep down, I

know he's right. Our house is already sold, and there's nothing I can do about it.

"It's always hard to say goodbye to the people and places we love. Your friends won't forget you." Mom hugs me close, and I sense she's struggling, too. I want to stay mad at her, but I know I can't.

"Your mother and I brought you here when you were a tiny newborn. We have so many happy memories. Right, Kate?"

"Yeah, like the day we brought this fella home," Mom says, rubbing Barney's ears.

Dad kneels next to my bed. "Don't you remember? He was such an adorable puppy. Mom and I thought you'd wind up killing him when you refused to let us take him from your arms. You carried him everywhere for weeks, and we swear he was bigger than you."

"And honey, remember the dance parties and talent shows you and your friends held in the backyard for the neighbors and Grandma and Grandpa? Those are the things our family will always hold dear, no matter where we live."

Like the wave of a magic wand, Dad reaches for my favorite dance book from an open box and places it in my hands. "Don't forget, Libz, we never leave love behind." My parents offer each other a consoling hug, and although I'm not thrilled to be going, at least I don't feel alone anymore. "Letting go is hard for us, too," Dad admits.

"We have some time before the movers get here. Rest a while longer, but then we should finish packing your room." Mom softly closes the door—her trail of sentimental tears not hidden in time.

For weeks, I've been bouncing around like an over-inflated beach ball, one day flying high and the next crashing hard on the ground. Today, finally, the agonizing wait is over. No tantrums can change the inevitable, and God knows I've had plenty. My only choice is to tough it out and hope for the best. When this emotional seesaw is on the upswing, I have to confess that living near Chicago will get me one step closer to my dream.

Everyone in my hometown of Riverfield knows I plan to audition for a professional dance company when I'm old enough. Even our neighbors gush, "Hey, Miss Leggy Libby, you're destined for bigger and brighter places. There's probably a star dancing around the moon with your name on it right now."

When dance master, Bill West, saw me perform last summer and invited me to assist and tour with his national organization, I was convinced they might be right. I wanted to do it, but my parents said I was too young, and because of Grandpa's poor health, the timing wasn't good.

Reality hits hard this morning. Right now I'm scared. I've always been a big fish dancing in a small pond at Miss Dana's School of Dance. In the city, I'll be a minnow swallowed by sharks. Goodbye spotlight, hello back row. I can't even think about starting at a different high school or finding my way through a new maze of hallways. What if everybody hates me? And worse yet, what if I never find another studio to love?

My dog and I snuggle. "Oh Barney, when you eat, sleep, and dream dance, it's sad to be a studio rat without a studio."

He nudges as though he wants me to read. Grateful for the distraction, I open the book *A Dance Through Time*, a birthday present from Grandpa Marcus. It's always had a calming effect. He'd given it to me shortly before he died, and it pulled me through some of my dark days watching him suffer. Grandpa understood how important dance was in my life; I'll never forget his chirping bird whistle, pride filled hugs, or the flowers he joyfully delivered after every recital. I still recall our last conversation.

"Grandpa, I wish I could make you better. I wish I could fix you."

"Libby, sweetheart, don't you know that every time I see you dance, I feel better? The dance of your soul is the medicine for mine."

I say a prayer, hoping he knows how much he's loved and missed. Although my dancing couldn't save him, Miss Dana and I still believe in its healing power. I love how she says a truly inspirational piece of choreography combined with the ideal music, costumes, and lighting can lift the performer and audience to a higher place.

Barney and I study the book's awesome photos of famous dancers from the past. Even my mom, a professional photographer, raves about the pictures. I flip through the pages, innately drawn to my favorite. For some reason, I'm obsessed with the dancer in this old black and white photo. Maybe it's her physical beauty or the extension of her legs and perfectly placed pointe shoes in the height of her seemingly effortless leap. It might be her naturally arched back and gracefully extended arms. I don't know. I gently run my fingers across the small print at the bottom of the page. "Daniella Devereaux performing *Giselle*, Paris Opera House, 1913."

I've always dreamt of the day my mother will take my picture in this exact pose. I wonder about the great prima's life. Am I anything like her? Did she love dance as much as I do? Did she bounce from one place to another or care about where her life's path would lead her next? I gaze at her picture, daydreaming until my eyes grow heavy, and I dance with her in my dreams.

Failli (fa-YEE) Giving Way. A fleeting movement done in one count. From fifth position, the dancer springs into the air, turns slightly and lands in demi-plié on one foot. Brushing the back leg from first through fourth position croisé, she finishes in demi-plié with her body inclined.

Chapter Three

I jump at the sound of Mom's voice, "Rise and shine, Libby. We'll have to pack you in your bed sheets if you don't get moving."

"Aw Mom, I was just about to get a standing ovation."

"Would that be your first or second, sweetie?"

I send my bedcovers flying with one strong kick, and she nimbly dodges the pink satin pillow I sail across the room.

We finish packing while tears stream. Our Victorian style home looks sadly barren, void of all the memories that until recent weeks lined its charming walls. Gone are my framed school pictures and dozens more from past recitals. Placing the last one in a box, the little girl I used to be looks back at me. She stands defiantly and technically correct in first position, unlike the other equally adorable young dancers who appear slightly awkward with raised shoulders, bent knees, and parallel feet.

"That's always been one of my favorites. I never get tired of your dance pictures. Even at the age of three, the intensity in your eyes was obvious."

I laugh when my mom tells me for the hundredth time how I turned pirouettes inside her womb and how her doctor always joked, "I'm going to call this one my tiny Rockette." I roll my eyes and join in, knowing the last line by heart. "She must be rehearsing for her Radio City Music Hall debut." I guess I was born to dance.

From the bottom of the stairs, my dad's voice booms, "The trucks are here! Are you ready, Libz?"

I wipe my tears and fake enthusiasm. "You bet, Dad! I just hope the windy city is ready for me!" I perform a chassé into three split leaps across the wooden hallway.

"Well, Kate, at least we don't have to straighten the picture frames anymore after her prancing around."

"At least Mom doesn't have to pick up any broken lamps like the last time you tried a leap, Dad. Besides, it's a small price to pay for the privilege of having a dance diva in your midst!"

"Will, she's your daughter! I hope there's enough room in the moving van for her extra-large head." My playful swats at Mom and Dad send Barney whirling and barking.

After the neighbors gather for an emotional farewell, we walk through our empty house taking a quiet moment to imprint its image in our minds. Even Barney hangs his head and whimpers. The instant the fully loaded truck leaves the curb; I know our old life is gone. We swing by my dance studio for the last time, and I'm surprised by a wonderful send-off. Sometimes I think Miss Dana is the only person in life who understands me. Friends often tease that the world doesn't dance, people do. But Miss Dana and I hold fast to the belief that Earth is in constant choreographed motion—and everything in it, part of an exquisite dance.

Miss Dana pulls me aside. "Libby, you've been my favorite studio rat for twelve years. Certainly, you're one of the most gifted students I've ever had the privilege to teach. I know dance is your passion, and I have no doubt you'll find success. Your talented toes are firmly grounded by your strong spiritual sense of the world. I'll miss you." Her eyes water, and I fall into her arms and cry. Miss Dana continues, "I've always known this day would come. Trust this move is right for you. As I told your parents, I've already called a friend of mine. I'm sure her studio, L'Esprit, will be an excellent fit."

"I love that word. It's pronounced 'le spree' and means 'the spirit.' I learned it in French class," I say, trying to regain my composure.

"Let's face it, no one possesses the true spirit of a dancer more than you."

The business card she places in my hand reads, "L'Esprit Dance Studios, Miss Aimée Harris, Owner and Director." I can barely read it through the prism of my tears. "Miss D, someday I hope to follow in your footsteps. I promise I'll never forget you." Before I leave, she hands me a gift. After more hugs, kisses, and laughter, we vow never to lose touch with each other.

As our family slowly drives away, we pass the cemetery where my grandparents rest. Avoiding eye contact, we privately grapple with our emotions. Once merged onto the busy southbound interstate, I open Miss D's ribbon-bound poster and breathe in its meaning.

> *Art rises above all barriers,*
> *stirring the depths of our souls*
> *in written words or pictures,*
> *paintings or music.*
> *The art of dance*
> *like the art of life*
> *connects us forever . . .*
> *as one.*

I show the poster to my mom.

"This is lovely, Libby. It could easily be you posing in the picture," she says. "I think Miss Dana wants you to understand that you two will always share something special beyond your love of dance."

As Wisconsin gives way to the patchwork landscape of green rolling fields dotted with weathered barns and grazing cows, I wonder if I'll always be connected to Miss Dana and the other dancers, like the awe-inspiring Daniella Devereaux. *Could the words on the poster be true? Do love and art truly transcend place and time?*

Écarté (ay-kar-tay) Separated. One of the nine positions of ballet in which a dancer's legs are open in the second position with the working foot held in tendu and the body placed diagonally. A dancer's position is thrown wide apart.

Chapter Four

France, 1927

Steel gray clouds roll wildly across the foreboding sky in the waning hours of the dreary day, perfectly matching A.J.'s sullen mood. Not even the lush greenery of the French countryside lifts his spirits. How he wishes the heavens would open and drench him with rain to wash his tears away. Cabriole becomes skittish at the first clap of thunder. Gently, A.J. leads the horse by its reins into one of the small barns nestled on the Devereaux estate behind the château, once Daniella's favorite home and retreat.

It now stands silently filled with empty echoes of their laughter and love. He dares a look from the safe distance of the barn; the enchanting home reflects her warmth and grace. Her presence in every object and room bound to be both comforting and painful. He wonders why the house hasn't collapsed in sadness and despair without her. It's been over a year since her death.

A.J. knows this will be the last stop on his solitary journey. He must find a way to pull himself together or give in once and for all to the ever-downward spiral of guilt that relentlessly tortures him. His Chicago colleagues, like a crew adrift without a captain, tenaciously manage his vast international holdings. He doesn't care. He fears to stop grieving is to stop loving her—as if letting Daniella go might erase her existence entirely. Was his return to this place a terrible mistake? As he sorts through his thoughts, God grants his earlier wish.

The rain falls in torrents. A.J. backs himself and the horse further under the barn's ancient roof just before a sizzling bolt of lightening strikes. The power of the charged flash lifts him off his feet and slams his head against the old stone floor with a sickening thud. Cabriole instantly rears and breaks through the door; shards of splintered wood scatter everywhere. A.J. instinctively rolls away from the path of the crazed animal. Stiffly, he pulls himself to his feet and stares into the storm in utter disbelief. Barely making out the horse's glistening black coat and beating hooves, he watches as it blindly races into the tempest.

A.J. rubs the welt already forming on the back of his head. When a sudden burst of flames erupts in an empty hay stall, he boldly confronts the fire and its mounting heat. "Not today, you devil," he snarls. "You won't win this time!"

Soaking a blanket in a nearby water trough, he flings it over the burning debris. With maniacal pleasure, he observes it quickly dissipating into harmless, wispy vapors.

He glares in disgust. "That's it! That's all you've got?"

Another thunderous clap causes him to flinch. He reaches for his hat. He hates hats. Dani always forced him to wear one for protection from the sun, cold, or in his opinion just to make him look foolish. With it tugged securely over his ears, he lowers his head into the whipping wind in search of Cabriole. The wet ground grips his riding boots. Cold, hard raindrops pelt his skin, stinging the back of his neck. He circles the garden desperate to stay on the slick, rutted path, but the wind forcefully steers him towards an unwanted destination.

"Cabriole can find his own way home if he's gone to the lake! I couldn't bear the sight of it," A.J. mutters.

After almost an hour without a glimpse of the sorry steed, A.J. grudgingly turns his bruised and aching body towards home.

With no warning, the sodden earth gives out from beneath his feet, sending him tumbling down the treacherous embankment that skirts the narrow path. He bounces over roots, rocks, and tree stumps. Shrubs flatten and branches snap as his body gathers momentum. After a sheer drop of nearly ten feet, he comes to an abrupt stop facedown in the dirt. Motionless for a few minutes, he tastes blood. Wiping caked mud from his eyes, he ventures a sweeping look. "This can't be happening!"

A.J.'s landed a few feet from the lake where his hat floats at the water's edge. It must have toppled on ahead of him. He manages to wriggle forward, dragging himself to his knees. He reaches to grab the hat before it has a chance to drift further from shore. A woman's reflection in the mirrored lake catches his eye. His head spins over his shoulder, but he's alone. In agony, he searches the water again, but sadly the image of Daniella is gone.

A.J. wills his unstable legs towards the bench he crafted for their fifth wedding anniversary. It sits tucked among a patch of wildflowers. He wearily pats its wooden seat and says, "At least I know you're real."

He fondly recalls the piece. In true Dani fashion, she received the gift as though given a priceless jewel. Resting his hand upon their roughly carved initials, he lovingly retraces each letter with his fingertips.

Of all the places on Earth, this had been her favorite. She preferred dancing in a field of flowers to any stage. She would come here to be inspired. The pas de valse of the swans gracefully gliding in tandem, the brilliant sunlight dancing upon the water, and even the pas de deux of the butterflies' fluttering patterns fed her spirit. She would feast on the abundance as though at a splendid banquet. The surrounding peace and goodness, like a church or sacred place, had the power to elevate her soul. Here they enjoyed picnics and wine, often paddling the old wooden boat to the middle of the lake where they read poetry aloud. In this private haven, they shared their most intimate secrets. And they shared each other.

A.J. steals an anguished look at the lake and smiles, remembering how they laughed when she insisted on calling it Swan Lake and how he teased it seemed a rather grand name, offering Duck Pond as a more suitable description. He momentarily wonders where the swans and ducks have gone. "I shouldn't be surprised if they show up and peck at me angrily for abandoning them."

He bends his aching head and presses it firmly into the palms of his muddy hands. Alone with his thoughts, filled with unbearable sorrow, he openly weeps. He cries for what seems like an eternity, repeating aloud the same questions he's asked every day since her death.

"Why, Lord? Why did you take her from me? She was so young! Why couldn't I have saved her?" His sobs grow heavier as he begs, "Dani, I love you! I know you loved me! Please help me now!"

Not knowing if minutes or hours pass before his pleading and tears finally stop, and fraught with despair, he implores God to take his life.

"I can't live in this world anymore without her." The angry

truth he's harbored can no longer remain suppressed. "You should have taken me instead. I should have been the one!" At the same time, his heart aches knowing Dani never faltered, even in her darkest hours. She'd want him to go on.

Tonight at Swan Lake—clearly a crossroad in his life—he can no longer run from the inevitable choice to live or die. He will either drown himself where he last saw her reflection or somehow find the courage to live again.

Deeply engrossed in his own mourning, A.J. lies on the bench, unaware that the storm is over. He gazes into the blackness of night, reconnecting to the present. The stars appear hazy as he silently contemplates the open heavens.

Vividly, one by one, the stars begin to shine. The fog of his heavy thoughts lifts. Whether dreaming or not, he's unable to say. He continues to gaze into the velvety sky and recalls the verse she had written when her beloved first dance teacher suddenly died. "A heavenly star sparkles because a dancer's spirit performs in front of it for the all the world to see." In that moment, her voice whispers quietly to his soul, not in a language spoken, but a language felt. The midnight breezes gently caress his face, and the rustling leaves tenderly soothe him. He swears the lilacs, her favorite flower, suddenly bloom. He sputters in confusion, "Impossible! The season is long gone, yet their heavenly scent fills the night air."

With all logic cast aside, he knows beyond a shadow of a doubt she's here. Her presence surrounds him with an over-whelming tranquility. He languishes in the surreal moment as a soft touch guides his head. His gaze shifts to the small beam of light glistening in the middle of the lake; its transparent glow gradually brightens.

"Daniella? Have you come for me? Are you my angel of mercy?"

Her mesmerizing white figure blissfully dances just above

the water's surface. Suspended in translucent rays, her delicate arms entrancingly perform graceful port de bras. The extension of their brilliant radiance encircles him, filling him with peace.

Enveloped by the light, A.J. suffers no fear, only love. And within the fire of that love, he finds the flames of renewal and inspiration he desperately seeks. Her unspoken message of forgiveness releases his guilt. Hugged by God's own healing angel, he's blessed with new inner strength, trusting that Daniella and her beloved studio, L'Esprit, will live on.

Avant, en (ah na-V$\overline{AHN}$) Forward. The direction of a dancer's movement in which the given step physically travels towards the audience.

Chapter Five

Springwood Hills, Illinois
Present Day

*C*hicago's historic *Tribune Tower* becomes Dad's home away from home. His picture below the byline of his column "Nobleton Knows" makes him somewhat of a local celebrity. When Dad is asked for his autograph that he says will never be worth the napkin it's written on, Mom and I marvel at the coveted chicken scratch. She and I quickly adjust to his long hours and keep busy settling into our two-story dream home on 510 Rosenberry Drive.

One of our favorite features is the wrap-around porch with its curved front walkway. The fieldstone home, which we amusingly dub "The Château," has an irresistible French country charm. Its floor plan proves easily spacious enough for a spontaneous chassé tour jeté. Mom falls in love with the brick hearth and fireplace, envisioning our family posing for the annual Christmas card. The day Dad ceremoniously hangs our brass-plated name sign on the lamppost in the front yard, we know we belong.

Spoiling the moment, a car full of rowdy guys dressed in baseball uniforms from the school I'll soon be attending drives by beeping and jeering. When the driver revs his engine and makes the tires squeal, one of the boys points and shouts, "I think I'm in love!"

Mom's frown wipes the smile from my face. Dad shakes his head and kids, "This is why you won't be dating until you're twenty-five!" Secretly flattered, I suddenly develop an interest in baseball.

Our days become a blur of unpacking boxes, painting bedrooms, and thanking well-wishing neighbors for the endless stream of "welcome to the neighborhood" goodies.

"Mom, will we ever finish? Looking for my stuff and eating brownies is getting old."

We press forward every day, each with our own priorities, and on Dad's first free weekend, he does his best to please us both.

"Will, remember your promise. This second-floor addition with its vaulted ceiling and skylight will make an excellent portrait studio."

"You're right, Kate. The previous owners must have known you were coming." I immediately claim the unfinished portion of the basement. "Dad, I'll have plenty of room down here for my own practice studio."

"Yeah, Libz, I think so, too. This time we'll do it right with a professional dance floor, mirrors, and sound system." My pulse quickens. "In fact, how about I sweeten the deal with ballet barres and a walk-in closet for your costume collection?"

My wide eyes and ear-to-ear grin give dad the only answer he needs, and I almost forget that I've been ticked off at him for months for uprooting the family.

When word spreads that Mom's an award-winning photographer, the steady ring of the phone soon makes me her official message taker.

"Hey, Mom, while you were at the grocery store today, our new neighbor Mrs. Farley called, asking if you do action shots. She has two sons she'd like photographed outdoors."

"Thanks! What did you tell her?"

"I told her yes but that you aren't very good and that your pictures rarely turn out."

"Did you tell her that's because you're in most of them?"

"Two points for the sharp comeback, Mom!"

"Not as sharp as the pain in my shoulders. Can you give me a hand with these bags, honey?"

After a quick lunch, Mom retreats to her studio, and I return to my bedroom that's easily twice the size of my old one. Determined to finish my never-ending chore of unpacking, I lift a box marked "Libby's favorite books" and plop the heavy carton onto my bed. I'm momentarily distracted by the tantalizing scent from my open window and stop to look outside. Our street is relatively quiet today. I wouldn't mind catching a glimpse of the cute baseball player who shouted at me. I draw in full breaths of the summery fragrance. A soft splash of pink and yellow pastels catches my eye, but the mounds of small forget-me-nots are my preferred shade of blue.

I turn to the open carton and reach for my treasured gift. The book automatically falls open to my dance idol, Daniella Devereaux. After studying her image yet again, my gaze drifts towards the lilacs that cascade in full bloom and gently sway in the warmth of the midafternoon breeze. I swear my room fills with their sweet scent. The incessant chime of the front doorbell interrupts my musings.

Through the sidelight of our front entry, I see a meticulously well-groomed woman. She peeks inside rudely with her nose pressed against the window. Obviously, the stranger is eager to greet Springwood Hills' latest arrivals. Behind her is a girl about my age, the woman's mirror image. She stands sulking with folded arms.

Cautiously, I open the door. The two uninvited visitors barge in as though I'm invisible and immediately survey everything in sight.

"Can I help you?" I ask, trying to hide my annoyance.

"Thank you, sweetie! You must be Elizabeth."

"Yes, I'm Libby . . . and you are?"

"I'm Carol Ruthers, and this is Whitney, of course." Both Whitney's eyes and mine widen when we recognize each other from last year's regional dance competition. Her backstage shoe-throwing fit after failing to place was unforgettable. She's an attractive blonde with bored blue eyes and a Barbie doll figure, sporting a trendy outfit from head to toe. She glares at me while smacking her gum and blowing big, pink bubbles.

"Say hello, Whitney." Mrs. Ruthers tugs the girl's arm.

"Hello, Whitney," she mockingly repeats. With an exaggerated roll of her eyes, she says, "Mom, don't you remember her? She's the one from that silly little studio in Wisconsin that got lucky and won best lyrical solo at regionals."

"Oh . . ." Mrs. Ruthers says, "you look different."

"Some girls aren't as pretty without stage makeup," Whitney says. "Isn't that right, Lizzy?"

Not sure how to respond, I reluctantly greet them with an open hand and an uncomfortable smile.

Taking the wad of wet gum from her mouth, Whitney sticks it into the middle of my palm. "Thanks. I was done chewing it anyway."

My eyes narrow, and I can't help but think she's a witch with a capital B.

"Whitney!" Mrs. Ruthers shrieks. "What in the world are you doing?" The equally shocked woman pulls a tissue from her Gucci bag. Taking care to guard her dangling diamond bracelet, she attempts to swab the sticky mess from my hand.

"Soooorry, Libby. My effort at humor has once again failed. Will you ever forgive me?" Whitney smirks devilishly, certain her mother doesn't see.

"Libby, I apologize." Mrs. Ruthers says, her tone not the least bit sincere. "Whitney's always been a prankster. She often teases her friends like that. I'm sure she didn't mean to offend you."

Discreetly wiping my hand on my jeans, I say, "Your welcome to the neighborhood is certainly different."

"My boyfriend Brad tells me that you prefer guys whistling at you on the street. He's the captain of the baseball team and the star quarterback." Whitney then warns under her breath, "Hands off if you know what's good for you."

Flustered, I ignore her. "Mrs. Ruthers, do you live in this subdivision, too?"

"Oh, heavens no dear. We live in the gated community of Highland Estates. We only want to say hello. You know, find out more about you and your family."

To my tremendous relief, my mother finally appears.

"Hi there, you're Mrs. Nobleton. Katherine, isn't it? I hear through the grapevine you're quite the photographer. Did you take all these pictures on the wall?"

"Yes. Do we know you?"

"I'm sorry, sweetie. You don't know me yet, but you will. My name is Carol Ruthers. I'm the high school drama teacher. This is my daughter, Whitney. I just know we're going to be fast friends." Mom's eyebrows lift as the aggressive woman moves toward the pictures. "Oh my! This isn't Libby dancing, is it?"

"As a matter of fact, it is."

"Goodness, she looks like a trained professional. Did you use some of your camera magic to make her bodylines look that exceptional? So much can be done when you know how to work the angles." Carol nudges my mother.

"No, Libby looks good all on her own," Mom says, pulling away from the overbearing snoop.

Mrs. Ruthers examines the photos more closely. "Darling, did you take a look at these?"

Joining her mother, Whitney's bored blue eyes tint an envious shade of green. "They're alright, I guess. Too bad, Elizabeth, tryouts for the varsity dance team already took place in the spring. Maybe next year." Whitney's whisper hints contempt with a faint scent of beer.

"Couldn't I schedule a private audition for the coaches?"

"Oh no! That's not possible," Mrs. Ruthers says. "I'm the head coach, and we have our rules. The team is already established for the season. You understand, don't you? Our squad is one of the top ranked dance teams in the region, and each dancer must be enrolled in formal technique lessons. My Whitney is in the most advanced level at B-BOP Dance Studios. Unfortunately, if you miss more than two of our summer practices, you can't be on the squad, and we've already begun. Look on the bright side, dear. You'll have a full year to practice."

"What a shame. Everyone who makes the varsity dance team instantly becomes one of the most popular girls in school. Don't worry, there's always color guard tryouts." Whitney laughs, reaching for the door. "Can we please go now? I'm missing the team party at Brad's."

"Whitney's not one to keep a good party waiting. Everyone invites her! It was lovely to meet you. We should do lunch sometime soon." Mrs. Ruthers hands Mom her business card. "By the way, is it true your husband works for the *Trib*? When the girls win state, he'll probably want to do an article on them. Be sure to have him give me a call."

The two intruders abruptly fly out of the house. Mom quickly closes and locks the door. "Are you okay, Libby?"

"Yeah, I think so. Were they for real? I sure hope the other girls at school aren't like Whitney."

"And I sure hope the moms aren't anything like the charming drama queen—I mean drama teacher—Carol Ruthers! Not to spread gossip, but Mrs. Farley warned me she's a busy bee but mostly a busybody masquerading as a happy woman. Apparently, her husband dumped her for a perky, country club debutant." Placing an arm around my shoulder, she continues, "I'm sorry about the dance team, honey."

"You know poms isn't my thing. And anyway, I don't care about dancing just to be popular or to bring home a trophy. Dance will never be about those things for me. Besides, I don't drink."

"You smelled it too, huh?"

"Having that woman for a mother would drive anyone to drink."

Mom giggles. "Libby, you never fail to amaze me. When did you get to be this perceptive?"

After the Ruthers' bizarre intrusion, Mom and I decide to clear our heads by taking a drive around our new community. Knowing that Dad's investigative nature will force us to explore every option, we keep our eyes peeled for nearby dance studios.

We spot my new school, Springwood Hills High. It impressively sits at the end of a tree-lined drive, looking more like an Ivy League college campus. Mom points to the auditorium's theatre wing, and I wonder if any studios hold recitals there. Mostly, I remain focused on the one thing I care about and recall Miss D's glowing recommendation of L'Esprit. Articles I've researched on the Internet and read in dance magazines often hype the success of the studio and its students.

Mom slows down. "Look, here's B-BOP Studios."

"You've got to be kidding! It means Miss Bea's Ballerinas On Parade. I think I wanna barf."

"It's only a name, Libby. And just think, you could walk to class after school. Don't you want to stop?"

"Are you crazy, Mom? This is Whitney's studio!"

"We owe it to ourselves to at least check it out. Your father and I only want what's best for you. And L'Esprit's receptionist told me we can't get an appointment for two weeks."

"What? Why not?"

"Because they're competing at nationals in Las Vegas. Libby, stop it! I know that impatient look of yours. Just because you've never been to nationals doesn't mean you're not every bit as good as they are."

"I hope so, Mom."

"I know so. You always dance with all your heart and soul. Plus, you've got the physical talent to match. Isn't Miss D the one who says center stage follows you everywhere? You even placed first over L'Esprit's top graduating senior at regionals, and don't forget, your lyrical solo beat Whitney's. Face it! With your stage presence and technical ability, any studio would be blessed to have you."

"You have to say that. You're my mom."

"That's true, but facts are facts."

"Now you sound like Dad," I laugh.

"Well, your father's usually right. And since he's paying the bills, he'll want to be certain we choose the best studio before moving forward."

"Okay, Mom. Do what you have to do. But I know L'Esprit's waiting for me!"

~The moment Elizabeth Nobleton holds her thought, the lights in the deserted basement of L'Esprit flicker wildly, casting sinister shadows upon its long-forgotten remnants.

Sickled Awkwardly curved. An incorrect position of the foot in relationship to the ankle. The toes are twisted inward while the heel protrudes out and back. A complete misalignment of the foot—not the proper placement.

Chapter Six

M*om, Dad, and I arrive* at B-BOP Dance Studios on a warm summer evening. My parents, aware of my reluctance, make me promise to keep an open mind. Crowded tightly into the corner of a busy strip mall with the constant flow of traffic, its parking lot is as hectic as any major-league ballpark on opening day. When a group of young dancers darts between the cars, I gasp.

"So much for safety first! They should call it Bumpers On Parade."

My parents throw each other sideward glances as we climb out of our minivan. "Just give the place a chance," they say.

"I'll try, but I want to go to L'Esprit."

"We know, and we will! Let's be sure first, okay?"

"I'm already sure."

"Libz, how can you be certain?"

"Like your column says, Dad, a Nobleton just knows." I wink as I point out several large, overstuffed trash bags stashed behind the bushes near the front door. "Charming, huh? Strike one."

On first impression, the reception area seems pleasant enough. Vanilla-scented candles burn in the foyer and large potted plants, lit with tiny white lights, frame the perimeter of the open space. Upon closer inspection, an unkempt boutique overflows with dancewear. The walls, decorated with random shelves of trophies and crooked pictures, look desperate for a dusting. A robust woman with coal black hair sorely in need of a root touch-up sits with her head lowered at a messy desk. Her puffy hands and long, red, fake fingernails rifle through a multitude of files covered in crumbs. The strong spicy odor of tacos hangs in the air as we wait patiently to be acknowledged. When finally greeted by her Botox-induced eternal look of surprise, she seems irritated by our sudden appearance.

"Hello, we're the Nobletons. My wife called last week. Our daughter has a seven o'clock audition with the owner, Miss Bea," Dad says. Before she can reply, an agitated dancer nearly knocks me aside, demanding a bandage as she nurses a bloody scratch on her right shoulder. The receptionist rummages slowly behind the counter, searching one drawer after another before standing up empty-handed.

"We must be out. You'll have to get some tissue from the bathroom." The dancer stomps off without another word.

The receptionist's anxious eyes search the parking lot as if stalling for time. Mom taps the counter impatiently. "What about our appointment?"

Reluctantly, the woman places a call to Miss Bea's office. She then picks up her stack of folders. "Someone else will be right with you," she mumbles as she scurries away.

"Am I the only one who thinks this is a little strange?" Mom says.

"No, more like *a lot strange!*" Dad agrees.

"Strike two!" I emphatically add.

I cringe when Whitney Ruthers sprints by in pursuit of the wounded girl.

"Look, Tia," we hear her say, "it's not my fault you were dancing out of formation again."

"I was not, Whitney! Haven't you ever heard of fingernail clippers?"

"Oh, get over it! We've been dancing together since we were three. Quit getting in my way! I'm sorry!"

"Sorry doesn't stop the bleeding."

"Maybe learning to dance in formation would."

Before the drama further unfolds, one of the teachers steps from the nearest studio and pulls the two girls into her classroom.

The unattended phone at the front desk rings constantly. When it finally stops, an attractive woman dressed in designer jeans and bright pink high heels approaches.

"Hello. Please pardon the wait. I'm Miss Gina, the office manager. Miss Bea is unexpectedly detained. Unfortunately, she's unavailable for your audition."

"But we've had our appointment for a week!" Dad says.

"I'll personally give you a tour, and Libby can dance for Miss Terri. Trust me. All of our teachers are qualified to evaluate a dancer's abilities for placement. I promise to discuss the results with Miss Bea myself."

Miss Gina directs me to take off my cover-up and escorts me into the same studio Whitney Ruthers just entered. She introduces me to Miss Terri, who politely greets us. After their brief discussion, Miss Terri appears slightly frustrated by my unplanned audition. Composing herself, she asks about my background while the class of snickering dancers—pretending to review choreography—listens skeptically. I'm uneasy when

I see some of the girls whispering. Whitney's body language clearly indicates that she considers me a threat, and her sour face shouts *you'll never take front and center from me.*

Whitney is instructed to show me the sixty-four counts they're learning. She explains them rapidly, leaving out as much detail as possible, but I manage to pick up every nuance of the combination within minutes.

"Libby, do you have the steps figured out already?"

"I think so, Miss Terri."

"Then, let's try it from the top with music."

I dance full-out, leaping higher than anybody else. When the other girls do a single or double pirouette, I perform a quad. Astonished, she asks if I wouldn't mind doing it again—alone this time. Although Whitney's and Tia's eyes shoot daggers, I refuse to be intimidated. Afterwards, the class half-heartedly follows the teacher's exuberant applause.

"Is jazz your forte, or are you equally adept at ballet and tap?" Miss Terri asks.

"I think I do alright with both."

Whitney mocks, "I think I do alright."

Miss Terri frowns while others in the class muffle their laughter.

"Whitney, you owe this girl an apology."

"Oh, Libby and I are old friends. She knows I was just kidding."

"Is that true, Libby?"

"We've met."

"Then let me apologize for her. Whitney, you can see me after class."

Miss Terri excuses the dancers for a short break and asks to see me in my tap shoes and pointe slippers. Tia, with a wad of toilet paper still stuck to the side of her shoulder, places a consoling arm around Whitney. The two exit with threatening looks but hang out in the doorway gawking. I ignore them and perform the two pieces I've already prepared.

"I know Miss Bea will agree. There's definitely a place for you in our highest level if you want it."

"What is your highest level? I thought it was this class."

"Yes, it is," Miss Terri sheepishly admits.

Strike three! You're out!

When the audition is over, we glimpse Miss Gina accompanied by a rather loud and animated woman. The loquacious new arrival, overloaded with shopping bags, is oblivious to my family's presence.

"Gina, I just had the best dinner with some dear friends, and I can't wait to show you the unique items I found for the boutique today." Miss Gina abruptly hushes her and pulls the woman into her office.

"Where have you been? Why didn't you call or listen to your voice mail? I called twice. Did you forget to check your appointment calendar again?"

"Why? Did I miss something?"

"Yes, your seven o'clock audition."

"Oh, no! Not again." The office door slams.

A gold convertible sits in the lot, parked dangerously close to our van. Its personalized license plate reads: MZB-BOP.

"I think we can safely scratch Bimbos On Parade off our list. I vote we keep looking. Besides, I can't imagine dancing every week with Whitney Ruthers and Tia, the sobbing toilet paper girl."

~Although the night is calm and windless, an unexpected gust suddenly blows Miss Aimée Harris' business card along with Libby's favorite book to her bedroom floor. Witnessed only by the silvery moon, the pages of the book flip one by one. When they finally stop, the black and white photo of Daniella Devereaux is fully exposed. Her image reflects brightly in a solitary, shimmering beam.

Place, sur (<u>sewr</u>-plahss) On Place. A term used to indicate that the execution of a step does not move. The position is fixed, remaining in one spot. The dancer does not travel in any direction.

Chapter Seven

*T*he following Monday, Dance to the Max becomes our family's second stop on our tour of local dance academies. Its sleek lines remind me of a carefully balanced dance formation. Miss Nancy, the owner, greets us at the door.

"Welcome! It's such a pleasure to meet you. You are the first of my three interviews this evening. I'll have to keep things on schedule if you don't mind. No one likes to be kept waiting."

"Amen to that," Dad says. He smiles at Mom.

The rushed tour reveals an extra-large, state of the art facility with six oversized dance rooms in full swing. Miss Nancy points out the stage styled lighting, specialty floors, and surround sound stereo system. She brags about the iPods and laptops each equipped with Internet access and music downloading capabilities. One studio even converts into a black box theatre that easily seats over one hundred audience members. No less than four professional dressing rooms line the halls for small, in-house performances.

Miss Nancy does most of the talking, allowing no room for questions. She lists her studio's successes, boasting that some of her dancers have even appeared on national television. In her office, she directs our attention to a framed *Tribune* article about L'Esprit and Dance to the Max. As she babbles, all I can do is stare at the photo of L'Esprit and wish I were there.

"As you can see, we're mentioned as one of the top studios in the country." Dad doesn't let on that he's with the *Trib*, and I chuckle when I realize she hasn't stopped talking long enough to give him a chance. "Although we have a rather large student enrollment, it's a very small percentage of dancers that get accepted into our competitive program. Do you think you have what it takes, Libby?"

"I've trained since the age of three at Miss Dana's School of Dance in Madison, Wisconsin."

"Oh yes, that's Dana Greenly's studio, isn't it? She occasionally does some decent choreography. Libby, I know you're eager to audition here, but don't get discouraged if it doesn't work out for you, dear. Our top dancers have been studying for many years at a highly intense level. Some girls like to dance for fun, and we have great classes for that, too. But our top dancers train as pre-professionals, and dancing in these extremely advanced classes is not for everyone."

"I'll try not to become too discouraged, Miss Nancy," I say, determined to prove her wrong.

She gives my parents a handful of brochures, tells them to wait in her office, and then escorts me into a smaller studio. "This is our audition room, Libby. We have so many dancers applying for admission that I found it necessary to always have a private space available."

She closes the door. "Since I'm on a tight schedule, go ahead and show me your prepared audition piece."

"In which discipline, Miss Nancy?"

"Oh, you brought more than one—good for you. Let's get a

look at you in ballet first."

"Classical or Lyrical?"

Miss Nancy doesn't mask her surprise very well. She must think I'm a country girl who doesn't know the difference. "Classical, dear. You can put your slippers on while I cue your music."

"May I show you on pointe?"

"If you warm up quickly and think you're strong enough."

I lace up my pink satin ribbons, tie my hair into a bun, and do a few stretches. Once the music starts, I take a breath and flow with the melody. I dance as if each note were written for my movements alone. My port de bras lace the air. With each attitude and arabesque, I stretch further over the blocks of my pointe shoes. My eyes spot Miss Nancy on every chaînés turn, never missing a beat. When I finish my last lingering port de bra, Miss Nancy clasps her hands to her chest.

"That was breathtaking. How long did you work on that piece? Did your teacher hire a professional choreographer?"

"No, Miss D let me choreograph it myself, and I created most of it in one of my improv classes."

"You have an amazing gift for someone so young. Why haven't I seen you on the national circuit of competitions?"

"My real passion is performing, not competing."

"Eloquently put, Libby, but nothing looks better on a dancer's résumé than a few national titles."

"To me, trophies or titles don't matter. I simply love the way it feels to dance, and it's nice to hear others say my performance is uplifting. I want to study hard and become the best dancer I can."

Miss Nancy harrumphs. She has me perform other combinations, testing my knowledge of ballet terminology and my ability to pick up new choreography. I dance tombé pas de bourrée, glissade grand jeté, croisé en avant close fifth, sissone doublée without demonstration, and I can tell she's impressed. Tap and jazz are the same. From pullbacks to syncopated rhythms or Fosse styled moves to hip-hop, I meet her every challenge.

"Let me guess. You can sing, too?" Miss Nancy smiles. When we join my parents, she says, "Mr. and Mrs. Nobleton, Libby has the technical skills required to make it in this industry. With at least fifteen to twenty hours of dance per week and your financial commitment, I can have her ready for a national title within a few months."

"Fifteen to twenty hours a week? It sounds more like a part-time job. She's already got a lot on her plate with starting a new high school in the fall. I'm not sure a title is what our daughter is looking for anyway," says Dad. "We want her to be inspired to succeed, not catapulted."

"What other considerations could there be for such a promising young dancer? We'll definitely push Libby to her full potential at Dance to the Max."

Push, I wince, not liking her choice of words.

"For the record," Mom says, "we've never pushed our daughter to dance. Libby dances because that's who she is. She's self-driven. We only want to encourage and support her in any way we can."

"We noticed your shelves mostly showcase mini, junior, and some teen national titleholders. Why aren't there more students in your senior division?" Dad says.

Miss Nancy hesitates. "Our enrollment at the older ages isn't as high as at the younger levels."

"Did any seniors graduate from your studio last year?"

"Of course," Miss Nancy snaps.

"Would you say more than ten or less?"

"I don't recall," she says defensively.

I fidget in my chair.

"You don't recall, or you'd prefer not to say? While waiting, we couldn't help but overhear how some of your teachers talk to the girls. Is it possible the young ladies are pushed too hard and burn out too soon?"

A look of complete annoyance covers Miss Nancy's face. "I'm not sure what you're implying. I won't make excuses, sir! We strive to groom our dancers to be the best. The cream of the crop rises to the top, as they say. Eventually, a crop gets weeded out, Mr. Nobleton. We may not have the largest enrollment in the senior division, but the few dancers that do graduate off of our stage each year go on to professional careers. Dance is a serious business. We want girls that are totally committed and willing to pay the price both physically and mentally."

"Not to mention financially. Your rates in this brochure are at least twenty-five percent higher than any other studio in the Chicago area."

"Sir, take a look around. We're not like any other studio in the area, are we? We offer the best that the dance world has to offer."

Mom grabs my hand. "We do appreciate your time and professional opinion. We'll consider your offer."

Miss Nancy gives Dad a contract. "Just understand that our classes fill up quickly."

"You're our second of three appointments, but we'll keep you in mind," Dad says.

I swear I see dollar signs flashing in Miss Nancy's eyes as we leave. In a hurry to escape her greedy clutches, my dad fights his temptation to thrust the contract into the hands of her next innocent victims walking through the door.

"Wow, Dad! That was extreme."

"Let's just say I don't appreciate people who can't tell you the facts straight-up."

On the drive home, I sink into the backseat and look out the window, yearning for L'Esprit to be everything Miss D promised.

Relevé (ruhl-VAY) Raised. A position of the supporting foot in which the heel is raised from the floor, and the dancer is balanced on the ball of the foot or toes, if on pointe. A dancer's lowered position lifts.

Chapter Eight

France, 1927

*L*ike a warm and gentle touch, the early morning sunrise cresting over the wooded ridge soothingly caresses A.J.'s sleeping body. No longer tormented by screams, as he has been every night since her death, A.J. sleeps deeply, his dreams sweetly graced. Brilliant sunrays streak through the treetops and cast golden hues upon the dew-drenched landscape. A.J. wakes slowly and squints in the dazzling reflection of light dancing off Swan Lake. The birds' cheerful songs echo throughout the forest— truly the start of a new day, a new year, and a new life. He lies motionless for several minutes, grateful for Cabriole's return. The horse, almost humanly puzzled by his master's actions, impatiently stomps the ground while nudging A.J.'s shoulder. Within an instant, A.J. becomes acutely aware of his every ache, bump, and bruise. Although damp and cold, he's also more alive *than he's been in a very long time, which is a good feeling after being lost for the past year.*

He stands, reaches for Cabriole, and strokes the horse's dark mane. "It's okay, fella, we're gonna be alright. You've missed her too, haven't you?"

Cabriole whinnies. A.J. takes another long, careful look around the lake as if searching for one last sign from its life-giving waters. Finally, he accepts the peace and serenity that surrounds him. He picks up his hat, dusts it off, and looks into the horse's eyes.

"The storm has passed—le ciel se dégage. Let's trust the light of a new day." He mounts Cabriole, guides him by the reins, and together they head towards the château. Cabriole trots leisurely up the gentle slope. A.J. turns away from the lake, mindful only of the pleasant morning sun upon his back.

The time to say au revoir to the French countryside and return to his life in America has come. With a bittersweet surrender, he lets go. He knows with indisputable certainty that living again is the only way to honor his one true love, Daniella, his prima in heaven, her name forever etched upon his heart. As he reaches the top of the ridge, he stops for one final glance at her private pond below. A.J. fondly breathes in every ounce of the splendid scenery, their private paradise, their Camelot. When the image indelibly penetrates his being, he quietly exhales a whisper of goodbye.

Within two days, A.J. books passage home on the next transatlantic liner. The estate's staff, although highly elated by his profound transformation, is equally saddened by the announcement of his sudden departure. They pledge loyally to continue in his service, maintain the property, and assure Cabriole's excellent care in his absence. Businesslike handshakes swiftly melt into teary-eyed bear hugs.

While in Paris, A.J. awaits his return to the states and spends his last few hours strolling along the color-infused streets. He dismisses his chauffeur and visits with vendors while browsing the wares they peddle. For the first time in many months, he smiles at strangers and takes pleasure in the day. Stopping at a quaint outdoor café, he casually sips strong black coffee and scans the business section of the London Times, pleased to see that the U.S. economy shows such strong signs of a healthy upward trend. After neglecting his finances for over a year, he's encouraged by the prospect of an expanding portfolio.

Just then, the red and white overhead awning snaps briskly. An unexpected gust picks up his papers and scatters them in every direction. Quickly racing down the street, he gathers the wind-blown pages. The waitress, noticing the generous tip tucked beneath his coffee cup, shouts, "Merci!"

A.J. offers a wave and continues the chase. The last page that he finds is firmly pressed against the window of André Bordeaux's Antique Shop. The breeze rattles a small, painted, wooden sign that hangs slightly crooked above the front entry. A.J. translates the French script, "New Customers Welcome for Very Old Things." He peers inside at a plump, elderly gentleman with thick, graying hair sporting a full mustache. With a friendly nod, the shopkeeper motions A.J. to enter.

In a sudden burst, the heavy green door flings open from the inside, and bells clang overhead. A.J. steps aside politely, and two exiting women blush as they encounter the ruggedly handsome stranger. He stands over six feet tall, with broad shoulders and striking features. His flawless smile, magnified by the dimple in his right cheek, makes him all the more endearing.

"Bonjour," he says to the two ladies.

"Bonjour," they reply in soft, singsong voices, both caught completely off guard by their immediate attraction. Neither

woman can avoid a backward glance, hoping to catch another peek at his irresistible face.

A.J. *steps inside and looks curiously about. Antique relics usually don't interest him, and he isn't even certain why he obliged the keeper's request. Further into the store, a feminine, life-sized, angelic sculpture immediately catches his eye. It stands alone, partly hidden behind several antique chairs, one of which slowly rocks, beckoning* A.J. *Without forethought, he moves the chair aside and stands transfixed.*

"*She's a real beauty, isn't she, monsieur? Broken and battered perhaps, but definitely possesses a charm all her own.*" *The shopkeeper eagerly adds that the piece had been abandoned, and its sculptor is unknown.*

"*I've seen something like this a long time ago on my travels to Italy.*"

A.J. *doesn't budge, unable to take his eyes off the statue. Suddenly, a bright flash illuminates the room. For a split second,* A.J. *remembers his vision of Daniella at Swan Lake. Realizing that the shopkeeper did not share the same experience, he silently keeps his thoughts to himself.*

"*Oui! There are a series of statues in Italy of a much grander scale that appear to be half finished—bound in marble for eternity. They were created by the genius, Michelangelo. I, too, have seen them.*" *Who,* A.J. *wonders, would dare to copy the master? He knows this could not possibly be one of the originals.*

"*What kind of marble is it?*"

"*The finest, Carrara!*" *André replies.*

"*It's definitely of high quality, and the craftsmanship is indeed exquisite.*"

When A.J. *reaches out and touches the statue to examine it more closely, it's as though the sculptor's chisel and hammer strike at his very core. The angelic-like figure, partly sculpted, looks as if it's about to burst free of the block of marble that encases its lower body and limbs. Is this a finished work, or did the creator simply stop? At first, it appears solidly grounded, totally immobilized. Yet, upon further study, it looks as though it could tumble out and break free of its bondage. How can this be? A.J. wonders. She's earthly bound yet dances heavenly free.*

The glassy, marbled eyes captivate A.J. as they stare into his own. The parallels between Daniella's life, his vision at the lake, and this statue are crystal clear. The mere realization practically takes his breath away.

When he finally speaks again, he proclaims, "I must have it, no matter the price!"

"It's yours, Monsieur Dalton." André springs into action. A.J., enraptured by his find, does not notice the shopkeeper calls him by name. André enlists the aid of his young apprentice. "Quickly, Jacque, I will need your help over here!"

A.J. oversees the packaging from start to finish, wanting to make absolutely certain nothing further damages the statue in transit to America. To his unexpected pleasure, as they work, André reminisces about meeting A.J. years earlier. He tenderly speaks of Daniella's frequent visits to the shop and his personal deliveries to their château. Sadly, he adds how much she's missed. After refusing to accept the condolences of others since her death, for the first time A.J. finds comfort in André's kind words.

The shopkeeper and his young associate take extreme care to meet every detail of A.J.'s requests. Arrangements are made for the crate to be delivered portside immediately. With a firm handshake, A.J. pays André handsomely and thanks him for his exceptional service. He steps to his waiting car. Jacque, holding an oddly familiar object in his hand, runs out of the shop. "Monsieur Dalton, your chapeau! I found it on the rocking chair. I thought you might need it."

Although he didn't remember wearing the hat earlier, it was most definitely his—the one she had given him. Slightly perplexed, A.J. puts the brown leather hat on his head and secures the straps tightly under his chin. He climbs into the back seat, gives a final wave, and smiles through the rear window as his driver maneuvers into the morning traffic. André and Jacque share a good-natured chuckle and return to work, thankful for the day's profitable start.

At the end of a pleasant day's drive, A.J. and his coveted acquisition arrive at the French port. With the crate safely loaded, he confidently boards the ship. A.J. knows for the first time in a year where he's headed. His life has purpose again. As the liner sails calmly across the Atlantic, he watches the evening sun set over its vast waters. Unequivocally, he knows—surely as the sun rises in the east—that he alone was meant to find the statue. He will rebuild the Grand Dalton House Theatre and her dance studio, L'Esprit. Their dream must endure. He will take this long-forgotten, chipped, and bruised sculpture home and restore it to its original beauty to stand as his testimony of his undying love for her.

This is how the legend of L'Esprit began so many years ago . . .

Terre, à (ah tehr) Grounded. The dancer's foot is completely pressed to the floor. Even in a typically raised dance position such as an attitude or arabesque, the foot remains firmly planted.

Chapter Nine

"*C*ould you drive any slower, Dad? We're gonna be late!"

"The roads are packed. Relax! Remember, we're not in Wisconsin anymore."

Mom says, "We're almost there, and you have plenty of time to make your audition."

"I just can't wait another minute to get started. I know this is it. I can feel it. There's L'Esprit. Let me out!"

L'Esprit's large, uneven stone façade reminds me of a castle. Instead of being set in a secluded fairy tale forest, it's tucked in the center of Chicago, and I envision a drawbridge lowering to allow me entrance. Through the wide-arched windows of the second story, dancers flow unmindful of the activity in the streets below.

Planted amidst the rush of pedestrians, I'm unable to break my gaze from the world above—the world I most want to be mine. My thoughts float upward and hang like a soft cloud in the midsummer sky until I'm grounded by my mother's voice.

"Honey, come over here! You'll want to read this!" Mom points to a bronze plaque solidly embedded in the wall just left of the main entryway. To locals, I'm sure it's a well-known but mostly overlooked memorial. As I touch it, a warm, tickling breeze subtly caresses my face. I sweep the hair from my eyes and softly read aloud:

L'Esprit
Original Site of the Grand Dalton House Theatre
Established in 1915
Rededicated in 1928
In Loving Memory of
Miss Daniella Devereaux Dalton
Prima Ballerina of France
Beloved and Devoted Teacher of Dance
May 5, 1890 – December 31, 1926

Shivers race through my body. *Daniella Devereaux Dalton, the beautiful ballerina from my book. How is it I never knew she danced here?* A smaller inscription at the bottom continues, **The dance of your soul has forever stirred the depths of mine. A.J.**

Uncontrolled tears roll from the corners of my eyes at the sting of L'Esprit's tremendous loss. Dad puts his arms around me while mom consoles. "She was obviously loved very much in her lifetime, and that is what is measured more than a hundred years lived." Mom cradles my face and wipes my cheeks with her thumbs. Suddenly, I'm aware of the weight of someone's stare. I look to the upstairs windows and search them one by one. Dancers move benignly in constant motion, yet I can't escape the uneasiness of being watched.

Dad reaches to open the doors. "C'mon, Libby. No time for tears! We've got people to meet, and I know that dancing in a studio again will help you feel better."

An elderly gentleman wearing a security uniform greets us. "Welcome. I'm Mr. Stan. You look lost. Can I help you?"

"We're looking for the dance studio."

"Are you two pretty sisters signing up for lessons?" Mr. Stan winks.

"Our daughter hopes to," Mom smiles.

"You can use the main elevator if you like, or take the staircase straight ahead. You can't miss it. It's a top-notch place. I know you'll love it. I'm always around if you need anything," he adds with a friendly nod.

The nearly century-old building is a timeless mix of the past and present. A water fountain decorated with stone fairies fills the center lobby. Beams of gold stream through the skylight and reflect the copper and silver coins that rest on its sparkling bottom like sunken treasure. Dance students race up and down the grand staircase that looks like something from a glamorous movie set with widely curved, white marbled steps and an intricately designed iron railing. Faint strains of music descend from the studio above. The upscale boutiques and eateries that line the left side of the main floor are filled with customers.

Mom tugs Dad by his arm. "Look, Will! It's a dance studio and shopping mall. Does life get any better than this?"

Children dart around us, eager to be first to the fountain.

"Heads up, Dad!"

Pennies and laughter fly with countless wishes, including my own.

A pleasant, gray-haired lady gently arranges a cart of multicolored, long stem roses outside the Summers' Floral Shop. She smiles and waves, and I return the greeting. Two pint-size dancers dressed in pink run to hug her.

"We love you, Mrs. Summers!"

"Love you, too! See you next week, my sweet dancing

petunias!" The girls giggle as they skip off in search of their mothers under the watchful eyes of the kindly shopkeeper.

"I'll bet this is where the dance recitals are held." My father points towards the doors of a theatre with gold lettering overhead that reads: *The Grand Dalton House*. It occupies the other half of the building.

My eyes gleam. "Can we get in there? I'd love to see it."

"Not today, Libby. The doors are locked," Dad says.

Mom is preoccupied with the dozens of black and white photographs that line the theatre's outer walls. I study the photos of the crowds dressed in the fashions of previous eras attending performances. *Who are these people? Had any of them known Daniella?* I'm fascinated by the images of dancers arriving with trunks, scenery, and props at the stage door. I can almost feel the anticipation of opening night, as if some of the energy is still trapped inside the building. I can imagine the buzz of the audience as the house lights dim while the orchestra begins its overture.

"Kate, this must be a picture of that statue my assistant told me about," Dad whispers.

"What statue, Dad?"

"Oh, we'll discuss it later." Dad checks his watch. "Right now, we'll be late if we don't keep moving."

As we charge up the stairs, I look back over my shoulder at the wall of pictures and see a light blinking above an old-fashioned service elevator. It's tucked near the theatre in the far corner of the main floor and apparently stuck at the basement level. My feet firmly planted on the landing at the top of the staircase, I observe the light flickering nonstop as if trying to capture someone's attention. It certainly has mine and gives me a slight twinge, but before I can speak, the flashing ceases.

~For the past week in the dead of night, as if waking from a long sleep, L'Esprit's old, empty elevator travels upward from the basement. The steady hum of cables resonates throughout the dark and deserted foyer. When its groaning motor comes to a clanging halt, the creaking of the metal gate echoes hauntingly. The door slowly opens, waiting for the next unsuspecting passenger.

August, 1927

"I could probably swim faster than this old tug," A.J. remarks to a fellow passenger, his patience sorely tested as his ship sails westerly at an excruciatingly slow pace. In direct contrast, the maelstrom of activity surrounding his stateroom provides an unending amount of gossip and speculation aboard ship.

Wires and communiqués are received and dispatched feverishly as the services of architects, builders, and interior designers of the highest caliber are enlisted. Dalton House and L'Esprit dance studio will rise again. He'll persuade Isabelle, Daniella's younger cousin and protégé, to accept its directorship. After all, hadn't she willingly immigrated to America in Daniella's most desperate time of need?

A.J.'s daily unconventional trips to the cargo hold to personally inspect the condition of the crate further compound the shipboard mystery. Finally, the ship docks in the New York harbor. A.J.'s managers stand somberly scanning the crowded deck for their boss. They sigh collectively as they spot him wearing an outlandish hat and a broad, confident smile.

A.J.'s back.

Chaînés (sheh-NAY) Linked together. An abbreviated form of the term "tours chaînés déboulés." These small quick turns are executed in rapid succession, beginning either with a piqué or tombé, and may be done on pointe or demi-pointe. Usually performed in a linear or circular motion, these connected turns are chain-like.

Chapter Ten

A dramatic floor-to-ceiling wall of glass gives me my first view into L'Esprit. I'm reminded of Daniella as I reach to touch the twin doors' delicately etched triple D design. Walking through, I immediately smell the light fragrance of freshly cut lilacs, but none are visible. The receptionist approaches us with a pleasant smile as if we're old friends. While my parents introduce themselves and chat, I'm distracted by ballet music coming from a nearby studio. Dancers perform barre routines that reflect in the mirror. I fight the urge to run and join them.

Miss Aimée Harris, a brown-eyed strawberry blonde, extends a hand to my parents and introduces herself as L'Esprit's owner and director. She's the exact opposite of the heavily made-up Miss Nancy from Dance to the Max. With a classic, timeless look, she resembles the movie stars from the old black and white films my grandfather always enjoyed.

Taking my right hand, she cups it gently in both of hers. "Hello, you must be Libby. I've been waiting for you since Miss Dana called."

"Yes. That's me!" I answer with a ridiculously huge smile. "You haven't been waiting nearly as long as I have. I love L'Esprit already; does it always smell like lilacs?"

Miss Aimée's eyebrows lift. "Funny," she says, "sometimes I think it does, but no one else ever seems to notice."

When we tour the facility, Dad begins his usual line of interrogation. "How did you come to own the studio?"

"It's always been in my family," she says. "I'm the great niece of A.J. and Daniella Dalton. In fact, Daniella is my middle name."

"I'm blown away! You're related to my favorite ballerina. I Googled her dance career. I want to know everything about her, like why she left France and moved to Chicago. She was so young when she died. What happened to her?"

"She's the reason this place exists at all, Libby." Before she tells us more, her small mixed terrier bounds along the corridor carrying a pink, plush squeaky toy in her mouth. The scruffy puppy has four white paws, one ear up, and a lazy one that hangs down. Her tail never stops wagging while we each take turns petting her. Miss Aimée tells us her name is Roxy. When I stand, I'm face to face with the old service elevator and a formal portrait of a woman, her expression chilling. Oddly, Roxy growls and scampers off.

"Just so you know, Libby, this elevator is off-limits to students."

We wait for an explanation, but none is offered.

Miss Aimée points to the portrait. "This is Daniella's younger cousin, Isabelle. Although a very distant cousin of mine, she raised me, and I refer to her as my aunt. She directed the studio for many years after Daniella's death."

"Why is her picture hanging here? Is she still alive?" Again, my questions go unanswered as the receptionist informs us that a studio is available for my audition.

"Libby, please put on your pointe shoes and take as long as you need to stretch. You can change in this dressing room."

"Okay, Miss Aimée, but before we get started, I want you to know I'm thrilled to be here. Thank you for this opportunity."

When I'm ready, I hand her a CD and cross my fingers behind my back in the hope that Miss Aimée trusts Miss Dana's recommendation. I'm positive I belong at L'Esprit. I walk to the middle of the floor, close my eyes, and think of L'Esprit's celebrated prima. "This is for you, Daniella," I whisper. Then I strike my opening pose, and the next few minutes are a blur. The music, the mirrors, the walls, and the space my movements occupy all connect. Although my piece is physically demanding, I dance strongly, effortlessly surpassing even my own expectations.

Miss Aimée, covered in goose bumps, says, "Mon Dieu! Are you for real? That was professional performance quality and excellent technique. I love the carriage of your upper body and seamless port de bras. I don't need to see any more if you're too tired."

"Oh no, Miss Aimée, I'm fine. Dancing again is the best! Tap or jazz?"

"Let's try jazz this time. Hurry before you cool down."

When Miss Aimée teaches me other audition combinations in rapid succession, I pick them up as though I've known them all my life. So involved in my dancing, I don't realize how often this ability to know choreography before it's taught is occurring. Miss Aimée, on the other hand, seems rather comfortable with the notion. Sipping her bottled water, she smiles and slowly scans the studio as if searching for someone.

When the jazz music begins, Miss Aimée joins me on the dance floor and is swept into the moment. We meld in absolute synchronicity. Unstoppable, we dance harmoniously as our energy fills the room. Time neither races nor stands still. Not able to explain it, I know we're living and dancing in the moment.

"Libby, I may have to create another advanced level just for you! We're done here, unless you feel compelled to show me your tap skills."

"I'm so inspired. I'd love to!"

"Then put on your taps. I'll give you five minutes to dazzle me, and I have no doubt you will."

I tap freestyle until Miss Aimée calls an official end to the audition.

"That was the best tryout I've ever had," I say.

"It's what occurs sometimes at L'Esprit."

"Usually I'm glad when it's over, but I don't feel that way now. I'd keep dancing forever if I could. Miss Dana was right about you and this studio."

"Let's go find your parents. You fit perfectly—like another link in L'Esprit's chain. When can you start?"

~When the Nobletons and Miss Aimée leave for the evening, Mrs. Summers prepares to close her flower shop. After putting the last of her roses to bed, she steps outside into the coolness of night. She blinks hard when a streak of light pierces through a cloud. It illuminates Daniella's memorial plaque, and she shivers as memories of L'Esprit's unsettled past stir.

United States, 1927

The train carrying A.J. and his precious cargo leisurely weaves its way through endless small towns and open fields. It rocks soothingly across rickety bridges perched high above flowing rivers and small streams, stopping occasionally to deposit or collect passengers. One such station yields a troupe of dancers traveling to their next performance. A.J.'s talks with them, and to his delight, many had either trained or performed with his beloved Daniella. They are eager to share their personal memories during the remainder of the journey. A.J., freed from his self-imposed exile, allows each wondrous recollection to nurture him like a reviving drink of pure, cold spring water quenching an impossible thirst.

Excitement mounts as the train approaches the city. The pounding of A.J.'s heart matches the gusto of the conductor's robust announcement.

"Next stop, Chicago!"

Assemblé (ah-sahn-BLAY) Assembled. Joined together. A dance step in which the working foot sweeps along the floor before being lifted into the air. The dancer pushes off the ground with the supporting leg and lands in fifth position demi-plié. A dancer starts with one foot and ends on two.

Chapter Eleven

*S*ummer dance starts today. *Still* reeling from my extraordinary audition and consumed with curiosity about Daniella's studio, I talk Mom into dropping me off at L'Esprit extra early. I'm dying to see the wall of pictures near the theatre again, and my plan goes off without a hitch. As soon as the car stops, I spring out.

"Bye Libz!" Mom says with a wave. "No hugs and kisses?"

"Get real, Mom. Those days are over. I'll see you later."

Her pout makes me stop in my tracks, and I give her a quick hug. "Thanks, I love you. Have fun!"

I enter the front door held open by Mr. Stan, who gives Mom a reassuring wave.

"Isn't your sister taking class today?"

"Oh Mr. Stan, you know that's my mom. Actually, she tried an adult tap class once. It wasn't pretty."

With a hearty laugh, he steps aside and ushers me in. "I'm sure she must have other talents."

"Photography's her thing. She loves taking pictures."

As if reading my mind, he says, "The Dalton House has a wonderful collection of old photographs that depict its legendary history."

"I know. They're awesome! I'm planning to get a closer look at them today."

"Rose Summers, my sweetie in the flower shop, practically grew up in this place. She can fill you in on many of the details. In fact, I think I see her over there right now," he says with a kind smile.

"I'm on my way. Thanks, Mr. Stan."

I sprint to the picture gallery. Before I know it, I'm lost among the hundreds of images. Some show old-time movie stars. Others chronicle a horrible fire that destroyed most of the building.

"The fire was awful." I notice Mrs. Summers standing at my side.

"Were you there?" I ask.

"No, but my mother and father were. I was merely a twinkle in their eyes then. Although I must say, sometimes it feels like I was there. I've heard the stories of that dreadful night so many times. Lives were changed forever. But life has a way of moving on, and now you're here," she says. "We haven't formally met. I'm Rose Summers. You must be one of L'Esprit's newest dancers."

"Yes, I'm Libby Nobleton. It's nice to meet you. I start my first class today."

Mrs. Summers offers a welcoming hug. "Most of the kids never stop to look at these old black and whites."

"That's funny. I can't wait to study each of them. I especially love the ones of Daniella."

"That's because you must share her passion for dance. She was bold and courageous. She belonged here, and I can already tell that you do, too."

"What are these over here?" I point to another group.

"Those are from the grand reopening of the Dalton House back in 1928."

I peer closely at a photo. "He's adorable. Who's the guy in the picture in front of the angelic looking statue?"

"The handsome gentleman you're looking at is Andrew James Dalton. And the statue was once erected in Daniella's honor."

"I wish I could see it better. Are there more pictures?"

"It was truly an inspirational piece of art. Unfortunately, the statue and the pictures all mysteriously vanished years ago. This spectacular place was originally his wedding gift to Daniella. After the fire, he rebuilt it in her memory and dedicated it to the many aspiring young dancers that would follow—including you, I suppose." She affectionately rubs my shoulder. "The woman next to him is Isabelle Agnès Devereaux, Daniella's younger cousin and companion."

"That's right. I've seen her portrait upstairs."

"She was a dancer too, although not as acclaimed. Eventually, she became Daniella's successor. Why Mr. Dalton hired her, I'll never know."

When a customer interrupts, Mrs. Summers bustles back to her shop. "Libby, my flowers are calling. I hope we can talk again soon."

Left alone, I view the gallery a while longer and wonder about her comments regarding Isabelle. The hair on the back of my neck rises when I hear piano music playing in the theatre. The melody has a waltz tempo, old-fashioned and unrecognizable. I wonder if a rehearsal is in progress or if there will be a performance soon.

Before I know it, the history wall ends, and I find myself

standing before the ancient, iron-gated elevator. Fortunately, today it sits quietly. I learned from the pictures I'd seen that it was operated by a smartly dressed gentleman. Certainly, it must have been safe enough at one time, but for whatever reasons the old contraption creeps me out. *I'll take the steps, thank you.*

As L'Esprit's glass door closes behind me, I'm greeted by the receptionist, Miss Megan, with a cheerful hello.

"Hi, Libby! Are you ready for your first class?"

"I'm *sooo* ready! I can't wait to get into my dance shoes again."

"Good! That's the attitude we like around here."

"By the way, Miss Megan, do we get to see the show they're working on in the theatre?"

"Show? What show?"

"I heard piano music and wondered if there might be a performance scheduled."

"Music? That's news to me. Maybe someone's just testing the sound system."

"I can't wait to get in there and see the theatre for myself."

"Trust me, Libby, once rehearsals begin for competitions and the recital, you'll be spending plenty of time on the stage—probably more than you'll care to." She points to her left. "You're in Studio 3 tonight. The door is marked."

I slide into the dressing room, where the floor is already littered with about a hundred dance bags. Finding a tiny unoccupied space, I add mine to the collection. Tap technique is first, and I'm eager to begin. Several girls throw me questioning looks when I step inside the studio. I take a spot along the perimeter of the oversized room and appreciate the sponginess of the dance floor beneath my feet.

The floor-to-ceiling mirrors are slightly smudged at the three-foot level, where the little dancers probably touch them as all little dancers in love with the mirror do. For a split second, I think I see a reflection of a feminine figure near my own. I turn, but no one is there. I shrug it off and instead take pleasure in the late afternoon sunlight that streams through the gracefully arched windows. My eyes trace over the double-leveled ballet barres encircling the room. The fifteen-foot ceiling allows ample space for leaps, lifts, and tall dancers on pointe. *This place is awesome.*

Miss Aimée motions me forward. She takes my hand and asks the class for their attention. Instantly, all eyes are on me.

"Class, I want you to meet Libby Nobleton. She moved to the Chicago area from Wisconsin. Many of you might remember her from our regional competitions. She danced with Miss Dana's Studio in Madison. Recently, Libby auditioned and earned a spot in this program. We're very happy to have you here," she says, wrapping an arm around me. "I'm sure everyone will make you feel welcome."

I nervously smile. To my surprise, Miss Aimée leans closer and gives me a hug. "They're nice kids. You're going to like them," she whispers. As she starts the music for the tap warm-up, I'm gratefully released from the center of attention.

A giant toxic rush of first day, new girl emotions threatens to overwhelm me, but it quickly vanishes as I take my place among the other dancers and do a few pullbacks to make sure my taps are ready. I grin at the two girls on either side of me and am rewarded with two bright smiles in return. Some of the others look at me rather intently. I understand. I have to earn their respect.

As I follow Miss Aimée's lead, I'm startled to see my reflection. I beam, looking slightly deranged. My cheeks ache from smiling. I want to do a cartwheel and yell, *I made it! I'm finally part of L'Esprit.*

Instead, I draw a deep breath and talk myself down. *Libz, this is it. Don't blow it!* Most startling, I find I'm dancing. *Wow! The music's on and my feet are moving. Am I doing what everyone else is?* Relieved, I find I'm in sync with the rest of the class.

I will myself to tune into the "dance channel" in my head, as Miss D used to call it, when her young dancers' limited attention spans began to wander. My focus immediately sharpens. I'm aware of the heightened energy level in the room as everyone pounds out the intricate rhythms, dancing full-out.

Miss Aimée is a wonderful teacher, firm and demanding, yet incredibly encouraging and positive at the same time. When she demonstrates a particular step, her footwork is the most accurate I've ever seen. Her timing impeccable, her taps ring with clarity. She gives new meaning to the phrase "dancing on air." Although Miss Dana will always be special to me, as I watch Miss Aimée, I fill with wonder, like a young girl falling in love with her first dance teacher again.

The assistant teacher, a big splash of color, is long and lean with red hair and emerald green eyes. Her freckled cheeks are rosy from the exertion of the tricky combinations. Best of all, she wears what I call a "real smile," not the kind reserved for school pictures. Equally impressive, she copies to a tee every detail of Miss Aimée's choreography. Miss Aimée refers to her as Miss C.C., and I immediately decide she's fun and someone worth getting to know.

As the class abruptly ends, I have the weird sense that I've been sucked into a time warp. It can't possibly be over already. I'm suddenly wedged in the crush of dancers as they rush to the door. Some of the kids are nice enough to stop.

"Hi, I'm Caroline, these rising stars are Lauren and Emily— great job today! And this handsome stud is Jarrell Jordan."

When I see him up close, my jaw drops; he's sizzlin' hot. He could easily be a GQ model.

"Welcome to L'Esprit!" Jarrell says. "How long have you been dancing?"

"Why haven't we seen you at nationals?" asks another dancer. Like a tennis player, I lob answers back and forth to their barrage of questions and try to mentally note everyone's names. I'm sure I'll remember Jarrell's.

When a sullen-faced dancer snidely mumbles, "Got milk, cheese-head," I pretend not to hear and refrain from mooing. She was the one girl in class who stayed in the back, straining to pick up choreography. I take the high road and simply disregard her.

"Don't mind her," Jarrell laughs. "We prefer milk over vinegar any day."

With a last few words of welcome, the rest of the dancers move into the hall. I go to join them, but Miss Aimée motions me to wait. I swear my heart stops cold. *At least I won't have to remember any new names. I'll probably be dancing in a lower level after all. Stop it! I know I did a fantastic job.* Putting on one of those fake smiles I detest, I bravely step forward.

"Libby, how did you like your first class?"

"I loved it, Miss Aimée. The time totally flew."

"That's good. I'm glad. Will you come to my office for few minutes after lyrical tonight? There's something I'd like to discuss with you."

"Sure, Miss Aimée," I say.

She nods and leaves the room. C.C., the redhead, finishes tidying the CDs and collecting the attendance sheets while a petite blonde girl scoops up the left behind dance clothes. I can't help feeling confused. *Do they know what Miss Aimée wants to talk to me about? Do I dare ask?*

"There! Miss Aimée likes everything neat and ready for the next class." They scan the studio, making sure everything's in order. Then turning their full attention towards me, they smile and introduce themselves. "Hi, I'm Cynthia Cunningham, but everybody calls me C.C. And this gorgeous prima is Brooke Allen. She assists in all the advanced ballet classes. We're glad to have you with us, Libby. You're *reeeally* good!"

"So are you guys," I say.

"Obviously, C.C.'s the tap diva. I do much better in my pointe shoes," Brooke says.

"You kicked some major butt today. Everybody stepped it up a notch because of you," C.C. says.

"Really? I mean thanks. I'm so impressed with everyone, especially Miss Aimée!"

"We know. She's L'Esprit's original studio rat; she's been here all her life. Talent must run in her genes! Imagine being the great niece of a world-famous ballerina," C.C. says.

"Some say Daniella danced like an angel and was divinely inspired. Others say she still performs among the stars at night." Brooke executes an impromptu piqué turn into a heavenly sauté arabesque.

On the way to our lyrical class, I think about her remarks, suppressing the tiny goose bumps that cover my arms and legs— my personal gauge that God's speaking. Like Miss D's poster, His message might be found in the lyrics of a song or a poignant moment in a speech or whenever music and choreography ideally blend.

After a full day of summer dance, I knew I had two new friends. We hit it off instantly. We chat and goof around like triplets joined at the hip. I'm excited to find out that we're neighbors and will be attending the same high school in the fall. I'm especially pumped when C.C. tells me she already has her driver's license and can pick me up if I ever need a ride or just want to hang out. Brooke then surprises me with a giant hug.

"I should've warned you. Brooke is known for her hugs!"

"She doesn't know her own strength!" I say.

"It's just nice to have a new friend," Brooke says, giving me an extra squeeze.

"Oh, I get it. I'm just too boring for you," C.C. teases.

"You know what I mean. We'll be like the three musketeers." Brooke wields her pretend sword.

"Or more like the three blind mice," C.C. snorts, grabbing her nose. In a muffled voice, she adds, "I think I just injured my adenoids."

"As long as they don't call you the three little pigs," Jarrell jokes as he rounds the corner. "You were amazing in lyrical tonight, Libby."

"So were you. I wish I could fly through the air as powerfully as you. Except for Trent Michaels, I can honestly say that I've never seen a guy perform a lyrical routine with such emotion and strength."

"Thanks a lot! Comparing me to Trent is a major compliment. Maybe you and I can pair up sometime." He hugs Brooke and C.C. goodbye. "I'll text you guys later; try to behave."

"He's a keeper," I say. "What's his story? Is he straight? Does he have a girlfriend?"

"He's a studio rat just like us, and yes he's straight. We've been dancing together since we were babies. I think he has a secret crush on Brooke," C.C. says.

"I always thought he liked you best," Brooke fires back.

"Whoever he likes is one lucky girl," I say.

"Sounds like he wants to hook up with you, Libby," says Brooke with a wink.

"Shut up, you two. I'm sweaty enough. All this talk about

Jarrell isn't helping."

"Hey, maybe we can do a trio together. Girls only!" I say.

"Classical ballet!" Brooke says.

"No, tap!" C.C. insists.

"It's gotta be lyrical!" I say.

"Then jazz it is!" We dissolve into another fit of laughter.

"Libby, we almost forgot. Miss Aimée's waiting. Her office is the second one on the right. Be sure to come and find us as soon as you're done," C.C. says, shoving me out the door.

Walking alone, the lights above begin to flicker. At the end of the dimly lit hall near the old elevator and Isabelle's portrait, I hear a low, rumbling growl. My apprehension lessens when Roxy darts out of the shadows. "Hey puppy, you're trembling. What's wrong? There's nobody down there. Is there?"

Unnerved, I run towards Miss Aimée's office, a jittery Roxy close at my heels.

Chicago, 1927

The joyous homecoming A.J. shares with family and friends equals the giddy exuberance usually reserved for a celebrated war hero. The staff bobs and curtseys comically until he threatens to have them all dismissed.

In truth, he has triumphantly fought his own private battle and won, returning not a hero but healed.

He has survived.

Étoile (ay-Twahl) Star. A title reserved for the leading female or male dancer of the Paris Opera.

Chapter Twelve

I timidly tap three times on Miss Aimée's office door and practice responses for any possible scenario. *Miss Aimée, I was a bit overwhelmed today. I'm sure I'll do better next time. I'm usually very focused.* They all sound lame even to me, but they're the best I can come up with on the spot. I listen to a soft, familiar tune. I recall it as the same melody I heard outside the theatre.

"Please, come in!"

I step into another time. Although the rest of L'Esprit has been modernized over the years, Miss Aimée's office is a reflection of the days of old. Sitting at her oversized, mahogany desk, she types on her laptop while speaking on the phone. *Hmm, no music.* With a wave of her hand, she motions me to take a seat. Roxy follows and jumps onto my lap. While I stroke her short scruffy coat, I admire an ornately carved fireplace. Its marble mantle holds a collection of small pictures. I recognize the face of Trent Michaels in one. Super famous and super cute, he's regularly featured in dance magazines and is always the top draw at any dance convention where he teaches. Every dancer, including me, has a crush on him. His classes are always filled to capacity with girls scrambling to get as close as possible. His is the only class we ever attend with full hair and makeup. Posed cozily arm in arm with Trent is a very content looking Miss Aimée. *Are they a couple? They sure look good together.*

Across from the fireplace sits a very comfortable loveseat. *Romantic.* I wonder if they ever cuddle together in front of a roaring fire. The wooden floor is partly covered with a thick, colorful, and heavily patterned carpet. Miss Aimée's tidy antique desk is decorated with a tall vase full of long stem red roses and a large snow globe. Encased in the clear ball are dancing figures of a woman wearing a flowing white gown held in the arms of a man, dapperly dressed in black tie and tails. Maybe the melody I heard belongs to the twirling couple.

My gaze finally rests upon the true focal point of the room, and instantly my unsettled nerves calm. On the large wall behind Miss Aimée hangs the portrait of Daniella Devereaux Dalton. Her eyes sparkle with a lively spirit as though she might stand and dance out of the picture. She sits outdoors dressed in a white chiffon, waltz-length ballet costume surrounded by wild bunches of lavender lilacs. A fresh sprig of flowers is tucked in a soft purple sash that hugs her tiny waist. Her radiant face tilts ever so slightly with loving eyes that focus on something or someone just beyond the artist. Matching pointe shoes add the finishing touch to the perfect ballerina every aspiring dancer dreams about. The signature "M. Doll" is scrawled in the portrait's lower corner. I cannot tear myself away from her soothing presence.

Miss Aimée concludes her phone call, snaps her laptop closed, and swivels in her chair. Together we silently study the portrait.

"She has the same effect on me," Miss Aimée smiles. "Sadly, we never met, but her legacy continues to motivate me every day."

"She's amazing! I've admired her since the first time I read about her in *A Dance Through Time*. I've always wanted to know more about her. Being here where she once lived and breathed is almost unbelievable. She was such a gifted dancer! Why isn't she in a magnificent ballet pose?"

Sadness clouds Miss Aimée's eyes, and she's silent for an uncomfortable length of time. "It wasn't spoken about often. Daniella never wanted to be defined by her tragedies. She preferred to be remembered as a passionate dancer and teacher. To me, she's a true and lasting star."

"Oh, I . . . I'm . . . sorry," I stutter. "I didn't mean to bring up painful memories."

"It's okay. Daniella never wasted a single day feeling sad. Self-pity was an emotion she refused to acknowledge."

We both take a moment longer to think about her. I accept Miss Aimée's vague response, but I know my inquisitiveness will never rest. *What tragedies? Did she suffer an incurable disease?* Common sense tells me that now is not the time to ask.

Miss Aimée folds her hands and looks me squarely in the eyes. I decide to take a preemptive strike, blurting out, "I absolutely love it here. I know I can do better!"

With a burst of laughter, Miss Aimée replies, "If you did any better you would have my job, Libby. I invited you here to ask if you had any interest in becoming an assistant teacher this fall. You could start training this summer with Miss Kali. With your talent and outgoing personality, you'd be an excellent helper. I know the dancers and parents would love you."

"For real? When can I start?"

"Hold on. I love your enthusiasm, but you should talk it over at home first and decide after checking your school schedule. Aren't you dancing on your high school's varsity poms squad? I'd need you here by four o'clock on Tuesdays and Thursdays."

"I'd like to be on the school's dance team; only the coach, Mrs. Ruthers, said I already missed tryouts. Besides, I don't mind staying as far away from Whitney as possible."

"Forgive me, Libby. I never talk about moms, but the mere mention of the Ruthers gives me a massive headache. I was plagued with phone calls for months after Whitney failed her audition at L'Esprit. She insisted I accept Whitney as an advanced level student and was furious when I didn't."

"She's scary alright. But I'm okay, and I'd rather spend my time here with you."

"This is a paid position. Our assistants usually apply their earnings towards regional and national competition fees." My head swims at the magic word *nationals*. I jump to hug Miss Aimée and nearly knock over her fragile snow globe. Miss Aimée saves it from falling.

"It's not broken, is it?"

"No harm done. It hasn't worked in years. I keep it because it once belonged to Daniella and played her favorite song, 'To Have, To Hold, To Love.'"

Her phone rings, signaling the end of our meeting. Roxy trails me across the room, her tail wagging.

"She's certainly taken a liking to you."

I reach for the door. "She's a darling dog." Giving Roxy a pat on the head, I quickly add, "I'll call you after I talk to my parents, but I'm positive it will be okay." Miss Aimée smiles and waves goodbye.

I race to the dressing room in search of C.C. and Brooke, my feet barely touching the floor. They greet my news with high fives and one more of Brooke's crushing hugs. "I'm ecstatic! I've been asked to assistant teach with Miss Kali."

"We know! We love her, and you will too!"

Clearly, this will go on record as being one of the best days of my life.

"Miss Aimée said I could put my earnings towards competitions. I've never been to nationals before. Where are they this year?"

"The Big Apple, New York City, baby! Don't you know, we're gonna be stars!" C.C. shouts.

This is truly more than I can stand. *Are all my dreams about to come true in one day?*

"Don't forget, we have to qualify first," Brooke reminds us.

I frown.

"Don't stress, Libby, we usually manage to qualify most of our routines. Haven't you heard? Brooke and I are national champions!" C.C. boasts.

I did know. I'd already seen the trophies lining the walls of the warm-up area and read about L'Esprit's many accomplishments on the Internet. "Somebody pinch me!" I say. "I'm part of one of the top dance studios in the country. Fall classes can't start soon enough."

Why did I ever resist moving to Chicago? Note to self— apologize to my parents when I get home.

We exchange phone numbers underneath the glow of the streetlight, and I notice Miss Aimée observing us from her office window.

We wave, and C.C. says, "Miss Aimée always tells us that the best thing about dance is the lifelong friendships we make. It's her favorite part of the business."

~Miss Aimée looks on, pleased with the girls' immediate connection. Her eyes drift to the portrait of Daniella, where they always rest at the end of her busy day. She thanks the stars above, knowing that Libby's presence is a gift to the studio, one to be treasured and nurtured. As she locks L'Esprit's glass doors, the snowflakes swirl inside the crystal globe on the corner of her desk. The key, wound by an unseen hand, sets the entwined couple slowly spinning. A tinny, old love song, the same music Libby's heard before, hauntingly lingers.

Dalton Enterprises, Chicago, 1927

A.J. proceeds to drive as fast as possible wherever he goes, as if making up for lost time after having been at the mercy of slow-moving ships and trains. Clouds of dust followed by the screech of tires often accompany his daily arrival at the office. He rushes through the reception area in an attempt to avoid his devoted secretary, Miss Olivia Winterset's look of mock disapproval and her usual stack of messages that require immediate attention. This game he always plays but never wins.

"Mr. Maxwell Doll is waiting for you," she announces to his fleeting back. "Here is his contract."

Mr. Doll, the renowned artist and sculptor, having already inspected the statue, is completely intrigued by its lifelike composition and most anxious to begin his work.

Brisé (bree-ZAY) Breaking. A dance step that travels in any direction with a small, broken movement of the feet. A brisé is an assemblé, beaten and traveled before landing in demi-plié in fifth position.

Chapter Thirteen

The cool, crisp morning air and burnt orange sugar maple in our front yard paints the ideal early autumn picture. I wake to the smells of Dad's Saturday pancake breakfast and tear through my closet dressing quickly in my favorite faded jeans and a soft, blue knit sweater.

I like my new school and with the help of C.C., Brooke, and Jarrell, I've almost learned to navigate the winding corridors without getting lost. So far, the faculty is likeable, except for my biology teacher who piles on a ton of homework every night. My classmates are mostly friendly and nothing like Whitney Ruthers. Turns out, she's well known but not well liked. Gratefully, we don't share a single class.

She'll probably kill me when she finds out her scumbag boyfriend, Brad, asked me for a date. After Friday's pep rally, he caught me by surprise at my locker and told me I didn't know what I was missing—like it would be a big deal to go out with a varsity athlete. When he saw Whitney's best friend Tia approaching, he had the nerve to plant a wet kiss on my mouth before escaping down the steps two at a time. Thank heavens Tia didn't see it, or I might be dead already. As if I'd go out with Brad Duncan anyway. C.C. and Brooke say he's been a real jerk since middle school, and like Whitney's other boyfriends, he only dates her for one reason. Jarrell promises to knock Brad unconscious the next time he comes near me.

Giving my hair a final brush, I dab on pale pink lip gloss and follow my nose into the kitchen. Barney isn't having much luck as he sits patiently waiting for errant table scraps. When I take my seat, he angles his big black snout as close to the maple-flavored bacon as possible.

"Morning, hon! Did you get any sleep last night, or are you too keyed up about starting another season of dance next week?" Mom kisses my forehead. "She's probably already forgotten about us. With her new friends and assistant teaching job, we've probably lost her for good."

"I hope not! Today's our big day together," Dad says.

"I didn't forget. I've been looking forward to spending time with you all week."

"Aw, thanks, Libz. That means a lot to me."

"Anything for you. Besides, if I can't hang out with my friends, at least it gets me out of doing chores with Mom." I slip Barney a small piece of bacon.

"How will C.C. and Brooke ever survive without you today?"

"They'll miss me, Mom, but they'll be okay. Brooke's brothers are taking her to visit their cousins in Milwaukee this weekend. They're big hockey fans, and they have tickets to an Admirals exhibition game. C.C. and her parents—now prepare yourself Mom because I know you're a huge fan—are going to Shelby Windham's for lunch."

"Shelby Windham? The queen bee of daytime television has her own restaurant?"

"No, Mom. They're having lunch at her home."

"Get out! Let me get this straight. *The* Shelby Windham is having them over for a visit?"

"I know. Isn't it cool? C.C. says Shelby is every bit as wonderful as you've ever heard and even more attractive in person."

"No doubt! Plus with her flawless complexion, she'd be the ideal subject to photograph," Mom says.

"All this Shelby Windham talk makes my father-daughter day plans seem shabby," Dad says with an exaggerated pout.

"No way, Dad! I'll feel like a VIP with my personal behind the scenes tour of the Tribune Tower."

For as long as I can remember, Dad and I have made a habit of spending one Saturday a month together. Whether a movie, a Badger game, or a long lunch at a favorite restaurant, we made a plan and stuck to it. I think Dad worries that eventually I'll outgrow our tradition, but in all honesty, I like it.

Mom says, "Libby, tell me again. What do C.C.'s parents do? How do they know Shelby Windham?"

"Remember, her dad's an architect, and her mother's an interior designer. They remodeled Shelby's Chicago residence and picked out just the right shades of green for her walls. That's her favorite color, you know. They've even been featured on the cable show *Glamorous Homes* and written about in *Architecture Today*."

"Good lord, you don't mean Curtis and Julia Cunningham? I've seen pictures of their spectacular designs. Didn't they, along with the Bailey Spice Company, recently build a community center for underprivileged kids?"

"That's right. C.C.'s grandfather is Preston Bailey. He's quite the philanthropist. He's worth a fortune, and C.C. and her parents are his only heirs. Mr. Bailey gave C.C. the nickname paprika—

except when her fiery temper flares. Then he loves to call her his red-hot chili pepper. Her face turns beet red every time he says it. If you ever want to get her mad, just call her that sometime."

"No thanks, I think I'll try to stay on her good side." Mom smirks. "You should too; maybe she'll get us tickets to the Shelby Windham show.

"Or at least some free spices," Dad says.

"What's Brooke's story? Don't tell me her parents are nuclear physicists?"

"No, Mom. Mr. Allen's a pilot, and Mrs. Allen is a doctor."

"You're kidding."

"Dad, don't freak! She's a veterinarian. Their house is wild. They have animals everywhere. Brooke's got two overly protective brothers—Ryan and Jack. Her tiniest twinge sends them into a tizzy. I don't understand it, but she tells me it's no big deal. Her mom's super nice. She even traveled to Miami after the last devastating hurricane. She volunteered with the Humane Society and started an online adoption service for the lost and abandoned pets."

"Sounds like you've met two fine families," Mom says.

After breakfast, Dad and I set off for the Tribune Tower on Michigan Avenue. He goes on and on about the building's history, telling me that the design had been selected in a contest to construct the city's most eye-catching structure. Completed in 1925, it was modeled after the Button Tower of the Rouen Cathedral in France. I personally like the gargoyle gutters and decorative supports called "flying buttresses." When Dad first said it, I envisioned the word as "flying butt dresses" reminding me of the wooden garden decorations that sprout up each spring in our old rural Wisconsin neighborhood. Surely the large woman bent over in her red and white polka dot oversized bloomers would never appear in our new subdivision! Dad explains that the tower contains actual stones from the moon, the Alamo, the Roman Coliseum, and the Great Wall of China. He's such a geek, but I'm proud of him.

At the security guard's desk, Dad flashes both his bright smile and employee ID. We sign in and head for the highly polished bank of elevator doors. The offices definitely have an air of power and importance. Dad's extensive tour ends at the desk of the editor-in-chief, where he and two writers huddle around a computer working on a late-breaking story. Although intent on their approaching deadline, they don't seem to mind our intrusion as they wait for a final fact-confirming phone call. Dad had apparently shared my recent good fortune of being accepted at L'Esprit.

"Miss Nobleton, it's a pleasure to meet you. You're even prettier than the pictures on your dad's desk. Those dance poses are stunning! We'll have to save plenty of space in our Arts section to devote to your future dance career."

With red cheeks, I thank them. When our visit abruptly ends with the ringing of the editor's phone, we make our way to Dad's office, where he surprises me with an unexpected announcement.

"Libby, I know how interested you've been in learning more about L'Esprit, so I thought you might want to see some copy I found. The place has a unique history. I could set you up in the archives while I use the time to verify a few facts for my own column if that's okay?"

"Dad, you're amazing! Of course it is!"

I sit in one of the many private cubicles with Dad bent over my shoulder helping me access the files. If not for the soft click of distant keyboards, I would have thought we were alone. I immediately submerge myself in the findings.

L'Esprit is listed as one of Chicago's most documented

haunted buildings. *Haunted? No way! It's a wonderful place, not scary at all. Why would anyone write such a thing?* I scan through rumors of strange noises and unexplained flickering lights. One article states that back in the late-1930s, a Russian dancer reportedly refused to return to finish the second half of a performance, claiming to have heard and seen things that were unnatural. *Unnatural? What the heck does that mean? Yes, it's an old building; the elevator gives me the creeps, but come on, haunted?* I backtrack even further, scrolling through the articles about the fire.

It was 1926 on New Year's Eve when the theatre was packed with partygoers. A dance performance provided the evening's entertainment, followed by a gala in the grand foyer. The photos I had seen with Mrs. Summers at the wall of history told merely part of the story. I never knew the extent of the tragedy nor how many lives had been lost—twenty-one people, including Daniella. Her body was found on the floor of the elevator, a broken bracelet clutched in her hand. *Dear God! That's how she died? Poor Daniella! I knew that elevator was evil.* The cause of the fire was never determined; it's speculated that a gentleman's unattended cigar might have set the blaze.

I press on, becoming more involved as I read. Many of the performers were among the injured, but fortunately all survived. Without the bravery of Andrew James Dalton, countless others would have died. *Why didn't he save Daniella? Why weren't they together?* In one picture, he looks emotionally distraught, and I find it hard to look at his face. Another shows the scorched grand staircase. I view the rest of them in rapid succession. People in torn evening clothes huddled, helpless and confused; costumed dancers covered with soot, totally grief stricken. My stomach aches as though I've been punched.

"Libby! What's wrong?"

I slump, hearing the concern in my father's voice.

"I never knew how brutal the fire was. I just hate that it ever happened. Can we please print this and take it home to show C.C. and Brooke?"

"Keep in mind, your mother may not appreciate me exposing you to the powerful details of the Dalton House fire. I don't think there's room enough for me and Barney in his doghouse," Dad says as he reluctantly hits the print button.

"Dad, is there more than this?"

"Yes, honey, but not now. I promise you can come back another day."

"But Dad, Daniella's life is like a giant jigsaw puzzle. I want to find the pieces and put them together."

"It must be my investigative gene that you've inherited. I understand, Libby. I do. But The Fudge Shoppe has two extra-large hot fudge sundaes with our names on them waiting for us, if you're up for it."

Shaking off my sadness like a dancer's unwanted injury when the show must go on, I concede. "Okay, as long as I get the one with the biggest cherry and the most whipped cream!"

"It's a deal, Libz. I'm watching my figure anyway."

~Pulling the copies off the printer, Will and Libby fail to notice the name *Daniella* filling the computer screen, duplicating itself into infinity. As they walk away, the undetected image brightly flashes one last time before the screen goes blank.

Chicago, 1927

A.J. is the first to arrive. He plans it that way. If his knees should fail him and buckle, he doesn't want an audience. His emotions are lined up in a row as if vying for attention. Dread at the sight of the burned-out elevator comes first, closely followed by unbearable sadness. As he surveys the ruins of the Grand Dalton House, he remembers what a perfectly clear evening it had been. The loss of Dani and the others was a tragedy beyond measure. Yet hope gallops across his heart like a flag-bearing white knight at the stunning sight of the grand staircase standing defiantly, as if daring to be restored to its original splendor. Yes. The Grand Dalton House will rise again. He owes it to Dani and all those he loved and lost on that terrible night.

Fondu (fawn-D<u>EW</u>) Sinking. A dancer's position is lowered by bending the knee of the supporting leg. Whereas a plié is done on both legs, a fondu is executed on one. The dancer's body appears to melt.

Chapter Fourteen

I wake slapping the button of my alarm before it has a chance to beep. I hit it so hard that the clock flies off the nightstand, landing in the wastebasket. *She shoots, she scores! I know it's going to be a good day.*

Crawling from beneath the warm covers and springing to my feet, I race through my daily ritual of stretching. Visions of today's classes fill my head. Humming ballet music in the shower, I wish I was already at the studio.

Today, I'll be studying with Trent Michaels in a dance intensive hosted by L'Esprit. We'll have Broadway's Tony award-winning choreographer all to ourselves.

According to C.C. and Brooke, Miss Aimée and Trent dated as teenagers at Chicago's School of the Performing Arts, where they fell hopelessly in love while starring in *Guys and Dolls*. Supposedly, the lengthy kiss they shared onstage caught everyone's attention, including Aimée's Aunt Isabelle, Trent's parents, and the school's stunned staff.

They were sadly separated when Trent's family moved shortly after graduation so he could attend Juilliard. Eventually,

Trent performed on the world's most famous stages, from Carnegie Hall to the Sydney Opera House. Teaching became Miss Aimée's passion. Many of her dancers received full scholarships to some of the most prestigious dance programs in the nation. Several even landed rolls on Broadway, while others toured with professional companies.

Isabelle, recognizing Aimée's gift, groomed her to run L'Esprit. When Isabelle's health deteriorated, Aimée became its executive and artistic director, dedicating her life to the students and studio she loved.

I hear Miss Aimée visits Trent regularly, but it's usually a trip connected with a national dance competition. In spite of his begging, Aimée won't leave L'Esprit, and she can't ask him to give up his dreams.

Their relationship, like a choreographed masterpiece that never found the spotlight, remains the studio's hot topic. Many of the moms hang out in L'Esprit's halls longer than usual whenever Trent's around, to sneak admiring glances at his tall, well-toned body, raven black hair, and dark eyes. With his classic good looks and Hollywood smile, posters of him advertising the Dance Intensive disappear at a staggering rate.

Everyone agrees he moves like no other male dancer they've ever seen. Jarrell admires his athleticism and showmanship; most girls simply appreciate the view. Brooke and I had the good sense to blush when C.C. boldly confided, "I'd watch the man sleep if I could. Anyone would have to be blind not to love looking at him, whether he's moving or standing still." My natural curiosity begs to see Miss Aimée and Trent together.

I shut off the shower as two droplets dance a pas de deux on the glass doors. They bounce back and forth off of each other before finally melding into one. *Like A.J. and Daniella. Are Aimée and Trent destined to do the same?*

At exactly 6:30 a.m. C.C.'s flashy, red convertible—a recent gift from her grandfather Bailey—quietly purrs in our driveway. As assistant teachers, our trio is expected to arrive early and help with check-in. With a quick note scribbled to my parents, I grab my bag and quietly let myself out the door. Brooke, half-asleep, gives a limp wave from the passenger seat.

"Brooke, are you feeling okay? You look a little out of it."

"I'm just tired."

"You're squinting," C.C. accuses. "Do your eyes hurt? Do you have one of those nasty headaches again?"

"Maybe a slight one, but I'm fine. No need to fret." She perks herself up. "Ladies, are you ready to jump and jive?"

"To boogie woogie," C.C. says.

"To rock and roll!" I add.

C.C. turns on the radio and immediately sings along, but when Brooke closes her eyes and turns her head away, C.C. adjusts the volume. She gives me a distressed look through the rearview mirror. We're both relieved when a few miles later Brooke asks, "Can you turn up the radio? I love this song."

We sing the corny lyrics at the top of our lungs for the remainder of the drive.

At L'Esprit, C.C. swings the car into her favorite parking spot. We're surprised to see another vehicle already there. The studio's doors aren't scheduled to open for another hour. Because of Trent's notoriety, alumni always come back, and qualified dancers from the surrounding area are welcome to attend. As we haul our bags from C.C.'s trunk, I wince when I recognize the two dancers in the silver sports car, Whitney Ruthers and her sidekick Tia. I stupidly offer a polite wave, but they totally snub me.

"Who's that?" Brooke wants to know.

"Unbelievable! It's Whitney and Tia. Don't tell me we'll be stuck with them all day," C.C. says. She puts her protective arm around my shoulders and shoots them a *don't mess with us* glare.

The Intensive attracts at least one hundred of the top area high school and college level dancers. L'Esprit alone has over forty students in its Senior Level that are required to attend. This is definitely an advanced workshop, and based on what I've seen at B-BOP studios, Whitney and Tia will never be able to keep up. In fact, I'm surprised Whitney's even allowed to participate. Miss Aimée must have caved to Mrs. Ruthers' demand. When we approach the building, Mr. Stan greets us.

"How are my three favorite dancing queens this morning?" He beams as if we're his own granddaughters. Holding open the doors with a dramatic bow and sweep of his arm, he grandly announces, "Miss Aimée and the Lord of the Dance await your arrival."

With our own goofy interpretation, we perform an impromptu Irish jig. Mrs. Summers gives a quick wave as we rush through the lobby towards the grand staircase. I stop at the fountain.

"Libby, what are you doing?" C.C. asks.

"A wish for luck, one for each of us." I toss three shiny pennies into the fountain.

"With your talent, you don't need luck," she laughs and tugs my jacket, pulling me by my arm.

While we chase up the stairs, Mr. Stan purchases three of Mrs. Summers' prettiest pink carnations.

"Rose dear, wrap these for our three dancing divas."

"You're a sweet old man, Stanley." Mrs. Summers delicately packages each one.

"And while you're at it, get me a single long stem, red rose from the cooler."

"And who might that be for?" Her cheeks brighten.

"You my dear, who else?"

"Stanley, you're a treasure. Now back to work with you."

C.C., Brooke, and I enter the studio undetected. Trent trails Aimée like a lost puppy as she prepares for the influx of dancers. "I miss you so much, Aimée. You get more beautiful every day."

"I miss you, too, but maybe you need to have your vision checked."

"Seriously, Aimée. Why won't you move to New York?"

"Why don't you move to Chicago?"

"Why do we have the same discussion every time we're together? Don't you know the mere sight of you makes me dizzy?"

She trembles and shyly looks away, but his gaze does not stray. I imagine she wants nothing more than to run into his arms.

Slowly he saunters to her and says, "We'll continue this conversation tonight over dinner." She reacts with a sigh when his breath tickles her neck.

"Only if you promise to buy me dessert," she says.

"You, my one true love, will be dessert."

Aimée presses her hands to the desk, and our six knees melt with hers.

"That's hot!" C.C. whispers.

"I know. I think I'm ready for another shower," I say.

"Yeah, a cold one this time," Brooke laughs.

We stick our heads in our dance bags, pretending to be invisible until Trent approaches.

"If it isn't my favorite clowns from last year. This new one looks familiar. She must be goofy if she's hanging out with the likes of you two."

"No, she's much worse!" C.C. says.

"I think I'm still officially the most deranged. If you don't mind, I prefer to draw my own conclusions," Trent says.

"It's an honor to see you again, Mr. Michaels, I'm Libby

Nobleton. I took some of your classes at regionals last year."

"Oh that's right, I remember. You were a standout and the well-deserved winner of the best lyrical solo."

"Thank you, Mr. Michaels." I blush.

"Please, Libby. Mr. Michaels is my dad. You can call me Trent, or should I say 'Mr. Trent' for studio purposes."

Walking into the changing room, Aimée says, "Since I can attest that you are certifiably insane, you can call yourself whatever you want, at least until the little men in white coats show up with your straight jacket. I already placed the call."

"I'll go quietly if you'll come along," Trent says with a grin and a glint in his eyes.

If Miss Aimée isn't game, the look C.C. gives us says she'd willingly volunteer to take her place.

C.C., Brooke, and I lead the way to the reception area. As expected, many of the dancers' moms, hoping for an encounter with Trent, find it necessary to walk their daughters into the studio. He does his best to give the crowd what they want, mingling freely and even signing a few autographs. I admire how he works the room, accommodating everyone. In the midst of all the commotion, Trent looks at Miss Aimée longingly when he thinks others are unaware. Something tells me the extra-bright smile she flashes isn't just for the paying customers this morning.

Class starts promptly at nine. The dancers scream and clap wildly when Trent is introduced.

"Welcome to L'Esprit's Dance Intensive. You must all be devoted studio rats if you chose to spend a sunny Saturday here with me," Trent says.

The dancers politely continue to applaud when the three of us are called forward to assist. Except for their icy expressions, Whitney and Tia pretend to ignore us. They're two mean-spirited girls, but I know who my real friends are, and we're here to have fun and dance.

When the music begins, I'm transformed, submerged in the workshop and unaffected by Trent's celebrity. I dance with pure unsolicited joy while other dancers act outwardly desperate for his attention. The scantily dressed Whitney and Tia are the worst.

Trent naturally pays attention to every dancer and is generous with compliments and positive corrections. We love his outrageous approach to teaching, and the class moves at a wicked pace. He invents nicknames for each of us. C.C. is "Fireball," Brooke is "China Doll," and I'm "Libby Lu." Secretly, Whitney and Tia are appropriately dubbed "Thing 1" and "Thing 2."

We snicker when Tia asks, "Mr. Trent, do we have the correct bodylines? Could you maybe adjust my hips?"

When Whitney asks if instead of a double pirouette, can she do a triple, Jarrell practically laughs out loud, mouthing, "She can barely do a clean single."

"Could we rotate more often? We can't see!" they whine. Before Trent has a chance to respond, they both force their way to the front, taking advantage of his easygoing nature.

"You two don't take lessons regularly at L'Esprit, do you?" he asks.

"That's right," Whitney answers. "I told you, Tia, we'd get noticed," she whispers.

"You've definitely attended conventions and workshops before, right?"

"Of course!" Whitney rolls her eyes.

"Then I'm sure you won't mind following proper dance etiquette. Your questions are welcome, but endless interruptions are not. Please understand that I need the most advanced dancers in the front so others can study their lines. It's in your best interest to step back and pick up more details of the choreography. I promise we'll keep rotating, but don't push anyone out of their spot again, or I'll ask you to leave." Whitney and Tia begrudgingly move to the back of the room as I hide my smile.

Throughout the day, Trent keeps us working hard and laughing harder. Several dancers catch his eye as being well above average in their discipline: Brooke in ballet, C.C in the tap combinations, and Jarrell in jazz. During a break, I'm flattered when Miss Aimée tells me that no one captivated him the way I did in the lyrical piece, and that I artfully brought his choreography to life. Trent even said I reminded him of Miss Aimée when she was my age.

We're all having a great time except for Whitney and Tia, who are definitely in over their heads. When Miss Aimée announces the lunch break, against my friends' advice, I approach them. "Hi, do either of you want any extra help with the combinations?"

"Look, 'Lizard Breath' or 'Lulu' or whatever it is, all we need from you are directions to the bathroom."

Your usual charming selves, I see. "The bathrooms are just beyond the reception desk."

Without another word, the two turn and leave with their noses in the air.

C.C.'s and Brooke's *we told you so* looks couldn't have been any plainer had they been written across their faces with bold magic markers.

Instead of turning towards the reception area, Whitney pushes Tia in the opposite direction.

"Where are we going? The bathrooms are over here," Tia says.

"Don't you see it?" Whitney asks.

"See what?"

"The elevator."

"No way. I'm not getting on that thing!" Tia points to the written warning. "Look, the sign says it's off limits to students."

"A dare is a dare. I never took you for a chicken, Tia. I've got my digital camera. We'll snap a few pictures to prove to the kids at B-BOP that we were in the basement. Besides, I could use a cigarette, and maybe we'll even figure out a way to get 'Loser Libby' once and for all."

Tia smirks. "There's a nickname Mr. Trent didn't think of. But Whitney, is it worth the twenty bucks to ride the elevator and snoop around?"

"I never lose a bet of any size. You're not afraid, are you?"

"Aren't you?"

"You know none of that stuff they say about this place is true."

"Then why do so many people say it?"

"You ask too many dumb questions. It's just an elevator ride. We've been here for hours. Have you seen or heard anything strange?"

"No, but . . ."

"But nothing, the place isn't haunted. Now let's go!"

When classes resume, C.C. and I wonder why Brooke hasn't returned. Trent notices her absence, too.

"I see Things 1 and 2 opted out of the afternoon session, but it's a ballet class, and I'm counting on my China Doll. Where's the Prima?" he asks.

"Maybe she's in the dressing room. I'll go check, Mr. Trent."

"Thanks Fireball. Libby Lu, if you would lead the warm-up routine, I can make corrections." Honored, I take my place at the front of the barre. Soon, C.C. and Brooke return. Although Brooke looks pale, she insists she's fine and apologizes repeatedly for being late.

"Are you sure you're feeling okay?" Trent puts his arm around her.

"Much better now." She winks at C.C. and me.

Brooke steps up to assist and flawlessly demonstrates the bodylines that every ballet dancer dreams of attaining. The class continues uneventfully until she loses her technique during a sequence of pirouettes and fouettés that she usually masters. This time, I notice she's spotting her turns with her eyes closed. When she falls off balance, Trent catches her.

"If you don't fall once in a while, you're not trying hard enough. It happens to the best of us," Trent says.

"What's up with Brooke today?" I ask. "I've never seen her wobble in a turn before, let alone fall."

"It used to happen a lot when she was younger. Her headaches were extreme, but then they stopped, or at least I thought they did," C.C. says with a worried look.

Miss Aimée rushes forward when Brooke's eyes turn glassy, and the color drains from her face. "Maybe she's dehydrated. Do you feel light-headed, honey?"

Weakly, Brooke nods. Miss Aimée gently escorts her out of the studio, promising, "After some water and a few minutes of rest, she'll be as good as new."

Trent finishes the lesson. Within the hour, Brooke rejoins the group, definitely looking better.

"Are you sure you're alright?" C.C. and I nervously ask.

"I'm probably just tired. I didn't sleep much last night, and I'm battling one of my stupid headaches. I'm fine now."

Unconvinced, Trent insists that Brooke sit quietly during the musical theatre class. She reluctantly agrees. Taking her by the hand, he escorts her to a folding chair at the front of the studio. She mugs a flirty face for our benefit, and C.C. and I can't resist a hidden giggle. How nice it would be if she were faking her headache for Trent's attention. Midway through the class, Brooke convinces Trent to let her participate, and he finally gives in. Once the three of us are reunited, we act out the skits and pantomime the vocals. C.C. delights Trent with her hilarious rendition of Winifred, from the Disney movie *Hocus Pocus*, but the fun turns to horror when ear-piercing screams erupt in the hallway.

Dalton Enterprises, 1928

Everyone agrees. The project is charmed. The reconstruction of The Grand Dalton House proceeds beyond all expectations, well ahead of schedule and under budget. Unfortunately for Miss Winterset, things aren't running quite as smoothly. She's come to the conclusion that the famous Maxwell Doll is either an eccentric genius or a raving lunatic after he storms into the office unannounced, demanding to know who else has been commissioned to work on the statue. When A.J. assures him that he's the only artist considered even remotely worthy of the precious restoration, he breaks down in a torrent of tears.

With eyebrows raised and mouths agape, they listen to Mr. Doll's rambling litany of unnerving occurrences. "It restores itself! The marble that should be cold to the touch is impossibly warm and pliable. Its color becomes more vibrant every day. I want answers!"

"I want a drink," A.J. mumbles as he pours two calming bourbons from his private stock. Miss Winterset shocks A.J. further by adding a third glass and downing hers in one gulp.

As they politely usher Mr. Doll out of the office, A.J. smiles, comfortable with the premise that the statue might indeed have qualities beyond the artist's earthly experience.

Glissade (glee-SAD) Glide. The dancer's working foot slides along the floor lifting to a strong point slightly off the ground. The opposite foot pushes away from the floor so that both knees are straight and both feet are pointed for a moment before landing in a closed demi-plié fifth position. The dancer's step floats on air.

Chapter Fifteen

Could this be one of Trent's zany tricks? His classes are famous for being out of the ordinary, and after all, we were performing Bette Midler's version of "I Put a Spell on You." Unfortunately, Trent appears as perplexed as the rest of us while the deafening shrieks grow louder.

Miss Aimée flies into the hallway in time to catch Whitney and Tia fleeing from the forbidden elevator. "Girls, what in heaven's name are you doing out here? Where have you been?" Miss Aimée sharply points to the ancient contraption. "Did I just see you get off that elevator? Stop screaming this minute! Tell me what's wrong!"

The two girls scramble over each other to get as far away from its closing door as possible. Not nearly as brave as before the ride, Whitney gasps, "Tia and I are leaving right now. This place should be shut down. It's possessed!"

"Why? What are you talking about?"

Whitney, close to a complete meltdown, fights tears. "Everything went dark, and then a menacing voice told us to leave."

Tia sobs, "It told us, *'Get out!'*"

"Girls, you're not making any sense."

"Something was after us down there. We don't know who or what it was, and we don't care. We just want out *this instant!*"

"Are you sure it wasn't someone playing a trick on you? You realize you had no business going where you don't belong, and once again you've disrupted the entire workshop. I don't know what you think you're doing, but I can promise you that you're absolutely safe. Nothing here would harm you."

Whitney and Tia look at each other. "Come on, Tia! If Libby and her friends were up to something, they'll regret it. Let's go! Trent Michaels or not, this workshop has been a big waste of time. Our place is at Ballerinas On Parade where we're appreciated. Besides, our studio isn't scary like this one. You'll be hearing from our parents, and they'll be expecting a full refund!"

The hyper girls scoop up their belongings and race through the reception area. Miss Aimée turns to the nosy students gathered in the hall. "Okay, kids. Back inside. It was probably just a harmless prank by Whitney and Tia."

"Yeah, a last-ditch effort for Trent's attention, I bet. They're pathetic!" Jarrell says.

Miss Aimée appears unsettled, and I wonder if it's more than rumors and phone calls she dreads. Does she suspect that something stirs within the walls of her beloved studio? The thought gives me chills. When Miss Aimée declares, "Never again. I'm done! Thing 1 and Thing 2 are officially blacklisted, banished forever," C.C. voices what we're all thinking. "Outstanding! It's about time."

A thunderous applause erupts when the afternoon session ends. Everyone immediately surrounds Trent wanting hugs and pictures. He graciously signs each request for an autograph and poses until the last camera is put away. After an hour, the studio empties out except for us.

Starving, we plan to hit the '50s-themed diner down the block where the servers sing and dance costumed like Elvis, Marilyn Monroe, and other celebrities.

"A cheeseburger, malt, and fries sound good to me!" I confess. "Too bad Jarrell had to take off. Do you think Mr. Trent and Miss Aimée would want to join us?"

"Did you really ask that? You saw those two this morning. They haven't been alone in months. I'm sure they have big plans of their own," C.C. says, "and they don't include three teenage girls tagging along."

"You're probably right. Let's just say goodbye."

Before we leave, Aimée and Trent catch us off guard by asking if we know anything about Whitney and Tia's escapade. We truthfully deny any knowledge of the bizarre event. Miss Aimée looks unsettled but shakes it off.

"You girls were outstanding today."

"Thanks, Miss Aimée. We loved every minute."

"I want to show my appreciation for your assistance," Trent says. "I have some influence around here. Maybe I can convince your teacher to let me choreograph a trio for you."

Our shrieks jolt the couple. "Are you serious, Mr. Trent? That's incredible!"

"We'll talk about it later. Right now all that matters is that you're feeling better, Brooke." Trent tweaks her chin. "It's been a long day; you three should get going." He politely guides us through L'Esprit's glass door.

"Have fun sleeping over at Libby's house tonight, girls," Miss Aimée says.

"I'll never understand why they call it a sleepover. Aren't they more like party-all-nighters?" Trent jokes.

"It's a girl thing. Try not to get into any trouble," Miss Aimée warns us over her shoulder.

"We'll have fun, but staying out of trouble is another matter," C.C. laughs. "Miss Aimée should follow her own good advice," she quietly mumbles.

We descend the grand staircase and are met by Mr. Stan, who hands us each a fresh carnation. "Of all the flowers that dance in the garden of L'Esprit, you three are the loveliest."

"At least the most fragrant. We've been sweating all day," C.C. quips.

Touched by his thoughtfulness, I thank him with a spontaneous kiss on the cheek. "Since when did you become such a poet, Mr. Stan?"

"Since my sweetheart, Rose, started reading poetry to me during my coffee breaks."

"We want to say goodnight to her. Is she still here?" Brooke asks.

"No, girls, she's left for the evening, but we have a luncheon date tomorrow."

"Way to go, Mr. Stan! Seems like love's in the air tonight," I say.

While walking to the restaurant, we fantasize about the growing romances and speculate about Whitney and Tia's strange shenanigan. "How weird was that ordeal, Brooke?" C.C. asks.

"Nothing surprises me when it comes to those two," she says.

"Do you suppose they actually did see something scary?" I ask.

"It couldn't have been anything worse than their own reflections," C.C. says. A guilty laugh escapes us.

"But don't forget," Brooke reminds C.C., "we've been spooked a few times ourselves throughout the years, especially when we've been there alone at night."

"Well, wouldn't anyone? It's an old building," I say. "Come

on, you saw how desperate they were for Trent's attention. They couldn't do it with dance, so they tried to get noticed any way they could. I'll bet they hoped to be rescued by him instead of Miss Aimée. I would love to have seen their faces when they got busted."

Once inside the restaurant, the aroma that greets us chases away everything except thoughts of stuffing our faces. Although tired from our exhausting day, we get a second wind and join the singing and dancing staff. The night manager offers us jobs on the spot, impressed by our ability to publicly make fools of ourselves. More interested in food than gainful employment, we finish dinner and head back to C.C.'s car.

As we drive away from L'Esprit's parking lot dimly lit by a scattering of street lamps, I glance up at the shadowy silhouette of a couple in an embrace. They seamlessly glide by the second-floor windows.

"Did you see them?" I ask.

"See who?" Brooke wonders.

"The man and woman dancing."

"Dancing where?" C.C. slows the car to look.

"Upstairs in the studio." I point.

"It must be Aimée and Trent," C.C. says. "I didn't see anything, but it had to be them."

We circle the block to get a better look, but on the second trip around, the pair has vanished. We continue our debate until we see Trent and Aimée exiting a trendy Italian restaurant hand in hand.

"Libby, it must be a night for wild thoughts. Yours seem to be getting the best of you, too," C.C. says. "There's no way that could have been them!"

"I'm telling you, I saw two people dancing in the shadows!"

"Maybe it was Mr. Stan and Mrs. Summers. He does have the

master keys to every business in the building," Brooke suggests.

"But Mr. Stan said she left for the evening," C.C. says.

"Yeah, you're right." I shrug. "And Mr. Stan shuffles when he walks. I'm guessing he's not the smoothest dancer either."

For the remainder of the drive, Brooke and C.C. gossip about Trent wanting to devour Aimée, his one true love, for dessert while I sink further into the back seat, the dancing phantoms gliding stubbornly through my mind.

Déboulé (day-boo-LAY) Rolling. The dancer executes a series of quick turns that spin, traveling forward in a single direction. The step rolls like a ball.

Chapter Sixteen

Pulling onto my street, Brooke nudges, "Libby, are you awake back there? You've been so quiet, we thought you fell asleep."

"No. I'm wide awake. My thoughts keep rolling in circles."

"Come on. You're not stuck on what you think you saw at L'Esprit, are you?" C.C. asks.

"I didn't think it, you guys, I saw it! And I know I'm not the only one who's ever seen or heard things."

"What do you mean?" Brooke asks.

"Just what I said. When my dad took me to his office, I read some articles in the old society pages. One Russian ballerina performing at the Grand Dalton House Theatre in the 1930s claimed the statue resembling Daniella scared her away."

"We've heard that rumor before. You mean to tell us it's true?"

"She said it singled her out and spoke her name. It upset her so badly she left in the middle of a performance and refused to dance at the Dalton House ever again."

"That's insane! She probably had to leave the company because she was pregnant."

100

"C.C.!"

"It's just too outrageous. Where's the proof?"

"Statue or no statue, there's always been flickering lights, and what about the piano music? Once, I even asked Miss Aimée if I was crazy. She hesitated and smiled oddly before responding, 'If you're crazy, then so am I.' I suspect she knows something about all the weird stuff that goes on there."

"And now we're going to have to put unexplained floating apparitions on the list," Brooke adds.

"Let's get inside before we worry my parents. They'll be wondering why we're sitting out here in the driveway. Be prepared. My mom will want to know everything about our day. *Every last detail.*"

"About the spinning, shadowy figures in the window, too?" Brooke asks.

"I think we better keep that to ourselves, at least for now. I'm warning you guys; my parents might pull me out of L'Esprit if they sense something's wrong."

After we regale my parents with the highlights of the day, Mom surprises each of us with a black and white photo taken at L'Esprit's recent open house. By using a special photographic technique, our pointe shoes appear in our favorite color. In Brooke's photo, she holds the most amazing penché wearing bright, rose petal pink pointe shoes.

"This is for you, Brooke. I love the height and extension of your back leg. And here you go, C.C. You're in flaming red shoes, blazing across the floor in a flawless grand jeté."

Before she hands me mine, Mom says, "Your picture has a grainy quality, Libby. There's a distorted image I can't explain."

"It looks like there's a shadow following you, honey," says Dad.

My radar shoots to high alert. *More shadows.* I can tell by their quizzical expressions that Brooke and C.C. pick up on it, too.

"But, I did capture you in the prettiest arabesque wearing powder blue shoes that match a cloudless summer sky," Mom says.

"Mom, these are amazing!" The three of us rush to hug her, touched by her thoughtfulness.

Before we go upstairs, I ask dad for the file on L'Esprit that rests in plain view on the kitchen counter. He reluctantly hands over the articles. "Now, Elizabeth"—Dad never calls me that unless he means business—"there's a lot of information in here. And there's even more boxed in my office. Remember how upset you were the last time."

"I know, Dad, but the fire took place a long time ago, and we still want to understand the full story. I wish you would have brought everything home."

"Libz, some of the events in Daniella's life are very sad, worse than anything you might have thought possible."

"What could be worse than a fiery death?"

Dad looks at Mom. "Oh, things like an old forgotten statue and the possibility of the place being haunted."

Not liking the direction of the conversation, I panic. "That's nonsense! Everybody loves L'Esprit."

Mom's attention turns to my friends. "You two have been there a long time. Have you ever experienced anything out of the ordinary?"

C.C. says, "Just the usual flickering lights and . . ."

My eyes scream *shut up*. "That's no big deal," I interrupt. "An old building's bound to have a few friendly ghosts." Grabbing C.C. and Brooke, I hurry them upstairs.

As we leave the room, my parent's whispers follow. *Haunted or not, I'm staying. I'd rather die than leave L'Esprit. Heaven forbid they send me to B-BOP or Dance to the Max.*

With the articles spread across my bed, we examine them

closely, sifting carefully through each one. Brooke stumbles upon a picture that commands our full interest. "I found something! Here's a clear photo of the statue of L'Esprit. It was spectacular." We crowd together for a closer view. "It looks exactly like Daniella!"

"I'd give anything to see the sculpture. I wish I knew what happened to it."

"Says here, Libby, it was brought to the United States from France by Andrew James Dalton and restored by an artist named Maxwell Doll. Evidently, it stood in L'Esprit's lobby for over a decade, but after Mr. Dalton's death, it just disappeared."

"I recognize that other name. Isn't that the same guy who painted the portraits of Daniella and Isabelle?"

"Good call, Brooke. You're right! The article says the statue taunted the artist, too. He said the thing practically repaired itself."

"Like it had special powers or something?" I ask.

"Personally, I think Mr. Doll spent too much time inhaling paint fumes."

"C.C.!" I laugh. "It could be true."

"Let's review our continuously snowballing story," C.C. says. "Your picture's wispy image, a piano that plays by itself, unexplained dancing shadows, and a vanishing statue that supposedly talks. Did I leave anything out?"

"Don't forget the flickering lights. We've all seen them," Brooke adds.

"And the strange reflections in the mirror—you know, the one I saw on my first day of class."

"Oh that's right, Libby, your first class. You did mention it. I almost forgot."

"What about the scent of perfume or lilacs? The fragrance is almost overwhelming at times."

"What? That's a new one," C.C. says.

"I couldn't be certain, but I've noticed it so often that I believe it's real. Don't forget, Whitney and Tia were certainly running from something today."

"Miss Aimée told me they were on the elevator," Brooke says.

"Are they nuts? I wouldn't go near that thing. You know that's where Daniella died," I say.

"We all know it," Brooke says, "but it's never talked about."

"I think it's time we take our own ride to the basement," C.C. decides. "I bet the storage room is filled with a ton of interesting things that might hold clues to L'Esprit's mysteries."

"It's a lovely plan," Brooke agrees, "except for the fact that we're not allowed on the elevator. Isn't the basement clearly off limits? No one's supposed to go down there!"

"Exactly my point, but why not?" C.C. wonders.

"Wouldn't it be simpler to just talk to Miss Aimée?" I ask.

"Don't get us wrong, Libby. We love Miss Aimée, but whenever we ask too many personal questions about L'Esprit, she gets tight-lipped—like she's hiding something."

"What would she want to hide—and why?"

"Trust us! She likes to keep the past in the past. I think if we want answers, we'll have to find them on our own. And here's breaking news. I've been in the basement before," C.C. says.

"You're kidding! When?"

"When I helped Miss Aimée and Mr. Stan carry costumes to storage. I saw a bunch of old junk down there, and I even remember a trunk marked DDD. I never gave it much thought, but with everything going on lately, maybe we should check it out. I don't think there's anything to be afraid of unless cobwebs and dust bunnies intimidate you. There's only one problem. We don't have the key to the storage room."

Just when the three of us agree it would be worth the risk, I catch the headline of another *Tribune* article from 1920. "Brooke, C.C., look! This must be what my dad meant!"

PRIMA PARALYZED
Tragic Accident and Failed Surgery Ends
City's Beloved Ballerina's Dance Career

Prima ballerina, Daniella Devereaux Dalton, accidentally injured during a rehearsal has failed to regain use of her legs after emergency surgery. Her new partner Sergé Lorenti, unfamiliar with the set at the Grand Dalton House Theatre, traveled too far downstage where he lost his footing. "Miss Daniella's hips slipped from my hands during a complicated lift. It was a poor decision on my part. I should never have been so close to the edge. I'll regret it the rest of my life."

Daniella fell from Lorenti's hold and hit her lower back on the stage before dropping five feet into the orchestra pit. Doctors at Chicago's Saint Claire Hospital worked through the night to repair the shattered vertebrae that severed nerves in her spinal column. Neurosurgeon, Dr. Walter Simms tearfully stated, "Nothing more can be done, the damage is irreversible. Tragically, she will never walk again."

The career-ending accident of our city's premier dancer is a loss felt around the world. The outpouring of love and support has been remarkably uplifting. Daniella reportedly holds

> *no anger towards Sergé, accepting the injury as
> part of God's plan for her life.*
>
> *Her husband, Andrew James Dalton,
> although grief-stricken by the event, tells the
> Tribune that even though his wife is in severe
> pain, she remains strong. "Daniella asks the
> people of Chicago and the world not to pity her.
> She dances in her heart and will continue to do
> so. As soon as her strength returns, she plans to
> resume her teaching schedule at L'Esprit."*

"My dad was right. This is worse than anything I've ever imagined."

"Us too, Libby," C.C. says.

"None of us dare to dream of our lives without dance—let alone the ability to walk," Brooke says.

"I'll bet it was her capacity to overcome tragedy that kept L'Esprit going," I say. "She must have been an incredibly strong person."

"If not for Daniella's inner strength, L'Esprit could have closed its doors forever, and the three of us may have never met," C.C. says.

"I feel like her life, lived nearly a century ago, is connecting with ours in this very moment," I say.

With thoughts of the prima spinning in our heads, I turn off the lights. We crawl beneath the covers and whisper into the early hours of the morning. Before I fall asleep, I offer a prayer of peace for the prima and wonder how God could have allowed her to suffer such a loss. I shudder and worry that Miss Aimée's studio might actually be haunted.

As the moonlight rolls across our sleeping faces, bittersweet images of Daniella dance with us in our dreams.

Dalton Enterprises, 1928

"Miss Winterset, get Isabelle Devereaux on the phone s´il vous plaît."

"Of course, Mr. Dalton, right away." She dials the number and blushes, thinking about her charming boss. Rather pathetically she confesses to herself, if he asked me in French to walk his dog, I'd do it in a heartbeat.

"Miss Devereaux is on the line, Mr. Dalton."

Reaching for the phone, A.J. realizes that if Isabelle chooses to accept this position, she will have impossibly big shoes to fill. Dani's already a legend. Her students will accept nothing less than the same loving guidance and inspiration that she showered on them with total generosity.

Admittedly, Isabelle (although equally beautiful) is not as gifted a dancer as Dani, and her disposition by all accounts is certainly not as sunny. Yet, she's his only logical choice to direct the dance studio. Dani loved her as dearly as a sister. He will force himself to do the same.

As if testing his resolve, her sultry voice involuntarily causes his stomach to nervously tighten.

"Hello, A.J., I've been waiting for your call."

Plié (plee-AY) To bend. A subtle lowering of a dancer's position through the bending of the knees that may be done *grand*, full bending, or *demi*, half bending. This exercise helps the joints and muscles become soft and pliable and the tendons flexible and elastic, while improving the dancer's sense of balance. Pliés enable the dancer to spring upward on jumps and leaps and protectively cushion her landing.

Chapter Seventeen

C.C., *Brooke, and I return* to our normal routine of attending high school classes together each day. The recent breakup of Whitney and Brad is all anyone talks about in the halls and on Facebook. Brad dumped her during the lunch hour, and Whitney's screeching hysterics annoyed everybody in the cafeteria. The epic scene finally ended when her fork full of mashed potatoes aimed at Brad's head splattered on a nearby teacher. Both were immediately escorted to the principal's office, with Whitney sobbing and Brad high-fiving his buddies. The YouTube video from someone's camera phone showed up on the Internet, getting thousands of hits. God help the guilty party who posted it, because Mrs. Ruthers is on the warpath and threatens to sue.

Although our school day is a drama a minute, the studio has been unusually quiet. At night, we continue to assistant teach and train in our dance classes while cramming homework in between. We search the windows every evening before leaving the studio, but no shadows dance in the dark, nor do the lights flicker even a single time. If not for the occasional scent of lilacs that follows only me, I might believe the past events were nothing more than my fanciful mind at play.

Just after three on a Saturday afternoon, L'Esprit's classes finish, and dancers scramble to catch rides home. Most rush down the stairway and scurry for the main entrance, eager to be free for the rest of the day. Wisely, Mr. Stan, avoiding what he and Mrs. Summers comically refer to as the "Saturday Stampede," takes cover behind the open doors as his polite reminder not to run falls on deaf ears. Miss Aimée also appears to be in quite a rush. Her black leather appointment book lays wide open on the reception desk. In bright red ink, she's scheduled a 3:30 haircut at a salon across town. In even larger print, enclosed in a circle is marked "Dinner at 8 with Trent."

"Girls, I need a big favor."

"Sure, Miss Aimée, anything!" Brooke says.

"Miss Megan, who usually locks up for me on the weekends, went home sick this morning, and I can't be late for my appointment today. Would you three be willing to pick up in the studios and lock the doors on your way out? It would be a tremendous help."

"Of course, we will! No problem. You know how much we love hanging out here, but we'll need the keys," C.C. says, the gears in her head already shifting.

"I'll give you mine," Miss Aimée says. "I know I can trust you three not to lose them. Thanks girls, you're lifesavers. Take as long you need." She tosses her keys to C.C and hurries away.

"Have a nice time tonight!" I shout.

"Yeah, be sure to give Mr. Trent a big squeeze from each of us!" C.C. says with a sassy grin.

While Brooke and I are lost in our romantic thoughts about the couple, C.C. double-checks to make sure Aimée's left the building. When certain she's gone, C.C. says, "Okay girls, opportunity's knocking."

She dangles Miss Aimée's keys in front of our faces. "These aren't just the studio keys. I also hold in the palm of my sweaty little hand our ticket to the basement storage room. Get my drift? It's now or never."

"C.C., what if we get caught?" Brooke asks.

"Who's gonna know? We're not doing anything wrong. We're just taking an innocent look around. After all, Miss Aimée wouldn't have given us the keys if she absolutely didn't want us to go down there. What's the big deal?"

"No, she gave us the keys trusting we wouldn't go there."

"Alright, Libby, but this chance may never come again."

"Okay," I reluctantly agree.

"No way!" Brooke says. "Are you two out of your minds?"

"C'mon, you know how many strange things have gone on here. Libby's sane and sensible! You read those articles, too. Don't you want to help her? Besides, you're as curious as we are!"

"Here, Brooke, if you're worried about getting caught, let's pick up some of these empty costume boxes. If we bump into Mr. Stan, we'll say we're storing them for Miss Aimée, and if that doesn't work, we'll just tell the truth—it's all C.C.'s big idea!"

"Aren't you the clever one?" C.C. throws me a devious grin along with an empty carton.

"I'll do it, but don't say I didn't warn you two if anything bad happens," Brooke says.

"That's the attitude. What could go wrong anyway? It's nothing more than an elevator ride into a basement filled with a bunch of old stuff," C.C. says.

We load our arms and make our way to the elevator, certain that our deception is an ingenious, foolproof plan.

"I'm glad the lights in the hall are working today. Sometimes it's as if someone's constantly flipping the switch," Brooke says. "According to Miss Aimée, Mr. Stan's attempts to repair them always failed miserably. Even the electricians he hired couldn't pinpoint the problem."

"I guess it's another one of L'Esprit's unsolved mysteries," C.C. says.

As we near the elevator, my knees weaken with every step. *I'm going to ride the creaky contraption—the actual space that had become Daniella's tomb nearly three quarters of a century ago.* I can tell Brooke's nervous too, but C.C. doesn't appear to be the least bit hesitant. I react strangely when I touch the black, metal door. Expecting fear, I'm instead filled with anger. I want to kick the old accordion-styled gate with all my might. C.C. puts her weight into pulling it open. Not exactly welcoming, the shabby, poorly lit space is drafty and much smaller than I expected. We step inside, and I keep myself distracted by reminding my friends about the other articles I've read.

"If I remember correctly, this elevator, the marble staircase, and the basement are the only parts of the Dalton House's original structure. Everything else was rebuilt after the 1926 fire."

Brooke tugs the heavy gate closed with a grunt. When I push the worn button marked "B," the monstrous thing awakens. Heavy gears grind loudly, and the floor moves with a jolt. *Please don't let the cable snap and send us crashing to the basement.* We stand awkwardly squeezed together with our oversized cardboard boxes as the elevator slowly chugs downward. The chipped brick wall of its shaft slides by in slow motion, and we edge closer to the forbidden. The snail's pace of our descent causes my chest to tighten. *Is this how Daniella felt? What's wrong with me? I can't breathe!*

"Libby, are you alright? You look sick," Brooke says.

Perspiration beads on my upper lip. "I think I must be claustrophobic. I hate this creepy thing! Can't you make it go any faster?"

"It's ancient, Libby. This is as fast as it goes," Brooke says.

"Does anyone else feel . . . feel hot?" I stutter.

"Libby, your forehead's dripping wet." C.C. comforts me while Brooke continues banging on the button.

Unable to speak, I clench my throat. The boxes tumble to the floor. My legs collapse, and I smack my head on the gated door.

"We're almost there!" Brooke braces herself while working to hold me up.

"Hang on!" C.C. screams.

"Libby, what's wrong? Answer us!" Brooke begs, tears in her eyes. "C.C., help her. Do something!"

An unfamiliar voice fuses with their cries, "Help me. Please get me out!"

Chassé (sha-SAY) Chased. A step in which one foot replaces another, literally chasing the first foot out of its original position. A chassé is executed forwards, backwards, side-to-side, or turning in the air usually at a fast tempo. A dancer's feet move quickly as if being pursued.

Chapter Eighteen

hen we finally reach the basement, Brooke and C.C. struggle to open the gate. Coughing, I fall to my hands and knees and fight to catch my breath. C.C. pounds me between the shoulder blades, and I drop facedown on the cold cement, damp with perspiration.

"Libby, talk to us!"

"C.C., should I run and get Mr. Stan? Should we call 911?"

Before C.C. can answer, I breathe freely and roll over onto my back. Inhaling the cool musty air, my lungs relax. Dazed, I take a few minutes to calm myself. "I swear I was fine one second and the next, I wasn't."

"Are you sure you're okay, Libby?"

"Can you get up? Are you dizzy?" C.C. helps me to my feet. I stand feeling absolutely normal except for the lump forming on my head.

"I don't know what came over me. I'm fine now, but for some reason my throat felt scorched, like it was on fire."

"That's awful!" Brooke winces.

"Maybe you *are* claustrophobic!" C.C. says.

"Maybe, but I've never been before. If it's all the same to you guys, I'd rather take the stairs when we're finished down here."

"You mean you want to stay? Shouldn't we just go? I knew this was a bad idea. I used to think we were safe anywhere in this place, but today I'm not so positive," Brooke says.

"You're sure you want to do this, Libby? Maybe this wasn't such a brilliant idea after all," C.C. admits.

"No, I'm fine. I think Daniella needs us."

"Libby, what are you talking about? How hard did you hit your head?"

"I know it sounds odd, but just when I thought I was going to black out, I heard a faint voice pleading for help."

"That was us, Libby!"

"No, Brooke, it was someone else's voice. Trust me. I'm not making this up!"

"We didn't say you were, but you're scaring us. How can we help someone who's dead?"

"I don't know the answer, but I won't stop now!"

"Alright. I'm in," Brooke says. "But so help me, if there's one more incident, I'm out of here—with or without you two."

"Let's get moving before we lose our nerve." C.C. motions us forward.

We pile the boxes to the side. Intent on scoping out the basement, I brush myself off and take the lead. Along the way, I turn on each light by tugging every string that hangs from the ceiling. Hitting a comfortable stride, we hike down the long, narrow corridor. I push the sickening elevator ride out of my mind knowing that my parents will never let me come back if they think I'm in danger—real or imagined. They're already upset by the weird image in my photo. If they find out about the dancing shadows and today's freakish incident, it might push them over the edge.

C.C. and Brooke trail behind whispering to each other.

"Do you get what just happened to her?"

"No, do you, Brooke?"

"Maybe this place really is haunted."

"Maybe it is, but why Libby? We've been dancing here for years."

"I hate to remind you, C.C., but remember that I started seeing blurry images in the mirror when I was six."

"That's right, I almost forgot. Everybody was convinced your nasty headaches made you see things."

"What are you two whispering about?" I ask.

"If it makes you feel any better, Libby, I used to see a strange reflection, too. I would move aside just to have my own mirror space. After a while, it simply stopped."

"Honestly? You too, Brooke?" I ask.

"Don't worry. Miss Aimée's been around forever. She grew up here, and she wouldn't stay if it wasn't safe," C.C. insists.

We quicken our pace.

"Wouldn't it be cool if these walls could talk?" Brooke says.

"That *would* be nice. They could tell us where to look for clues," C.C. says.

"Some of Daniella's forgotten belongings have to be hidden somewhere," I say with determination.

"I'm telling you guys, I saw all sorts of things covered with tarps. Anything could be stashed down here," C.C. says. "Even a dead body."

"Knock it off, C.C.! We're frightened enough," Brooke says.

Bravely, we forge ahead. Unfortunately, the basement becomes dingier and grayer the further we journey. Cobwebs hang in practically every corner of the ceiling. Even the basement's musty odor grows on me after a while. As the three of us walk single file, we each note the stage props and theatre backdrops lining both sides of the walls. The basement is deep underground, and the passage stretches endlessly. With no natural lighting, I'm thankful that each bulb is in working order. When I give the next cord a good yank, I accidentally pull the string off the chain. The bulb makes a loud pop, causing us to flinch.

When the light eerily flickers, Brooke asks, "Libby, what was that?"

"Nothing," I say. "I just pulled too hard on the cord." I place the broken string on the canvas tarp that covers a wooden table next to me.

"We better tie this string on, or someone will figure out that we've been down here," Brooke says, maneuvering her way into the middle of the pack.

"Okay, we will! But let's get to the storage room first before we change our minds," I say.

Pointing ahead, Brooke discovers at least fifty ballet costumes hanging on brass hooks, each completely protected in a thick, opaque, plastic garment bag. She stops to ask, "Who do you suppose wore these?"

"Probably dancers from L'Esprit's original productions," C.C. says.

"I wonder if years from now someone will be admiring our old costumes," Brooke says.

"Maybe your tutus, but I'll still be wearing mine for sold out performances," C.C. quips.

"You mean as an aging circus performer, don't you?" I mock.

"Oh, very funny," C.C. says, "and this coming from someone I call my friend."

We come upon dozens of pairs of frayed pointe shoes that line dusty shelves. I speculate about their times on stage, compelled to touch each of them. We see stage sets, fascinated by the designs that are virtually storyboards of distant productions. As I study the old scenery, I observe a carved forest and behind it a palace with golden sconces adorning its two-dimensional walls. These pieces that once graced the stage of the Grand Dalton House Theatre now stand alone, neatly stacked and completely abandoned. Everything else we pass remains hidden under heavy tarps. We peek under a few.

"Just more props, sets, and old lighting equipment," C.C. reports, unimpressed.

As the passage angles around the last corner, we see the storage room that C.C. initially described. She unlocks the door, and we split into three separate directions. Our eyes adjust slowly to the soft glow overhead, and we immediately try to make sense of the numerous containers stacked about the room. The first lid we open instantly excites C.C. and Brooke. It's filled with brightly colored boas and ridiculously oversized plumed hats. Like little girls playing dress-up in their mother's closet, my friends can't resist wrapping the boas around their shoulders, delighted with their find. When a tiny mouse scurries from a small, chewed-up corner of the box, their frenzied screams end their imaginary playtime.

"Was that a rat?" Brooke cries, clinging to C.C.

"No, just a tiny mouse," I laugh as they whip off the offending boas and frantically spit feathers. Their flailing arms send the suspended light bulbs swinging in circles.

We eventually return to the task at hand. Which container might hold some answers, we don't know, and I doubt if we'll ever be able to sift through them all. I'd hate to miss something important. As we complete our inspection, we arduously push each box back into place. Between the curled centipedes, dead spiders, cobwebs, and constant fear of another mouse, it becomes an even more difficult challenge.

"Finally! Here's something interesting," Brooke says.

"Hallelujah!" C.C. says. "What is it?"

"It's a bunch of photographs, some older than others."

"How can you tell?" I move closer.

"The styles and the quality of the pictures. Most are badly faded."

"What are they of? Do we have any idea who these people are or how they're related to Daniella and L'Esprit?" C.C. crowds tighter, snatching a few from Brooke's hand.

"I think a lot of them are the same people we've already seen on the history wall upstairs," Brooke says. As I examine the photographs, I notice they have something uniquely in common. Besides belonging to different decades, these snapshots definitely have a single thread tying them together.

"Brooke, C.C., look! It's not the people in them. It's something else. Can you see it?"

C.C. takes the pictures and feverishly flips through the stack. "I don't get it!" C.C. says. "What am I missing?"

"Look again. Somewhere in every photo, you can see the statue of L'Esprit. Here it's in the background of the lobby. In this one, it's very small and off center."

"You're right, the famous vanishing statue." Brooke hands me a more detailed photo. "Like the one in the *Tribune* article you showed us, the sculpture looks exactly like Daniella. Her face is angelic."

"It looks like she's trapped in the block of marble. Why aren't her legs finished?"

"I'm not sure. Could it be because Daniella lost the use of her legs? Maybe it's meant to represent her heavenly spirit and her earthly body."

"That's a pretty deep thought, Libby. You could be right."

"Why are these pictures hidden in the basement?" Brooke asks. "Why aren't more of them on display?"

"I say we keep digging. We're bound to find something else," C.C. says.

Box after box reveals subtle clues about the history of L'Esprit. We're pleased to find the original blueprints of the building that date back to the spring of 1915, as well as those drawn up for its renovation after the fire. Old programs from Daniella's performances rest among the withered, handwritten customer lists from 1928. The name "Sarah Summers" immediately jumps off the page. *Was she somehow related to our Mrs. Summers?*

As we continue the search, C.C. opens another carton containing several bundles of brown edged thank you notes. All are addressed to Andrew James Dalton and are tied together with pale blue ribbon. After Daniella's untimely death, he evidently offered scholarships in her name to young dancers unable to afford professional training. Touched, we read some of the outpouring of appreciation from the many students and even recognize a young woman who went on to have an exceptional solo career.

> *Dear Mr. Dalton,*
> *You are as kind as you are generous. To be the recipient of the Daniella Devereaux Dance Scholarship is an honor beyond description. Your wife's legacy inspires me every day, and her example will always guide me. Thank you for this life-changing gift. Because of you, I can follow my life's passion for dance.*
> *Sincerely,*
> *Melissa Montegomery*

Although grateful to learn something of the early days of the studio and its founder, all we have to show for nearly an hour's work are the photographs of the statue and perhaps the name Summers.

We make our way back somewhat discouraged. I wonder what I'm doing down here. What did I expect to find anyway? My steps quicken when I realize C.C. and Brooke have managed to get several feet in front of me. I race to catch up, passing the spot where I first laid the broken string.

In one alarming instant, the basement falls into absolute darkness. I can't scream. My feet become heavy, as if stuck in quicksand, and my stomach sinks like a rock. C.C. and Brooke scream wildly as if chased by demons. The rustle of dead leaves caught in a howling whirlwind rushes at me. I clench my teeth and hold my breath. A forceful gust of cold wind chases and tosses me aside. Clearly, the same stranger's voice from the elevator whispers, "Libbeeeee. Stop!"

Entrechat (ahn-truh-SHAH) Interwoven. A movement in which the dancer jumps into the air, beating her feet while rapidly crossing her legs in front and back of each other. Dancers' motions are braided together and connected with quickness and strength.

Chapter Nineteen

*I*mprisoned in blackness, my prayers are answered when electricity sizzles overhead, casting fleeting moments of light. I exhale with newfound courage, "Who's there? What do you want?"

The driving wind races toward me again. My pulse skips erratically, and I tremble as I stumble backward. I clutch the nearby canvas to break my fall but hit the ground hard. When the lights are fully restored, I find myself peering into terror-stricken eyes. Brooke and C.C. tower breathlessly over me.

"Libby, who were you shouting at? What's going on?"

"The power failed. That's all! The basement just lost electricity, right?" The panic in Brooke's voice matches the fear in her eyes.

"Didn't you guys feel it?"

"Feel what, Libby?" C.C. demands.

"I don't care what it was. Can we just get out of here?" Brooke pleads.

"It was too dark to see anything, but first I felt someone or something brush by me, and then just before the lights came back on, it whispered."

"Whispered? Libby, you're not making any sense," C.C. says.

"I thought I heard my name, and it wanted me to stop right here, like whatever it was didn't want me to go any further."

Brooke's voice quivers, "This is nonsense. Nothing came near us, and we can see down this corridor for miles in both directions. Look around. I'm telling you, there's nobody here but us!"

"Maybe. But as sure as I'm in front of you—I swear on my mother's life—we're not alone." Small pools fill the corners of Brooke's frightened blue eyes.

With the lights on, nothing appears out of the ordinary or for that matter, even remotely threatening.

"It had to be more than my imagination."

"Okay, Libby, if you say so. We can't deny that something unexplainable is going on."

The dusty tarp I grabbed had slid to one side, partially uncovering an old, wooden, leather-strapped trunk. We huddle for a closer look. Without another word, our impulse to run is gone. As we touch the trunk's lid and see the tarnished bronze emblem it bears, we collectively gasp.

"DDD. Daniella Devereaux Dalton."

"I told you," C.C. says. "This is it! It's not quite where I remember, but this was definitely Daniella's."

Gently unbuckling the worn leather straps, I open the creaking, arched lid of the antique. Very carefully, we sift through the contents. Brooke delicately lifts a small bouquet of dried lilacs and wildflowers tenderly pressed between aged papers. Beneath, lay a white chiffon dress with lavender ribbons tied at the waist. I hold it reverently for each of us to admire.

"This is Daniella's, isn't it—the one from the painting in Miss Aimée's office."

"You're right, Libby," says C.C.

I hand the dress to Brooke who clutches it tightly. "I can hardly believe this was hers. It's almost as if she's right here." When she spins in circles, a slightly tattered and creased handwritten floral card drops from the folds of the gown.

> *Dear Miss Devereaux,*
> *No flower blooms as lovely as you.*
> *Although we have never met, I*
> *feel eternally connected.*
> *You dance from your soul, and mine*
> *has been forever changed.*
> *Thank you for touching my heart. - A.J.*

Paris, France, springtime, 1913

Andrew James Dalton's business trip to Paris is highly successful but proves exhausting. With a free evening, he accepts an invitation and is delighted to attend the Paris Opera House Ballet. Those closest to him tease that he harbors a secret desire to be on stage. Privately, he admits to loving genuine applause and never holds back a well-deserved ovation for someone else.

Tonight is different. When the audience erupts into reverberating cheers, A.J. sits completely and unexpectedly mesmerized. Having seen numerous ballets, including the premier performance of Anna Pavlova in the United States in 1910, he feels he has seen the best the ballet world has to offer. But this evening he's drawn hopelessly to the young prima. She captivates the entire theatre—including himself—with her grace and beauty. Her movements sing to his very being. She dances his every emotion as if her artistry is interwoven with each of his unspoken feelings.

In the weeks that follow, he tries to forget her but cannot. Before leaving Paris, he sees her show nine times. And each night as she takes her final curtsey, the stage is showered with red roses. He spends every spare hour seeking to find out everything he can about the prima of his dreams.

Discovered at age seven by the LaCoussierres, directors of the Paris Ballet, Daniella was a delightful child born into a ballerina's body. She was graced with a natural ability to perform technically correct chassé tour jetés without ever being taught. Madame LaCoussierre developed an immediate fondness for her and convinced the Devereauxs to let the young prodigy study in Paris. Daniella sorely missed her parents, younger brother Lucien, and baby cousin Isabelle; the sacrifices she endured were as great as the gifts she possessed. As she grew, rave reviews followed her every performance. Not the typical temperamental ballerina, locals praised her love of children and many charitable works.

A.J.'s behavior is completely out of character, and he knows it. Interrogating the theatregoers, trying to catch glimpses of her in street clothes after an evening's performance—what is he thinking? He has successfully dodged the advances of some of the world's most intelligent and seductive women, but now, nearing age thirty, he finds himself hopelessly obsessed with the young dancer.

He decides he must stop his preposterous notion of wanting her. Attending one last performance, he anonymously sends her a simple bouquet of freshly cut wildflowers.

At the end of the evening, Daniella requests that all the flowers delivered to her dressing room be donated to the children's ward at the hospital—all but one. She is sincerely touched by the card's poetic expression and intrigued by the initials A.J.

Who was this insightful admirer who knew that her favorite flowers were freshly cut lilacs? Every night someone tried to impress her with outrageous, exotic blooms. Yet it was this small, simple bouquet tied with a lavender ribbon that left its indelible imprint.

Passing around the treasured memento, the three of us are swept away by the card's romanticism. We're thrilled to know that the first time Andrew Dalton had ever seen Daniella, she was dancing!

"It was love at first sight for A.J.," C.C. sighs.

"Yeah, like he knew she was his soul mate," Brooke says.

"I wonder how they finally met."

"I don't know, Libby. But thank heaven they found each other, especially for the sake of L'Esprit and Miss Aimée," Brooke says while furiously digging inside the trunk. "Now I *have* to know more! Let's see what else we can find."

~In a distant corner of the basement, in a spot that has remained unoccupied for more than half a century, the air settles, and a draped figure waits.

Pas de deux, grand (gra̅hn pah duh <u>duh</u>) Two dancing together. Differing from a simple pas de deux, this dance is created in five parts: the entrée, adage, a variation for the danseuse, danseur, and the coda. The grand dance of two would not be attainable for the ballerina without the aid of her partner; the dancers work together as one.

Chapter Twenty

C.C., *Brooke, and I reach* deeper into the chest and retrieve a cream-colored, leather book.

"It's a diary! This must be Daniella's! We'd know for certain if I could get it open. How can a lock hold on something this old?" C.C. vigorously tugs at the catch. "Maybe she doesn't want me to read it!"

Brooke takes a turn, working impatiently on the journal's stubborn lock before giving up. "I must not be meant to see it either."

She tosses the diary to me and buries her head with C.C.'s inside the trunk in search of the key. Catching the book, I'm amazed when its small keyhole mysteriously disintegrates sending gray wisps of ash spiraling upward. I gently tap the tiny lock once with my finger, and it instantly springs open before dropping from my unsteady hands.

"Whoa, Libby. I guess you're the one with the magic touch." C.C. and Brooke pull their noses from the trunk and see the book's pages exposed on the cement floor.

I look intently at the entry marked *March 30, 1914* and delicately touch the upper corner of the paper covered with Daniella's flowing hand-scripted words. With every sentence, the past lives.

Never away from my beloved France before, the only places I've experienced are the ones created on stage. I'm sad to be leaving my family and friends behind, but I know traveling abroad will be a grand adventure. The LaCoussierres have booked performances from New York City to San Francisco, with a final stop in Chicago. Little Isabelle wants to come along. Father says she dances continuously, always pretending to be me.

We're fascinated to learn about the uprooted young woman who wasn't much older than ourselves. I quickly decide her words could easily be my own, and I especially identify with her anxiety over starting anew. Randomly, I read another excerpt.

I have dreamt of dancing all my life. No matter how many audiences for whom I perform or how loud the applause, it is not the real reason I dance. For me, art is the universal language of all people, and I wish to communicate beyond the physical boundaries of words. If my dance can touch another—a complete stranger—like my unknown A.J. a year ago—then I know that I have truly lived a life of purpose. This is the desire that continues to stir within my being. Somehow, I'm more connected to life when I dance. Every color under the sun shines brighter, music echoes lovelier, and every emotion experienced is felt more intensely. Why would you walk through life when you can dance? I know there is a higher meaning to this gift; I just don't know what it is yet or where it will lead. I trust God would not have blessed me with such a talent if I were not meant to share it with the world, and hopefully, one day with someone special. Wher-

ever I go, I hope my dance and I will be embraced.

"She was such a remarkable person," I say.

I flip through more pages, and several yellowed newspaper clippings drift to the floor. They land at Brooke's feet. Collecting them, Brooke says, "Looks like she received glowing reviews everywhere she went."

"The *London Times* said she rivaled the ballet stars Taglioni and Pavlova," C.C. says.

"It doesn't get much better than that, does it? Look! Here's a quote from Madame LaCoussierre, 'A performer is never as good as her best review or as bad as her worst.' As if Daniella needed help staying grounded," I say.

"I don't know. It could be easy to get stuck up in the midst of such constant praise," Brooke says.

"Words to live by! I'll have to remember them when my name is featured in the *New York Times* for winning my first Tony Award," C.C. says.

"Oh, in your dreams!" Brooke scoffs. "You poor, misguided fool. Your name's more likely to end up in the tabloids squeezed between UFO and Elvis sightings."

We laugh when C.C. strikes an Elvis pose and mumbles, "Thank you. Thank you very much."

"Hey, June fifth is my birthday. Let's read this one," I say.

June 5, 1914

My dance partner, René Vernau, informed me that our opening performance in Chicago is sold out. Our cast and crew are invited to attend a formal dinner dance afterwards. The event is to be held at the Palmer House, hosted by Mr. Andrew Dalton, whom I am told is a wealthy philanthropist. Society's upper echelon is expected to attend. René, who is always the most knowledgeable and up to date on social events and company gossip, tells me the festivities will include a silent bid auction. A pair of my worn pointe slippers have been requested. I'm willing to oblige, but who would want them? I'm pleased to learn that all the proceeds are slated to benefit the area children's hospital. Personally, I look forward to meeting this Mr. Dalton. I picture him to be an older man with a generous nature.

June 9, 1914

Chicago's opening night was a spectacular event. I surely danced the best performance of my career. Each movement flowed without effort, every turn and leap flawless. René and I partnered every pas de duex seamlessly, and the lifts and escorted turns were executed to perfection. I have never felt more on top of my pointe shoes. God must have given me wings. The audience stood for three ovations before the curtain drew to a final close. After a brief celebration backstage, we hurried to dress for dinner. Starving, dinner can't come soon enough.

Later . . .

The Palmer House ballroom glistened. Over 250 people were in attendance, yet I'm certain I'm the one who experienced the most memorable evening. Crisp white linens, fine china, and gold- plated silverware were neatly arranged at every table. Soft glowing mirrored candlelight and freshly cut flowers, including lilacs, formed each centerpiece. Even in my simple lavender chiffon gown, I felt pretty among the elegant ladies dripping in jewels who were accompanied by distinguished, tuxedoed gentlemen.

René and I were seated at a table next to the LaCoussierres. The hospital's administrator, his wife, and an American diplomat also joined us, along with a very charming Chicago couple named Wrigley. I thought it unusual that there was one empty place setting next to mine. As the evening continued, the most handsome man I have ever seen approached the podium to speak. Introducing himself as Andrew Dalton, he eloquently greeted the assembled guests and thanked the LaCoussierres and our ballet company for being in attendance. He then extended his arm and with a heart-melting smile introduced René and me. I stood with René and waved while the room rose to their feet for another exuberant round of applause. I blushed when I looked back at Andrew Dalton and realized his gaze had never left me. The rest of his welcoming words were lost as I toiled with my flustered emotions. This wasn't the Mr. Dalton I expected.

When he returned to the floor, I saw his eyes seek out our table. René insisted his attention was for me alone. I shyly turned away. Mr. Dalton traveled about the room visiting with the multitude of seated guests. René teased that I must have done something to keep him away. My appetite vanished, and my meal remained untouched. "Do they starve their dancers in France?" my dinner companions asked.

"Heavens no, we let them eat once a month," Madame LaCoussierre teased.

Although amused by the humorous banter, I couldn't stop my focus from shifting to wherever Andrew Dalton was standing in the room. It seemed he stopped to personally mingle with everyone. Was he avoiding our table for some reason? Was he avoiding me?

The orchestra started, and the couples in our group made their way to the dance floor. René suggested as we followed them, that perhaps I would rather be dancing with Mr. Dalton. Was it that obvious? Just as the music ended, I felt a gentle tap on my shoulder.

"If it is acceptable to you Miss Devereaux, may I have the next dance?"

Suddenly, I had two left feet. I found it difficult to make eye contact with this exceedingly handsome man. When I finally did, his warm brown eyes were desperately searching my face.

"Good evening, I'm Andrew Dalton."

René prodded me forward. I felt like a toddler learning to take her first steps. From behind Mr. Dalton's back, René wiggled his eyebrows, winking with a boyish grin. As Mr. Dalton took me in his arms, I trembled. No one would have ever believed that I was a professionally trained dancer. I stole a quick glance at his smile. It lit up the ballroom and made me dizzy at the same time.

"Your performance this evening was truly exceptional," he said. "You are the most gifted dancer I've ever seen, and I can't thank you enough for agreeing to attend tonight's gala."

I stammered, "I'm honored to be here, sir."

As we waltzed in circles around the floor, I was moved when he added, "Many children at the hospital will benefit because of your performance."

"As I'm certain they will from you, Mr. Dalton, for hosting such a worthwhile event."

Our conversation continued effortlessly and without pause as a new song began. I couldn't help but notice how beautifully we fit together. With my tiny hand in his, I examined his left finger for a wedding band. I wasn't sure how long he had been talking when I blurted, "Is there a Mrs. Dalton?"

"Besides my mother?" He looked genuinely surprised. "I hope there's a Mrs. Dalton out there somewhere in my future."

Embarrassed beyond description, I blushed furiously. His muscular arm tightened around my waist, silently absolving my faux pas. His smile broadened and revealed a deep-set dimple in his right cheek that I hadn't noticed before.

My emotions swirled about as we danced to an enchanting melody that I will never forget. When I finally had the courage to lift my eyes to his again, I asked if he knew the name of the song. He stopped, leaned over, and softly whispered in my ear,

"To Have, To Hold, To Love." It was a good thing that his arms held me securely, or I surely would have swooned at his feet.

A thousand eyes were upon us as he escorted me back to my table. A palpable murmur circulated around the room, and I suddenly realized we had been the center of attention on the dance floor. Could everyone see how attracted I was to him? Could he? As the next song started and the guests released us from their stare, I nervously sat, but not before accidentally knocking my handbag to the floor. As we both bent over to retrieve its scattered contents, we unceremoniously bumped heads. With all sense of decorum lost we laughed together, robustly and with abandon. When we finally stopped, his eyes locked with mine. In that very moment, I know my heart locked with his for eternity. Gathering each item, I heard a heavy sigh escape his lips, and he looked at me in total disbelief. After he handed me my most valued possession—the floral card from a year ago—he spoke.

"You did get my flowers."

"That's got to be the most romantic story I've ever heard," C.C. sighs.

"I feel like I was standing in that very room. Couldn't you see it unfolding right in front of you?" I press the cover of the diary closed. "I know it doesn't make sense, but I feel like I was there, like I was Daniella."

"Maybe it's just wishful thinking. You know we all hope to find that perfect someone," Brooke says.

"I know I do," C.C. says, "and he had best be looking for me!"

"Be sure to shove us aside when he rides in on his white horse!" I pout.

"Who knows, Libby. Maybe he'll show up with two buff friends," Brooke says as she returns to her tenacious search of the trunk. We rummage through Daniella's old programs. C.C.

counts nine ticket stubs printed in French, each from the same production of "Giselle" at the Paris Opera House from 1913. I slip on Daniella's purple pointe shoes that fit like a glove. "These are in the portrait too, aren't they?"

"They don't look very worn, just old." Brooke examines them more closely. "They're not even broken in."

"It's probably because she never danced in them after her partnering accident," C.C. sadly states. "It's heartbreaking. Where was René? Why did she have to get a new partner anyway?"

Still looking, I retrieve a gold bracelet from the bottom corner of the trunk. It has a tiny heart-shaped locket that hangs like a charm. "Look, I think I found a piece of her jewelry."

"This thing is a real antique," says C.C. "Too bad the clasp is broken."

"It seems familiar. I swear I've seen it somewhere before." Brooke watches as C.C. delicately opens the locket. Engraved inside are the initials "A.J." "This definitely must have been Daniella's."

Fascinated by our find, we each take turns trying it on. I'm the last to wrap it around my wrist, and it instantly scorches my skin. "Ouch! What kind of gold is this anyway?"

"Why? What's the matter, Libby?" Brooke asks.

"Oh my gosh! Look at the red welt. It didn't do anything like that to Brooke or me. You must be allergic!"

"Here we go again. Now I'm claustrophobic *and* allergic!"

Unlike the first time I touched Daniella's trunk and felt protected and close to her, once the bracelet appeared, my safety net vanished. I wonder if the others feel the sudden chill that sweeps across the basement like a dark cloud as I swiftly place everything back exactly as we found it.

"Daniella's haunting L'Esprit. I'm convinced of it, but what is she trying to tell us?" I ask.

"My mom says a haunting occurs when someone chooses to remain earthbound. Some die too young or too quickly and haven't accepted that it's their time to cross over. Others can't rest because they have unfinished business or a message that they want to reveal."

"I've heard that, too," Brooke says.

"If it is Daniella, I wish she'd do it without hurting me. She's got my full attention."

"Ours, too!"

We close the trunk and notice the pictures that had mysteriously blown out of my hands earlier were not strewn chaotically as we expected. Instead, they're arranged in a line, like a Hansel and Gretel trail of breadcrumbs for us to follow. As we pick up the photos, we reexamine each of them and their common link, the statue. Did these pictures mean anything? I reach for what I think is the last one and spot the edge of yet another. It's slightly hidden beneath a long drape in a shadowy alcove. Stepping closer, we're startled by a human figure lurking beneath the cascading cloth. Without hesitation, C.C. gives the heavy tarp a sharp tug.

"Wait! Stop!" Brooke's pleas come too late.

Allongé (ah-lawn-ZHAY) Extended. The dancer's bodylines are long and reaching. Whether through the length of the leg and foot or in the delicate placement of the fingertips, the dancer's extension is at its fullest.

Chapter Twenty-One

*T*he exposed figure looks blankly into our bewildered eyes. One hand rests on her chest while the other stretches outward, daring us to step closer. Mesmerized, we stand face to face with the elusive, legendary statue of L'Esprit.

The photographs did not do her justice. I'm compelled to touch the surprisingly warm marble. "C.C., Brooke, don't be afraid. Come closer. Isn't marble usually cold?" My fingers remain on the statue's outstretched arm as my two friends timidly approach.

"It does feel warm." Brooke places her hand next to mine. "It's truly lifelike. She's breathtaking."

"Look at her face, it's smooth and delicate. It looks painted rather than chiseled," C.C. observes.

"Is it the lighting down here, or is this really Daniella we're seeing?" Brooke asks.

"If her legs weren't encased in stone, I think she could step right out," I say.

"She looks trapped," C.C. says with a tinge of sadness.

"I know. It's as if she wants to burst out of the stone and dance," I agree.

"Why is this piece stored in the dark, dingy basement?"

"I don't know, Brooke. Maybe someone's trying to hide something," I offer. "In any case, this is a *major* discovery."

"Libby! Look at your wrist!" C.C. points to the red, blistering mark left by the bracelet as it fades before our eyes.

"I'm officially spooked! It doesn't sting anymore either!" I nervously rub the wound in disbelief. When the burn completely disappears, we look at each other dumbfounded.

"Maybe Mr. Doll was right, and the statue does have special powers," Brooke says on the verge of tears.

"It's probably the most unique piece of artwork I've ever seen, but hiding something like this doesn't make any sense. I wish Miss Aimée would explain it."

"Do you guys want her to find out we've been snooping around all afternoon? Who knows, she might be the one who put the statue and the pictures in the basement in the first place," C.C. says.

"I don't want to risk it." Brooke wipes her eyes. "Isn't there anyone else we can ask?"

"I know!" C.C. says. "Let's ask Mrs. Summers. She's been around forever. She must know something."

"I'm not sure what she knows, but she'll absolutely freak when we tell her what we've found," I say.

With our plan set, we reverently cover the sculpture. Interestingly, in comparison to the other objects in the basement, both the cloth and the statue are free of dust and cobwebs.

"We're not all caught in the same dream, are we? This is real, right? It will still be here when we come back, won't it?" I ask.

We reluctantly abandon the lifelike statue and set off on our mission, determined to rescue her from the bowels of the basement. C.C. pulls each light cord as we go, and we cautiously look over our shoulders. We dash around the elevator, and I shiver as I run. *No way!!!* "I'm not getting on that thing ever again."

"Me neither! C'mon, the door is this way," Brooke says.

"Pick up the pace, ladies, I'm in the rear, and once I pull this last cord it will turn pitch black down here. Hold the door open," C.C. orders. We fly up the stairs, chased by silence.

~Alone in the abyss, a soft white aura radiates from the statue. Not quite home, but getting closer.

Grand Dalton House Foyer, 1928

With Daniella gone, every remaining day of A.J.'s life has become bittersweet, but none more than this particular anniversary of her birthday. Dressed in white tie and tails, he places himself on the grand staircase and surveys the upturned faces of his invited guests, knowing that the one he most seeks will not be among them. Yet, he stands tall and warmly welcomes one and all to the reopening of the Grand Dalton House and L'Esprit Dance Studio.

Being a true visionary, he built shops and boutiques under the cover of the roof and proudly assures the ladies that no longer at the mercy of the elements, they can enjoy the new experience of shopping indoors. More importantly, for the first time in public, he speaks of Dani and her legacy. Many of the women dab their eyes with dainty, lace-trimmed hankies, and several gentlemen with unintended comic relief, gustily make use of expensive, monogrammed handkerchiefs.

Much to the annoyance of Miss Winterset and some of the others in A.J.'s inner circle, Isabelle is dressed in a tight, crimson, low-cut gown, and positions herself next to him, assuming the role of hostess for the evening. Since her appointment as the studio's director, she's become unbearable, attaching herself to A.J. whenever possible. She demands that business meetings take place at fashionable restaurants and public places. She even manages to have photographs placed in the society page of the newspaper to make it appear as if they are a couple.

As A.J. directs everyone's attention to the pièce de résistance, a hush descends. For months, rumors circulated about an objet d'art that was to be unveiled. Covered in white satin, it stands on a pedestal in the center of the landing just behind him. Rather than try to convey his feelings regarding the unique power of the statue, he instead declares, "I'll let this remarkable piece speak for itself."

Mr. Doll winces at these words, knowing that they were truer than anyone could ever comprehend. He has heard it speak his own name more than once—a fact that he has kept to himself, especially after the debacle in A.J.'s office in the early stages of his work. An audible gasp rises as the draping cloth is ceremoniously removed. The angelic figure in its magnificent splendor completely personifies Daniella, leaving everyone spellbound. Finally, a smattering of applause grows to a resounding fanfare. A.J., immensely pleased, fades into the background. Isabelle, ready to explode from having been artfully abandoned, feels the massive white shroud land squarely on top of her. It fortuitously hides the anger blazing in her eyes. She barely avoids the crush of the curious as they rush forward, eager for a closer look.

The museum-quality statue of L'Esprit becomes an instant celebrity. Chicago area residents possessively regard it as their personal treasure. No one can deny that it inspires a plethora of emotions, and many even claim that it pulses with a lifelike energy. Those compelled to touch the marble often linger in its loving presence, basking in its aura of mystery.

Tombé (tawn-BAY) Falling. The dance movement appears to fall forward or backward onto the working leg finishing in a demi-plié. A dancer falls.

Chapter Twenty-Two

*M*rs. *Summers, primping in her* display case mirror, is caught off guard by the thunder of our stampeding feet. Startled by our windstorm entrance, she nearly knocks over a tall vase of bright, yellow daffodils.

"Girls, what's the matter? You scared me half to death."

Toppling into each other, we come to an abrupt stop.

"Brooke, dear, you look pale. Why are you girls still here at this late hour? Don't you three darlings have big dates waiting for you?"

"No, not us, Mrs. Summers. You and Miss Aimée are the only two getting asked out on dates these days," C.C. says.

"You girls are so pretty you must intimidate the boys. And you're always dancing, they probably think you don't have time for them."

"You're too sweet, Mrs. Summers," I say.

"Yes, but I'm also right. Now, what brings you into my shop acting like the devil himself is after you?"

"C.C., Libby, and I were just wondering if you could answer some questions about L'Esprit."

"I could certainly try, Brooke. After all, it's a subject I know quite a bit about."

"We don't know where to start," I say.

"Just start at the beginning, and I'll see if I can help. I go back a long way, you know. My mother was one of the first employees at L'Esprit Dance Studios."

"Was her name Sarah?" C.C. blurts.

"Why yes, how did you know? Did Miss Aimée tell you?"

"Not exactly," Brooke evasively replies. "We didn't know your mother worked at L'Esprit."

"She did indeed. As a young woman, she enrolled in ballet classes. Mother soon discovered she was cursed with two left feet but became indispensable as the studio's receptionist and Daniella's personal assistant. The two struck up a lasting friendship—kindred spirits, I suppose—especially after poor Miss Daniella's accident."

"We read she was dropped during a rehearsal and broke her back," Brooke says.

"It was tragic," Mrs. Summers says. "Daniella's dance ambitions were ended along with her cherished dream of starting a family. Mother said she never saw a couple more deserving of children or more devastated by their loss."

"How did she ever find the courage to go on?" I ask in a small voice, realizing for the first time how hopeless Daniella must have felt.

"With God's grace she found the strength. Daniella considered it a privilege to be entrusted with the care and guidance of the hundreds of children that attended L'Esprit," Mrs. Summers says. "She mothered each dancer in ways she might not have otherwise done. Even though the nerve damage was extensive and excruciating, she accepted the accident as part of heaven's grand design and inspired everyone that knew her. Of course,

Mr. Dalton didn't spare any expense for the best doctors' care, but operations and medical technology weren't what they are today. An experimental, high-risk surgery was her best chance. Unfortunately, it was a splintered bone fragment that severed her spinal cord; the damage was permanent. When she awakened, she still experienced pain, but only from the waist up. I'm told she never felt her legs again."

"They must have been destroyed." C.C. frowns.

"One would think. But not Daniella Devereaux Dalton. A.J. had an elevator immediately installed, and before you knew it, she returned to L'Esprit in a wheelchair with her head held high. Her performing career may have ended that day but not her teaching career. She'd roll alongside the ballet barres, instructing her students from her new vantage point. It seemed she could get a better view of their hips, legs, and feet, making it easier to offer corrections. Whenever she missed performing, she'd simply close her eyes and dance within herself—where all the real dancing is done anyway."

"That's true. I always dance better in my head than I do with my feet," Brooke says. Solemnly, we nod in agreement.

"At a young age, Daniella was blessed with an inner wisdom most people never attain in a lifetime." We hear the admiration in Mrs. Summers' voice as she speaks. Just as the pages of the diary had been intimately revealing, her recollections of her mother's memories make Daniella even more real to us.

"Daniella's legacy taught me that during life's many twists and turns, God is always there. I wanted to be just like her," Mrs. Summers says, "but when I tried dancing, unlike you three, my body didn't take to it as naturally. As you eloquently expressed, Brooke, my best dancing was always in my head, too. Of course, I didn't have the best dance teacher."

"Why? Who was your teacher, Mrs. Summers?" C.C. asks.

"Miss Isabelle. She was attractive and could definitely be charming at times, but trust me, she was nothing like the Daltons. It's difficult to comprehend that she could be part of the same family tree as Daniella and Miss Aimée."

"How was Isabelle related?" Brooke asks.

"Not *was* my dear child, *is!*"

"Isabelle's still alive? She must be over a hundred years old," C.C. says.

"She's as old as dirt, but she's not buried in it yet. I guess the earth doesn't want her either."

"Where is she now?" I ask.

"She's living in a nursing home on the outskirts of the city. Miss Aimée visits her, although I'm not sure why. Isabelle loved her as a small child, but she was so hard on the poor girl as Aimée grew older. Never had a kind word from what I can remember, and unfortunately, when Aimée's parents perished in a car wreck, Isabelle became her last surviving relative."

"What brought Isabelle to L'Esprit?" Brooke asks.

"Daniella invited her to America for a visit. She was an aspiring ballerina but never earned a principal role. She said it was because the LaCoussierres suspected she would leave the Paris Opera Ballet just as Daniella did. Truth be told, she never measured up, and I think Daniella pitied her." Mrs. Summers locks her cash register and throws a questioning glance at Brooke, who swipes her beaded forehead. "Mother said Isabelle worked hard and was allowed to perform like a prima, a role she greatly savored. With her attitude of entitlement, she eventually convinced Daniella to let her stay and teach classes of her own. But she coveted the prestige of the role more than the duties involved. She wasn't very good with children; she seemed more preoccupied with her reflection than interacting with her students. She treated my mother like a servant but softened her demeanor whenever Mr. Dalton was nearby. Honestly, it was mother who kept L'Esprit running after Daniella's death. Isabelle, of course, took all the credit."

"She sounds like a mean person," I say.

"More like a wicked witch," C.C. says.

"I can't disagree with you, girls. When mother wanted to quit, Mr. Dalton couldn't blame her. Grateful for her service, he financially backed The Summers' Floral Shop. It's been in my family ever since."

"This is like a modern-day soap opera!" C.C. says.

"I like to think the bad memories fade and the good ones live forever," Mrs. Summers says.

Well, something's still living in the Dalton House. "If you don't think me too rude, Mrs. Summers, why did Daniella die alone? We know she was lost in the fire, but why wasn't she with her husband? He saved dozens of others. How come he didn't rescue her?" I ask.

"He would have moved heaven and Earth to save her, but when the flames broke out there was complete pandemonium. He couldn't find Daniella anywhere. The elevator was stuck and the staircase impassable. And Libby, you're right. While frantically searching, he saved countless others, including my mother and father who almost died that ghastly night."

The blood in Brooke's face drains.

"Daniella wasn't found by anyone until it was too late. She had fallen from her wheelchair and was trapped on the elevator floor. Mr. Dalton was unaware that at some point during the party, she had gone up to the studios of L'Esprit alone. For what reason, we will never know."

"He must have gone insane with grief," I say, sensing Mrs. Summers' escalating emotions.

"He did! Although he managed to achieve much in his

lifetime and keep her legacy alive, the light in his world permanently dimmed the night Daniella died."

"Thank God for Andrew Dalton!" C.C. says.

"What happened to him, Mrs. Summers? Did he ever fall in love again? How did he die?" I ask.

"Some say it was a heart attack, but most believe as I do, that he died from a broken heart. He never remarried, nor had any children of his own, although many women, including Isabelle, attempted to win his favor."

When Brooke stumbles into me, the pictures I had gathered in the basement accidentally drop from my hands and scatter across the floor of the flower shop. Before Mrs. Summers strains to see the fallen collection, I scramble to brush them into a pile and present the photos to her.

She peers through her pink-framed reading glasses. "Where did you find these? They haven't been seen in years."

"What do you know about this statue, Mrs. Summers?" we ask.

"Mr. Dalton found it in France shortly after Daniella's death. It inspired him to rebuild their dream after the fire. Supposedly, during Mr. Doll's restoration, it took on Daniella's face all by itself. I never tired of looking at this sculpture. I truly thought Daniella could dance right out of the marble. Sounds silly I know, but it was so lifelike that I actually thought it was possible. And here's a secret I rarely share. When I was a child, I swear I heard it whisper my name."

The three of us exchange glances. I beg her to continue.

"When the Dalton House reopened in 1928, the sculpture was placed on display in the center of the lobby as a tribute to Daniella. It stood there to remind everyone that she was the reason the Grand Dalton House existed."

I softly repeat in French, "L'Esprit's raison pour être."

"Yes. Daniella was and still is L'Esprit's reason for being! Mother said the statue represented her strength and courage after the accident. Even wheelchair-bound, she danced from within, her choreography never more creative or inspiring. Mr. Dalton might have hoped the statue would inspire others to overcome their own adversities. And perhaps it served as his daily reminder to never give up. Sadly, after his death, the statue disappeared without a trace. Some say it was stolen, while others say it mystically left on its own. Personally, I think Miss Isabelle had something to do with it."

"But that's what we came to tell you, Mrs. Summers. The statue of L'Esprit is . . ."

We're horrified when mid-sentence, Brooke falls lifelessly at our feet.

Renversé (rahn-vehr-SAY) Upset. The upper torso is forcefully bent during a turn in which the normal balance of the dancer is disturbed yet the equilibrium is maintained. The body bends from the waist to the right, left, or back with the head following the movement.

Chapter Twenty-Three

The constant tick of the clock on the sterile white wall echoes disturbingly in my head. I want to cry, scream, or at least kick something, but all I can do is sit quietly as C.C. and I spend yet another miserable day at Mercy Hospital with Brooke's family, the Allens. The hours move in slow motion, every sound and smell irritatingly magnified. Brooke, tiny and still in her hospital bed, shows no signs of regaining consciousness. I quickly learn the meaning of the word surreal as my life takes on the quality of a very bad dream.

The doctors say the tumor is inoperable. They've done everything within their power to relieve the pressure on Brooke's brain, but no one knows for certain if she'll ever wake, and if she does, if she'll ever be the same. C.C., Jarrell, and I cling to hope and to each other. We keep it together for the sake of Brooke's family. Incredibly, the Allens are rocks, consoling us and looking out for each other. All we can do is wait and have faith. Why is it we seem to have it the least when we need it the most? It's awfully hard to trust in God when your friend is dying.

C.C. and I visit the hospital chapel constantly and beg God and all the angels and saints for a miracle. I'm not above making a deal with God. What does He want? I'll do it! As the hours drag, we worry that her chances for recovery are growing slim. Is God even listening?

"I just want to smash something!"

"I know, me too! In fact, I already did. I totally lost it last night in front of my parents."

"Oh, C.C., I know you've been best friends with her forever."

"Where are Brooke's hugs when you really want one? Thank God I have you, Libby. I'd hate to be going through this alone." She clings to me, her face wet with tears. "Do you think Brooke even knows we're here?" C.C. sobs, desperately searching my face for reassurance.

"Of course she does. Love is always felt even if it can't be spoken or heard."

"We just have to keep praying, right? Miracles happen; doctors are human, sometimes they make mistakes, too. She'll get better, won't she, Libby?"

"She's gonna wake up, C.C. She'll be okay. We have to keep the faith!" We repeat this same conversation every day.

Last night when Brooke's breathing became shallow and irregular, Miss Aimée reminded us that even when Brooke was little, she looked like a feather, but in reality, she was tough as nails. "It's not in Brooke's nature ever to quit," she said with a calmness that took away the sting of our terror and tears. God knows we've cried buckets, especially when Mrs. Allen held on to her daughter for dear life, her fierce embrace devastatingly sad to witness. For the first time in the Allens' presence, we let ourselves cry. Miss Aimée gathered us into her arms, and although I couldn't voice my deepest fear—even to C.C.—I was scared out of mind that Brooke would leave us.

As word of Brooke's condition spreads, her hospital room fills with loving relatives and neighbors. School and studio friends arrive in droves. Her room soon overflows with balloons, stuffed animals, ballerina dolls, and flowers of every kind and color.

We're shocked at the unexpected arrival of Whitney and Tia. "Mr. and Mrs. Allen, we feel bad about Brooke," Whitney says. "She's not going to die or be brain damaged, is she?"

We suck in our breath. Even Tia has enough sense to be mortified.

C.C. pulls Whitney aside. "Shut up! Don't you ever think before you speak?"

"I'm just as concerned as everybody else."

"Yeah right. Concerned for yourself and your competition at regionals," Jarrell accuses, clenching his jaw.

"Get real! Regional competition is the last thing on our minds. We just want Brooke to get better. Don't we, Tia?"

"Whatever you say, Whitney." Tia shrugs.

"You've never been the warm and fuzzy types. Forgive us if we're having a hard time taking you seriously!"

"Think whatever you want, C.C. Tia and I came to pay our respects."

"This isn't a funeral. You can go now, everybody's seen you." Jarrell roughly shoves the unwelcome pair out the door.

"Calm down, C.C. You're frightening me," I tell her. "I'm not trying to defend them, but sometimes it's hard to know the right thing to say."

"Quit making excuses, Libby. Nobody can be that stupid. Did you see Mrs. Allen's face? I could kill Whitney for upsetting Brooke's family like that."

"Yeah, and I'll be first in line to help!" Jarrell says, tightening his fist.

"Let it go, you two. They're not worth it. Besides, they're gone now," I say.

Fortunately, the delivery of a spectacular bouquet of flowers helps to diffuse the ugly scene. We tease Brooke that if Trent's personal message doesn't make her wake up, then nothing will.

To L'Esprit's Darling Prima,
Hurry and get well.
Center stage and our hearts are empty without you!
With Love,
Miss Aimée and Trent Michaels

After another week, the hospital staff knows C.C. and me by name. We become regulars in the chapel. We're encouraged when Brooke's breathing stabilizes, and the doctors assure us that she's resting comfortably. On the rare occasion when we're left alone with Brooke, we each stroke her hair and chat nonstop. C.C. begs her to wake up, believing that if she speaks loudly enough she'll get her to snap out of her coma. I don't know if this is true or not, but I'm open to any theory that might work.

"Brooke, I know you can hear us. We have no intention of saying goodbye. We need you here. Come on, you can beat this thing. Haven't you ever heard the expression 'heaven can wait?' God doesn't need you right now, *we do!* Aren't the three of us going to do a trio this year? You've got to help us solve the mysteries at L'Esprit. I think the place is definitely haunted. What do you think? Anytime you care to wake up and join the conversation would be fine. As a matter of fact, *it would be great!!!"* C.C.'s shout draws the attention of a passing nurse who promptly shushes us. Lowering her voice, she continues, "You agree with me, don't you, Libby? Let's just admit it, L'Esprit has ghosts."

"You don't have to convince me. I know at least one dances around L'Esprit, and I'm certain it's Daniella's."

"But why would Daniella haunt L'Esprit? Wouldn't she want to be in heaven with A.J.?"

"I bet it has something to do with the statue. Think about it, C.C. We were practically led straight to it. We were literally trapped in the basement until we found it."

"If her ghost is truly around, then there must be a good reason. There must be something she wants us to know."

"Or do."

Our conversation is interrupted by the return of Brooke's parents and her two brothers. Their blank faces are unreadable, marked only by exhaustion.

Reading the misery in our eyes, Mrs. Allen says, "Girls, your friendship means the world to Brooke, and we hope you know how much your support means to our family. C.C., you're like a sister to her, and Libby, you've been an absolute angel since the first time she met you. We can't thank you enough, but it's not healthy for the two of you to be here day and night. We're certain your voices are comforting to her, but we know Brooke wouldn't want you to stop living. Miss Aimée tells me you haven't even been going to dance class. You've missed a lot of regional rehearsals, haven't you? Brooke knows you love her, but remember she's the one in the coma, not you."

"Mrs. Allen, we want to be here in case she needs us. Besides, rehearsals aren't any fun without Brooke. We love her," C.C. says.

"Of course you do, honey. I promise to call immediately if

her condition changes. It's a nice Saturday morning. You two should do something special today in honor of Brooke. Do something that you think Brooke would rather be doing right now if she could. Tomorrow you can come back and tell her all about it. Please don't feel guilty about leaving. We'll be here for her."

Kissing Brooke's forehead, we take her fragile hands in ours and tenderly squeeze.

"Hang in there, prima girl. You'll get through this!" C.C.'s mascara smudges beneath her bloodshot eyes. "Look at me, Brooke, I'm a mess again. Every time I visit you, I end up looking like a raccoon. Don't you wish she could get up and come with us, Libby? She looks really pretty and peaceful, doesn't she?"

"Yes, she's beautiful. Maybe she's having a wonderful dream and doesn't want to wake up yet." As we leave, I send a quick text to my dad.

"What are you doing?" C.C. asks.

"I have a plan," I say. "Come on! Follow me. I agree with Mrs. Allen. Brooke would want us to dance, and we'll go to the studio later for regional rehearsals. But first, I have a surprise."

Emboîté (ahn-bwah-TAY) Fitted together. The dancer springs lightly into the air from a fifth position demi-plié alternating from one leg to another and landing with a bent knee that must move beyond the supporting leg during each exchange. The step moves forwards, backwards, or turns. The tightly connected footwork fits like a lid upon a box.

Chapter Twenty-Four

I take C.C.'s arm as we enter the lobby of the Tribune Tower. My dad eagerly awaits our arrival, glad for the chance to provide a distraction from our bedside vigil. After consoling C.C. and me, he escorts us into a small conference room adjacent to his office.

"Here, girls. These files chronicle events that took place after the Dalton House fire. Why don't you start with these, and I'll see what else I can find."

We're committed to researching the details surrounding Daniella's death and hope to confirm our suspicions of L'Esprit's possible haunting. If we're lucky, we might even find some information about the mysterious statue hiding in the basement.

C.C. opens the large, covered box, removing the yellow sticky note on its lid. She laughs for the first time in weeks as she reads aloud, "Happy haunting! Go get 'em my dancing P.I.s." We share a smile at Dad's humor when we see the crossed-out letter "a" knowing that he intended to spell "hunting."

We tackle the task of sifting through the reports, wishing Brooke could be with us. The diversion helps us gradually escape from the troubled present into the unknown past. After we learn about the locals' stunned reactions to the fire and skip through numerous listings of pending memorial services, we become increasingly intrigued with the coverage of Mr. Dalton's actions. One article, dated January 12, 1927, revealed this insight:

Following the funeral services for Chicago's beloved Prima Ballerina, Miss Daniella Devereaux Dalton, it is reported that her husband Andrew James Dalton has left the country. Miss Olivia Winterset, his personal secretary, is quoted as saying, "Although his current whereabouts are unknown, Mr. Dalton has issued assurances that his unscheduled departure will not affect the daily operations of his business. The loss of the jewel of our city, The Grand Dalton House, is a tremendous blow both financially and emotionally, but our board of directors insists that Dalton Enterprises remains solvent and in good hands. Mr. Dalton is in deep mourning and will not be available for further comment. He asks that you kindly respect his privacy."

We search further through the pages. Fire Chief Seth Jamison was first to report to the scene of the fire.

"Mr. Dalton is a real hero. If not for his gallant efforts, many more lives would have been lost." When asked about the possible cause of the inferno, Jamison offered two possibilities. "Since the point of origin is yet to be determined, faulty wiring might have been the culprit. In a gathering of this magnitude, of course, we can never rule out an unattended cigar. Our investigation remains ongoing and inconclusive at this time."'

As we read on, I make a quick mental note of how this clipping corroborates Mrs. Summers' version of the tragedy.

"Our city's prima died alone. She was found on the floor of the elevator next to her wheelchair, clinging to a gold bracelet. The small, attached heart-shaped locket was engraved with the initials A.J. When I tried to re- *turn it to Mr. Dalton, he claimed never to have seen it before, insisting it wasn't hers. The poor man was so upset, further questioning was pointless. God bless him and all those who suffered that terrible night."*

"Do you think it's the same bracelet we found in the trunk, the one that burned your wrist? Remember?"

"How can I forget? What do you think it means?"

"I wish I knew. Isn't it odd? Why didn't Mr. Dalton recognize the bracelet?"

"Why was she clutching it in the first place?" I say. "If you were trapped in an elevator and battling to escape a fire, would you be mindful of your stupid jewelry?"

"Maybe it was special to her because it was a gift from him. Maybe it broke off when she was trying to escape. I bet she fell out of her wheelchair when she reached to pick it up," C.C. says.

"That's my point. When you're fighting for your life, why would you care about a bracelet? Besides, it couldn't have been that special if Mr. Dalton didn't even remember giving it to her."

"Yeah, you're right. It doesn't add up. Grief-stricken or not, you'd think he'd recall it, especially since it's inscribed with his initials."

"Great. More questions!" We both sit somewhat deflated until my dad reenters the room.

"Girls, you're gonna have a field day with this information. It's interesting, I'll admit. I'd hate to think that L'Esprit might in fact be haunted. And your mother will definitely have second thoughts about you dancing there if it is. You know, Libby, your safety and well-being are our top priority." He places another cumbersome file on our rapidly accumulating stack. "It turns out my colleague is quite the avid ghost hunter. She's been collecting articles on local hauntings in Chicago and southeastern Wisconsin for years. She's explored many of the places herself and has even appeared on a Halloween special with Shelby Windham. Apparently, there's also mention of the Whispering Statue of L'Esprit. It disappeared years ago, and its whereabouts have never been determined."

C.C. and I lower our eyes and gulp simultaneously. We're grateful when the cell phone clipped to my dad's hip vibrates. Recognizing the number as the contact he's been waiting for, he winks and leaves us with our project.

"Phew! That was close. I'm warning you, C.C., if you ever want to see me again, never tell my parents what's going on at the studio."

"Don't worry. My lips are sealed, at least for now."

"It seems my connection to L'Esprit and Daniella gets stronger every day. I don't understand it myself. I just know Daniella needs me. Remember, Will and Kate are on a need-to-know basis. And right now, they don't need to know."

We split the stack fifty-fifty, although I tease that C.C.'s half looks a lot smaller than mine. Without hesitation, we rifle through one unsolved legend after another.

Resurrection Mary was a young high school student who died after leaving the Willowbrook Dance Hall in 1921, after her date left her for another girl. While walking home in the dark, she was killed by an oncoming car. Residents claim the distraught woman can still be seen in the late-night hours wandering aimlessly up and down Archer Avenue. In recent years, a man unfamiliar with the urban legend picked up a girl fitting Mary's description. From his rearview mirror, he saw the woman vanish from the backseat of his car at the same point where Mary was struck. The driver, a nonbeliever in the paranormal before, believes in ghosts today.

In 1933, the country's first interactive museum was built in Chicago. It was at the Museum of Science and Industry that Clarence Darrow made a promise to his son. When he died, he would come back and give a sign that he was okay. On March 13, 1938, the son had his father's ashes sprinkled in the Jackson Park Lagoon. To this day, people claim to see a man's ghost dressed in a camel-colored coat and a hat styled from the 1930s walking in front of the museum. As recently as October 31, 1995, a group of seventy tourists witnessed such an event and even videotaped the man's image. They say it is Clarence looking for his son.

Other articles tell of Chicago's Great Fire in 1871 that destroyed over five hundred buildings. Hundreds-upon-hundreds of lives were lost. Some say many of their spirits still roam the streets today.

The Excalibur Club, built in 1892, stands atop a burial ground. Patrons swear that souls from beyond inhabit the building. On July 24, 1915, the S.S. Eastland ferry boat overturned in the river nearby, and more than eight-hundred people drowned. The Excalibur was turned into a makeshift morgue. Medical examiners, unable to keep up with the overwhelming demands of the tragedy, pronounced many victims prematurely deceased. They lie helpless in the building for days until they died. It's said that their moaning pleas for help still echo through the hallways. One owner, having spent the weekend in the building, was awakened by desperately pleading voices coming from the mysteriously illuminated basement. He claims angelic auras hovered over him whispering, "We're watching you," and he now believes in the world beyond.

These stories, although far-fetched, have a ring of truth. We continue scrolling through other paranormal activities documented for years throughout the Midwest.

The scorned Lady in Blue floats through the Country House Restaurant in Clarence Hills, Illinois waiting for her lover. In Wisconsin, Pinky, a former local actor and ghostly prankster, walks around slamming doors at the Sunset Playhouse. Strange occurrences at Heaven City Restaurant, built in 1917 atop an Indian burial ground, have unnerved patrons and employees alike. A large statue of a young girl in the La Belle Cemetery drips a red substance some are convinced is blood. Those who claim to have witnessed the event now avoid the cemetery at night. Even the ill-fated Rainbow Springs Grand Hotel and Carroll College's MacAllister Hall list details of their ghostly inhabitants.

"Incredible! Is there any place on Earth that isn't haunted?" C.C. asks. "This is getting way too weird!" One unexplainable account follows another, and then there it is in bold, black letters.

"Libby, this is it! Here's the story you told us about the night of the sleepover."

THE LEGEND OF L'ESPRIT AND THE WHISPERING STATUE

March 3, 1938

Opening Night Cancelled! Disappointed Sell Out Crowd Sent Home! Rumors continue to surround The Grand Dalton House Theatre and its famed statue. Revered Russian ballerina, Krystina Ramonakov cut short her tour of the states, claiming mental fatigue and physical exhaustion. Fellow dancers who adore the kind and caring prima speculate that L'Esprit's statue might have been the cause of Krystina's abrupt departure. She alleged that the statue tormented her with its eerie stare and the whisper of her name when she was alone in its presence. She claimed that the Grand Dalton House is haunted, and that the statue is possessed. Artist and sculptor Maxwell Doll lent credence to her remarks when he attested to the statue's powerful energy and strange glowing aura. The sculpture's unearthly nature continues to be a source of constant speculation. According to other troupe members, lights flicker, and strains of piano music play in the deserted corridors of the building. Could the Grand Dalton House be haunted? After all, twenty-one people did perish in a raging inferno when the original structure burned to the ground in 1926. Is the whispering statue of L'Esprit merely a hoax, or could the statue be a conduit, a medium through which the spirits from beyond communicate? Those special few that hear it whisper have never stayed long enough to search for answers or to unravel the meaning behind this phenomenon.

"This proves it. You're not alone. I take back what I said about the ballerina at the sleepover. She was clearly singled out, and so are you."

"I knew it, C.C. It's true. I might be afraid, but I'm not running away."

"I'm with you no matter what. But with Brooke so sick, I couldn't bear to lose you, too."

Touched, I promise C.C. that I'll be fine with her at my side. "Look, here's more. Check out this article dated 1940."

WHISPERING STATUE VANISHES WITHOUT A TRACE

Once again, mystery surrounds the Dalton House and its legendary statue. Police received a call from Miss Isabelle Devereaux who reported the disappearance of L'Esprit's priceless sculpture from the Grand Dalton House lobby. It apparently vanished during the night. An extensive search of the grounds revealed no leads or clues as to its whereabouts. Miss Devereaux adamantly claims that several museum curators have tried to acquire it in recent months. Was the disappearance one of thievery or a well-executed plan to keep the curiosity-seekers coming to the theatre? Many hypotheses have been put forth, but no conclusions drawn.

In subsequent articles written decades later, Miss Aimée's name appears, supporting the belief in the statue's power. Although it vanished years before she was born, she has honored it as part of her family's personal legacy. She denied claims of a hoax, adding that its disappearance was a tremendous loss to L'Esprit. Isabelle Devereaux—confined to a local nursing home—was unavailable for comment.

"Libby, this is too good to be true! Miss Aimée won't be mad at us. She'll be glad we found the statue. Won't she?"

"I hope so, but we'll have to let it go—at least until after regionals. We can't be late again. Rehearsals start in a half hour."

1940, The Dalton Estate

A.J. opens the door and slips politely out of Isabelle's way. "Thank you for agreeing to meet with me," he says as she sweeps in full of confidence and high expectations. She scans the foyer for the ever-present Miss Winterset. As if reading her thoughts, A.J. informs her that Olivia has the day off. He does not see the smug expression cross her face as she digests this welcome tidbit of information.

"I'm sorry to hear that. I always look forward to her company. Such a lovely woman," she lies, always jealous of the amount of time he spends with his attractive and highly regarded secretary. Isabelle takes advantage of their privacy and hands him her coat. She allows her seductive touch to linger on his arm.

Being alone with A.J. was all she ever wanted. She has loved him forever, loved him in her opinion, more than her dearly departed cousin the sainted Daniella ever could. Hasn't she devoted her career to L'Esprit and those insipid, talentless children? One day he will realize her sacrifice and finally fall in love with her. Never married, she's more than willing to wait for the only man she ever loved.

A.J. interrupts her thoughts. "Sit down, Isabelle, we need to talk," he says, the palms of his hands ridiculously sweaty. He's negotiated million-dollar deals with the moguls of finance and industry on a daily basis. He's dined with presidents and royalty and sits on the boards of some of the most prestigious foundations in the world. No one affects him as she does.

Isabelle sits as instructed, straight-backed and perched on the edge of her chair. Her adoring eyes focus squarely upon him. Clearly, he has something important on his mind. Daring to wonder; can it be? Has he finally come to his senses? Are his lips about to speak the words she's longed to hear?

A.J. knows no other way but the direct approach. There will be no turning back now. Steeling his resolve, he plunges ahead.

"I want you to know how much I appreciate you and all you've done for L'Esprit," he begins.

"Thank you, A.J. Yes, it's true. I always wanted to please you. To tell you how much I lo . . ."

He abruptly cuts her off.

"Isabelle, you must listen very carefully. There have been complaints—too many to ignore. Enrollment is dropping, and Dani's legacy is becoming tarnished. I have decided to remove you as the director of L'Esprit, effective immediately."

The smile slowly fades from Isabelle's face as she replaces one mask with another. Anger beyond anything she's ever felt consumes her. She's on fire. Letting me go? What does he mean? Calling upon all her strength to control her rage, she calmly defends herself.

"I don't understand, A.J., I've never let you down. I've always been there for you and L'Esprit."

"My mind is made up, Isabelle. I've delayed this decision far too long already. Students leave your lessons in tears, and the studio suffers because of you. The quality of instruction, your instruction, has diminished. This is a business of feelings and emotions. It takes a person with feelings and emotions to run it. Worst of all, the children's love of dance is being destroyed, and that is unforgivable. It cannot continue. There is no love or passion in your work."

On her feet and furious at his words, Isabelle screams, "Passion! What do you know about passion? How can you expect me to love those spoiled, sniveling brats?" *Her mind races as she sees her hopes and dreams die before her eyes.* "What am I to do?"

A.J., shocked by her transformation, tries to reassure her that she'll remain on retainer for the rest of her life and will always be taken care of out of respect for Dani. She refuses to be comforted. Her resentment mounting, she pushes all reason aside. The mere mention of Daniella's name proves to be the proverbial last straw. Her face darkens. "I don't want to be taken care of. I don't need your charity. How dare you! The almighty A.J. Dalton. You think you can buy me off?"

"Isabelle, you're family. This is business. I know you've tried to do your best. L'Esprit is sinking, and I can't let it continue."

"And I can't let you do this to me!" *She speaks with the wrath of a scorned lover, albeit an imaginary one. She reaches under the collar of her blouse and shows him a locket that hangs around her neck. She snidely asks if he's ever seen it before. A.J. tries to keep pace with her emotional leap, focusing on the heart-shaped locket hanging from the necklace.*

Losing patience, he asks, "What is this, Isabelle?"

She coldly replies, "It matches my bracelet."

A.J. narrows his eyes, confused.

"For such a brilliant, powerful man, you're rather slow. You know, A.J., you've seen it before; it's the one that was found with Dani in the elevator."

Recognition dawns on his face. "Your bracelet? Now I'm the one who doesn't understand."

"There are a lot of things you've never understood. I've been in love with you since the first day we met. If you had only given me a chance, I could have made you happy. I was the last person she saw, you know. She said to tell you goodbye. I had to leave her there. She grabbed for my hand and ripped the bracelet off my wrist. What could I do? I had to save myself. There was no sense in both of us dying."

A.J. can take no more.

"*Damn you, Isabelle. You left her there? What kind of monster are you?*" The revelation of what she had done sickens him.

"*Don't you see? I had to save you. I did it for us, A.J. We were meant to be together.*"

"*There is no us! She trusted you! She loved you like a sister!*"

"*Oh yes. A sister to do her bidding. An errand girl. I wasn't the crippled one; yet I was the poor cousin to be pitied. How do you think I felt always living in her shadow—left in the wings every time she stepped out on stage for another ovation or left behind every time you took her out to dinner or a party? Even her paralyzing accident didn't stop her. She was still revered. The talented prima, loved by all. She had everything. She had you. Were you blind? Could you not see how much I wanted you?*"

"*Isabelle, you were only a child.*"

"*But I grew up.*" Isabelle stops talking and wages the battle of a lifetime within her. Does she dare speak the unspeakable?

"*I'm telling you, Isabelle, for the last time, we will never be together.*"

Her heart broken beyond repair, she maliciously drops the final bombshell. With flashing eyes, she flippantly remarks, "*Oh speaking of children, did you know Dani was pregnant when she died? She planned to tell you at midnight. Romantic, don't you agree? I see by the look on your face that you didn't know. Don't feel too badly. Maybe it wasn't yours. Hadn't her old dance partner René recently been in town for a cozy visit?*"

A.J.'s legs can no longer support him as he recalls Daniella's promise to surprise him at the stroke of the New Year. He collapses into his chair. His head throbs, and he feels as if he's been physically beaten. He intuitively knows the truth. Daniella died pregnant with his baby.

It's more than he can bear, and Isabelle knows it's over. She has gone too far. The words she has spoken cannot be erased. The

secret she's held for so long has spilled out in her mindless fury,
and she's lost him forever.

The door slams. She leaves his estate, and although he hopes
he'll never lay eyes on her again, in his next breath, he asks God
to judge her mercifully.

Quick and almost painless, the warmth spreads throughout
A.J.'s chest as he sits with his eyes closed. His breathing becomes
shallow as a vice-like pressure constricts his heart. There's no
fight left. His last thoughts are of his beloved Dani. He can see
her, smell her, and hear her sweet voice. When he opens his eyes,
an astonishing, brilliant light surrounds him like it had many
years ago at Swan Lake. This time when he sees Dani . . . she's
really there.

Pas de chat (pah duh shah) A cat's step. From fifth position, the dancer's toe raises behind the side of the opposite knee that is bent in demi-plié. The supporting leg then springs upward to the side to mirror the other, and for a brief moment both legs pass each other in the air. The dancer's feet land almost simultaneously in demi-plié fifth. This movement is named because of its similarity to the leap of a cat.

Chapter Twenty-Five

*A*ll week long, Miss Aimée drives her dancers hard, keeping everyone focused. The intensity of the rehearsals acts like a pressure valve that releases our overwhelming thoughts of Brooke, and somehow our numbers manage to pull together despite the big holes in the formations caused by her absence. True to her word, Mrs. Allen texts us a daily update on Brooke's condition that, so far, remains unchanged. We push away the grief and dance through it, although Brooke is always on our minds.

Our regional competition takes place less than ten miles from Brooke's hospital bedside. If the downtown Chicago hotel were any farther away, C.C. and I might have felt compelled to drop out. The Stairway to the Stars Dance Convention is one of Miss Aimée's favorites. It's mine too. This is where my lyrical solo placed first with Miss Dana's studio last year. Only the top-rated dancers from the Midwest attend. Even Dance to the Max and B-BOP prove to be worthy competitors, often entering pieces that qualify for nationals.

While most of the L'Esprit dance company opts to arrive the night before, Jarrell, C.C., and I hang back to visit Brooke. Her darkened room is somber—the quiet broken only by the intermittent beeping of monitors. Although she's neatly tucked in her bed and resting only inches from us, we can tell she's miles away. The sight of our unresponsive friend rips C.C.'s heart out again. She physically crumbles.

"It'll be okay, C.C. Brooke will be with us in spirit," I say.

"I know. I've just never competed without her before." She covers her face with both hands, and I hug her close. When I'm about to lose it, too, Jarrell steps in and tightly wraps his arms around us.

"Stay strong, girls. Remember what Miss Aimée said, 'Brooke's a fighter.' Isn't that right, Brooke?" he says, taking her tiny, lifeless hand in his. "You do your best to wake up." Wiping his wet cheeks with the back of his sleeve, his voice trembles, "We'll dance our best for you, I promise."

Catching her breath in a heavy sob, C.C. sniffles, "Bye, Brooke, I love you. It won't be the same without you."

We leave the hospital with the Allens' blessings and a fresh determination to keep the faith.

At 7:30 the next morning, the hotel's impressive lobby is already crowded. We check in with Miss Aimée, who gives us our wristbands, and then follow the parade of dancers into the main ballroom for warm-ups. Whitney Ruthers races by, bumping the dance bag from my shoulder, obviously on a mission to get to the front row.

"I'm going to pretend that was an accident," I tell C.C.

"Wise up, Libby! Everything Whitney does is intentional. Anyone wanna guess how long she'll last up there?"

"I give her five minutes tops!" Jarrell laughs.

Just then, Tia walks by, giving the three of us an ugly scowl. She joins Whitney and whispers in her ear. The two turn to stare us down. C.C. smiles and waves as if they're best friends, and I can't stifle my laughter when Jarrell blows them each an exaggerated kiss. Whitney's eyes narrow, and Tia's face reddens. We dismiss the insufferable pair with a shake of our heads.

True to form, Whitney and Tia don't last long. Once the serious choreography begins, they fake headaches and sit on the sidelines. They giggle and critique all the dancers, especially me, their rude snickering obnoxiously loud. When I nail the instructor's combo and earn verbal praise, they skip out completely. After the lunch break, Jarrell informs us they're rehearsing their solos at the pool wearing skimpy bikinis.

"Whitney's got a hot bod, but Tia's looking a little chunky these days," he remarks, patting his stomach.

"Solos! That's not fair. We'd all like to be working on our solos," I say. "It would be a shame if one of them slipped and broke her leg."

"Yeah, a real tragedy. I hope Whitney doesn't fall in!" C.C. says, piling her sarcasm on top of mine.

"With what I saw, they seem more interested in flirting with the local boys. You know the type. The guys that show up at every convention eager to gape at you girls," he says, adding, "I think Whitney was practicing a pointe number, but it was hard to tell."

"That would make sense," C.C. agrees. "She probably figures with Brooke out of the picture, she might actually stand a chance to qualify her solo for nationals this year. Won't she be surprised when she finds out that Miss Aimée put you in as a late entry?"

When classes end, we hurry to get ready for the evening competition. C.C. and I are bummed because we can't perform the awesome trio Trent choreographed for Brooke, C.C., and me. But Jarrell, always the comedian, cheers us up.

"Hey, you two, no sour faces. You'll get to do it next year. Besides, you need to pour your energy into our trio. As it is you can barely keep up with me," he says, pretending to stand in the glow of his own personal spotlight. "After all, I'm the big cheese of our studio rat pack."

"That's laughable! Without us, you'd be nothing," we tease.

With a pretend tear and fake pout, Jarrell marches off. "If you need me, I'll be in my dressing room. The one with the big star on the door."

"You dreamer, you're in the men's restroom as usual," I shout, making a mental note to cut out a star and decorate it with toilet paper later.

Two of the hotel's ballrooms are combined to create a makeshift theatre. The stage—a raised platform—is heavily draped with a dark blue skirt. The backdrop features the words "Stairway to the Stars" written on an illuminated staircase surrounded by a thousand twinkling lights that remind me of the elegance of L'Esprit's grand staircase. The judges' table faces the stage and sits about twenty feet away. Matching blue cushioned chairs occupy the rest of the floor and quickly fill with family and friends.

We pile into the dressing room that's nothing more than a smaller ballroom shared by each of the studios. Chaotic, it's scattered with an endless array of costumes, makeup kits, and dance shoes. We see our studio gathered in the far corner and cross the floor that's already covered with a ton of sequins, feathers, and hair pins. To add to the insanity, Miss Nancy and her Dance to the Max students hog the practice area while noisily working on their routines and marking formations. When someone's hairpiece rolls across the floor looking like a crazed rodent, half the room screams while the other half laughs. I felt bad when Miss Nancy scolded the dancer who retrieved it.

"Oh the poor kid, let's hope Miss Nancy isn't packing a staple gun." C.C. nudges me.

"Shhh, C.C. If she hears you, she's liable to staple both of us to the wall." We forge ahead but not before the sound of a sharp slap catches our attention. To our astonishment, we overhear Whitney Ruthers berating her mother.

"Leave me alone! I can do my own makeup, Mom!"

Mrs. Ruthers rubs the red mark on her hand. "I know you can, but you always make a mess with those false eyelashes."

"That's because you're constantly hovering over me. What are you doing in here anyway?"

"I'm only trying to help, baby. You want to look perfect, don't you?"

"You can help by taking your seat in the audience with the other parents."

"Alright, I'm going."

Tia blocks her path, struggling with her costume.

"Here, let me help stuff you into that thing. Maybe you should lay off the mac and cheese, sweetie." Mrs. Ruthers gives the zipper a final tug before stomping away.

Tia, stung by her comment, nervously pats her stomach and snarls, "Typical, Whitney. You tick her off, and I get yelled at."

"It's not my fault. She's right! Your costume did fit better a month ago."

"Shut up, Whitney! You're such a brat," Tia says, folding her arms across her body.

"So are you!"

"Just what we need, more backstage drama," I whisper.

"We should keep moving before they turn on us." C.C.

quickly pushes me along, saying, "That girl should think less about gluing her false eyelashes and cement her lips together instead."

Like a breath of fresh air, I spot Miss Dana and my old friends from Wisconsin. When they see me, they scream my name, and I'm suddenly caught in a whirlwind of hugs. Texting and Facebook are fun, but seeing the gang again is so much better. Even though Miss D and I email frequently, I suddenly realize how much I've truly missed her.

"Miss D, I'm so happy to see you!"

"Me too. Miss Aimée tells me you're doing an exceptional job at L'Esprit. I knew you would. Your friend Brooke is in my thoughts every day."

"Thanks Miss D. She's in mine, too. I do love it here, but I'll always love you and your studio!"

"I appreciate you saying that Libby, and I can't wait to see you dance again."

We chat about everything until I notice C.C. standing uncomfortably alone. "C.C., come over here. I want you to meet my first dance teacher."

"Cynthia Cunningham, isn't it? Your performances are always delightful. I'm sure you have another fabulous tap routine in store for us tonight," Miss Dana says, extending her hand.

"It's nice to see you again. Libby talks about you all the time."

Miss Aimée joins our group. "Sorry Dana, you can't have Libby back. She belongs to L'Esprit now. Run along girls, you need to stretch. Jarrell's waiting for you in the wings. You're up right after B-BOP's ballet trio."

Dana and Aimée leave to take their seats. "They're like two peas in a pod," I say.

"Just like us," C.C. agrees.

We hug.

"You had me worried for a second. I forgot you belonged to another studio full of friends before you met Brooke and me."

"Yeah, but you two are the best. Truly, C.C., I wouldn't trade our friendship for anything in the world."

C.C., Jarrell, and I quietly wait backstage while Whitney, Tia, and a lanky, awkward boy perform a bizarre ballet.

"This is like watching a train wreck," Jarrell whispers.

The girls' drab costuming doesn't help the lengthy piece. While they attack the dance with intense passion, it sadly lacks any technical skills—a fact that even their long peasant skirts can't hide. The nerdy diva guy, costumed in gold lamé pants and matching shirt, portrays his role of the wealthy merchant to the extreme. At least, I think that's what he's supposed to be. They all begin over-dramatizing their parts, unknowingly crossing the line between serious art and humor. Setting the ballet world back years, C.C. and I don't know if we should feel sorry or embarrassed for the dysfunctional trio. When they run off stage, the boy wildly fans his face with both hands, demanding a tissue that he uses to dab his sweaty brow and dripping armpits. We're grossed out when he leaves the disgusting tissues on the floor for the stage crew to pick up. Meanwhile, Whitney and Tia trip off stage, landing in an exhausted heap. Rubbing their bruised knees, they scream for water.

Stepping over the fallen pair, C.C. snidely remarks, "Ballerinas down."

"They didn't name it Stairway to the Scars for nothing," I mumble as we strike our opening pose.

Our A-game is on. We ace our lyrical trio despite Whitney and Tia's distracting presence backstage. When the two finally recover, they crowd the wings so tightly that they're practically on stage with us. Their taunting glares and pointing fingers hidden from the judges' view fortunately do not ruin our number. C.C. and I remain focused on maintaining our clean lines and emotional execution, but it's Jarrell's sheer strength and physicality that wows the audience. His shirtless, muscular body moves gracefully across the stage like a large stalking cat, and the females in the audience react to every powerful leap and acrobatic turn that he makes. Our number ends in a show-stopping pose that showcases Jarrell. He holds me with one arm in a double stag lift high above his head, his large hand pressing securely into the small of my back. My torso arches while my arms and head drop towards the audience. Even from this inverted position, I can see the wide-eyed faces of Miss Dana and my parents. C.C. completes the picture as she balances in a back-bend position between the floor and the grasp of Jarrell's other hand as he holds her one leg high in the air. Her bodylines fully extended, mimic my own. The lion has caught his prey. When the applause erupts and the judges rise to their feet, Whitney and Tia slink away.

As the night progresses, the competition heats up, and my lyrical solo goes off without a hitch. Although Miss Aimée tries to convince me otherwise, I'm still not sure it's good enough to beat Miss Nancy's best senior soloist: a flexible gymnast whose dance is amazing. I hear her older brother is a dancer with a famous New York company. No one comes close to C.C.'s performance. Her tap routine rocks the house. Miss Aimée and the L'Esprit dancers are overjoyed when Jarrell's self-choreographed hip-hop production gets an unprecedented standing ovation. On the other hand, B-BOP's hip-hop entry renders us speechless. Its strip-club sleazy antics display more belly button rings and cleavage than style. I'm thrilled when all of Miss Dana's numbers look sharp and energized, leaving no doubt they'll qualify for nationals.

When I make my final costume change and return to the

stage dressed in Brooke's pale pink tutu, my stomach flip flops at the sight of Mrs. Ruthers primping over Whitney's makeup again. Spotting me, Whitney chokes on the water she's sipping and sprays her mother.

"What the heck are you doing here?" she sputters.

"I'm a late entry. I'll be taking Brooke's spot."

"Mom! Miss Bea! She can't do that. Can she?"

"Technically she can. Doesn't she look pretty, Whitney?" Miss Bea says, fluffing my tutu, totally oblivious to the Ruthers' ever-growing resentment.

"Don't get frazzled, dear. She's no Brooke Allen. Libby's no threat to you," consoles Mrs. Ruthers. "You've been rehearsing this solo for over a year. Just go out there, and show her how it's done." Once Whitney takes her place on stage, Mrs. Ruthers shoves me aside. "Step back, Libby. Don't you know it's rude to gawk in the wings?"

I bite my tongue. *That's a rule you should teach your own daughter.* I fume to myself.

Surprisingly, Whitney's pointe solo, although simply choreographed, isn't half bad. For whatever reason, her technique is passable this time, and I even find her stage presence more pleasing. The only things that mar her performance are her inability to get completely over her blocks and the false eyelash that dangles from her lid like a dead caterpillar when she takes her final curtsey. Furious over her makeup malfunction, she bolts off stage not even pausing long enough to see the soloist from Dance to the Max. When I take the stage, I'm glad she's gone. Jumpy as a kitten and missing my friend Brooke, I know pointe isn't my strongest discipline, and I momentarily second-guess why I even agreed to do it. I ask Daniella for inspiration, hoping that I can represent both L'Esprit and Brooke admirably. When my performance ends, I hear Brooke cheering. *Libby, I knew you could do it!* The applause feels almost as good as one of her crushing hugs.

Though ten o'clock at night, we're pumped for the awards presentation as we pile onto the stage, every dancer scrambling for a place to sit. Miss Nancy, anticipating winning most of the awards, naturally directs her students to gather at the front. B-BOP Studios, led by Whitney and Tia, bulldoze their way downstage desperate to be seen. As tradition dictates at every competition, the L'Esprit dancers mob the right upstage corner furthest from view. Happy when the dancers from Miss Dana's school sit next to us, I yell my head off when they win the spirit award. I'm proud they're considered the friendliest studio at the competition.

The solo awards come next. C.C. takes first in the tap category, and all of L'Esprit goes nuts. Whitney's extreme disappointment is apparent when she grudgingly accepts the third-place trophy for her pointe routine. She snatches the prize without a word, refusing to even look at it, and slumps back to her space on the stage. Mrs. Ruthers is totally shocked and leaves the ballroom in a huff. I nearly pass out when my name is announced as the first-place winner in the pointe solo category. This time Miss Dana's school joins our celebration. Unaware of the developing drama, Miss Bea cheers along raucously, keeping her dancers in the excitement of the competition. Their hateful emotions unsupported, Whitney and Tia openly seethe.

Many other dancers and studios get recognized during the night. I can tell Miss Aimée and Miss Dana are amused every time Miss Nancy accepts an award with a beauty queen wave. The highlights of L'Esprit's night are when Jarrell wins the best student choreography award and when Miss Aimée takes top honors for the small group lyrical piece she created in tribute of Brooke. We hope Brooke will someday be healthy enough to see us perform it.

Our arms loaded with trophies and ribbons, we set out to our hotel room ready to celebrate. Unfortunately for us, Whitney and Tia occupy the last elevator.

Looking squarely at me, her expression bordering on demonic, Whitney chides, "Bet you're glad Brooke's on her death bed."

"What a brainless thing to say. If my arms weren't full, I'd slug you," I shout.

"Admit it! You'd never take first place if she were here," Tia says.

"Yeah, and you two would be even bigger losers!" C.C. says, lunging at Tia.

With a back flick of her hand in C.C.'s face, Whitney yells, "Cynthia, chill! Nobody's talking to you."

I corner C.C. before a violent catfight starts. "Drop it, C.C., they're just jealous."

C.C. angrily frees herself. "Stay out of our way the rest of the weekend, or I swear that you two will be the ones on your death beds!" Fortunately, the elevator door opens, and Whitney and Tia leap off before C.C. can do any physical damage.

We spend the next morning taking classes and dodging the guys Jarrell warned us about. Whitney and Tia are nowhere to be found.

"They're either off chasing boys or shopping on Michigan Avenue," C.C. guesses.

The rest of us dance our butts off, looking forward to the late afternoon faculty show that customarily marks the end of the convention. Minutes before it's about to begin, the ring of my cell phone stops us cold. I fumble to find it in the bottom of my dance bag. I recognize the number immediately. "Oh my God, C.C., it's Mrs. Allen!"

Changement, grand (grahn shahnzh-MAHN) Big Change. The dancer's feet literally change position in relationship to each other while in the air. This movement begins in a deep demi-plié and requires a strong push off the floor in order to lift the dancer higher. The goal is to remain grounded the shortest length of time while suspended in midair for as long as possible.

Chapter Twenty-Six

B *reathlessly, we burst into Brooke's* hospital room to find her bed completely surrounded by family and no less than a dozen medical professionals. Amidst a flurry of activity, Mrs. Allen spots us. Her look of elation says the news is good. We timidly crowd closer and see Brooke's fingers twitch. We're told she squeezed her dad's hand just moments before we arrived. I swear her pale lips curve into a soft smile at the sound of our overjoyed voices.

Four doctors usher the Allen family into the hall for a private consultation while the remaining medical personnel tend the equipment tracking her vitals. After several minutes, the two of us are left alone with Brooke.

"C.C., do you realize what this means? God heard us."

"Thank goodness. These last few weeks have been horrible. It's the worst thing I've ever experienced."

"Me, too! I never wanted to give up. It's a true test of faith, isn't it, C.C.? It can't be explained, but count me in as a believer. My grandpa said that, like a loving parent, God is always with us in our joys, and that if things turn out badly, He'll never abandon us in our sorrows."

"I like that thought. Maybe that's how the Allens survived this depressing ordeal."

"Maybe faith is what gets us through anything."

"Now we know something of what A.J. went through," C.C. says.

"No, that was much worse. Besides Daniella's death, there was all that mystery surrounding the fire."

Our conversation eventually turns to regionals and our excursion at my dad's office last week. We never notice Brooke's eyelids flutter as C.C. and I discuss our award-winning routines, the wild catfight with Whitney, and our findings from the *Tribune's* archives. We unintentionally become louder and more animated.

"It's like we're living a game of Clue! Daniella died in the elevator holding a bracelet her husband didn't even recognize."

"Yeah. Except it's not a game. It's real!"

"I know. And what about the statue? It can't just disappear and reappear, can it?"

"Tell that to the statue, because that seems to be exactly what it does."

"Why now? It hasn't been seen in years!"

"I wish I knew."

"Do you guys ever shut up?" Brooke's tiny voice rasps. "Can I get a word in?" Our heads spin in stunned unison as we practically leap out of our shoes. "If that's all it took to get you two to be quiet, I'd have done it sooner," she says.

C.C., overcome with emotion, breaks down in tears while I charge out of the room to find the Allens. My outburst attracts the attention of the entire floor. Thinking the worst, every available hospital staffer descends like a swarm of angry bees. Mr. and Mrs. Allen nearly faint from relief when they realize their daughter is alert and speaking coherently. I retreat to a corner chair and silently talk to God. *Thank you for sparing our friend.* Mrs. Allen smothers Brooke's face with kisses while her dad holds her hand in his, their composure completely lost.

In the days that follow, Brooke patiently allows the testing, prodding, and poking that the doctors demand. The results of a battery of medical tests and lab work are all negative with no earthly explanation. One minute near death, the next healed. The hospital's lengthy roster of physicians finds every excuse to examine her.

Brooke's the only one who knows for certain that she's completely cured, and she does her best to reassure C.C. and me. In time, her strength gradually returns. The hospital seems reluctant to let her go. The doctors are perplexed by the fact that she flatlined twice in the ER. Brooke is immediately placed on an accelerated course of physical therapy and endures the sessions because she knows that each one moves her discharge day that much closer.

"I never realized how bad my headaches and blurred vision were affecting my balance. Don't tell anybody, I nailed a pirouette today when the doctors weren't looking."

"Brooke, are you insane?" I scold. "You could have hurt yourself!"

"I'll tell your mother if you try that again," C.C. warns.

"Listen to me! The tumor is gone, and I want my life back."

We talk about studio gossip until C.C. poses the questions everyone's been dying to ask. "What was it like when you were in the coma? Could you hear us? Did you know we were even here?"

"I did. I've been waiting to tell you something." Brooke guardedly glances at the door.

"What is it? What's wrong? Is your headache back?" I ask, perched on the edge of her bed.

"Will you stop? I told you I'm fine!" She then speaks softly and motions us closer, "It's just something I've been thinking about ever since I woke up."

"Just spit it out! Don't keep us in suspense," C.C. says.

"Okay, here goes. It would have been so easy for me to let go and stay in the best dream of my life. You guys, I think I caught a glimpse of heaven. I've kind of been keeping it to myself because I wanted to remember it exactly as it happened."

Brooke gathers the covers around her, plumps the pillows at her back, and then slowly begins. "While I was asleep, I had this most incredible dream; except it felt more real than any other dream I've ever had. I was drifting somewhere between the heavens surrounded by a wondrous blinding light. Then someone held my hand, and I smelled lilacs. When she spoke, I recognized her voice although I had never heard it before. It was Daniella wearing the costume from her portrait. You know, the one with the purple sash. We danced beside a secluded lake. Two white swans glided across its glass smooth surface, creating swirling patterns that we copied like skaters on ice. Suddenly, we were dancing in the studio at L'Esprit. For a moment I thought I saw you, Libby, standing with the statue in the doorway. You watched us before vanishing in a misty cloud. L'Esprit looked very different—like in the olden days."

I shiver when my old recurring nightmare flashes before my eyes. *Could the teenage girl and ghostly image have been a premonition of Brooke and Daniella?*

"Daniella said heaven's gate had been stormed by the prayers of many. I was spared and granted an exceptional gift, a true miracle," Brooke says.

"I told you, C.C., prayer is powerful, and prayers are always answered."

"Go on, Brooke. Tell us more!" C.C. begs.

"I asked her, why me? What have I done to deserve this? She said, *'It's not what you have done; it's what you are yet to do because it is my miracle too. In time you'll understand.'* She stroked my hair, and her arms felt soft like feathery angel wings. I could have stayed with her forever. That's when I knew beyond a shadow of a doubt, I was healed. Again I asked why I was given this great gift. She replied, *'I am not yet at peace. Go home to your friends, and find the answers that will help put more than just my soul to rest.'* When she spoke for the last time, I thought I heard her say . . ." Brooke bites her lip.

"Heard her say what?" I ask.

"This is the most peculiar part of the dream. She said, *'Isabelle deserves . . .'*"

"Deserves what?" C.C. demands.

"I know this sounds outrageous, but she said, *'to die.'*"

C.C. and I gasp. "I don't get it. Why would she want Isabelle dead? The woman hasn't been part of L'Esprit in years. She's nothing more than a harmless old lady," C.C. says.

"She can't possibly want us to kill Isabelle, can she?" I ask.

"The harder I tried to listen to Daniella, the more her voice faded. I begged her not to leave me, but she was already gone. Libby, she spoke to me in heaven, but I think she's been trying to talk to you here on Earth."

Overcome with emotion, I say, "We *have* to put the pieces together so she can finally be at peace, and so can we."

We sit quietly for a few minutes until Brooke breaks the silence. With a mischievous twinkle in her eye, Brooke announces, "Daniella isn't the only one with a secret. When you see Miss Aimée, ask about hers."

"I can't take anymore secrets," C.C. says. "Can't you just tell us?"

"Trust me. It's good news. And it will be more fun if you hear it from her."

"But you were asleep in a coma," C.C. says, "how could you possibly know anything about Miss Aimée?"

"Before I was taken away by the white light—and promise you won't laugh—I was floating above the room. I noticed something about Miss Aimée that no one else did."

"Welcome to the twilight zone," C.C. says with a laugh.

"Whatever you saw, I believe you!" I reassure her.

When we say goodbye, we can tell that Brooke's her old self again by the power of her hugs. C.C. crinkles her nose and sticks out her tongue when Brooke playfully adds, "Tell Miss Aimée that I'm happy for her."

1940, Chicago Tribune Obituary

The untimely passing of one of its favorite adopted sons rocked Chicago. Andrew James (A.J.) Dalton, financier, real estate mogul, and philanthropist, died unexpectedly at the age of 52.

Dalton died Friday at his suburban Chicago estate of an apparent massive heart attack. Olivia Winterset, his longtime secretary and personal assistant, found him unconscious. She tearfully reported that all attempts to revive him were futile.

Dalton, born in Lake Geneva, Wisconsin, was the only child of English immigrants Mary and Joseph Dalton. He loved to joke that he was either born in a stable or on the Mayflower. He attended the University of Wisconsin where he earned a degree in finance and briefly tried his hand at acting, earning much of his college tuition by building sets and operating lights and sound for the University's theatrical productions. An accomplished, self-taught pianist and modest singer, he was often employed as an entertainer at local fraternity parties. A wise investment in a small parcel of land on the outskirts of Chicago became the cornerstone of his real estate empire.

In 1915, he married the renowned French prima ballerina Daniella Devereaux. Her studio, L'Esprit, rivaled the famous dance schools of France and Russia, excelling in technical and artistic training. After the tragedy of Daniella's death in 1926, Dalton, a visionary with a Midas touch, became involved in many entrepreneurial ventures, including aviation and photography. As an investor in the newly emerging motion picture industry, he was often photographed with leading ladies on his arm. By his own admission, his heart belonged to Daniella, and he never remarried.

His philanthropic efforts were legendary. During America's great depression, he opened Dalton House to the homeless and hungry, temporarily closing the theatre and dance studio. He funded pioneering medical research in the field of spinal cord injuries, and his magnanimous grants afforded educational opportunities for countless dance students. His employees often found themselves beneficiaries of his generosity. No matter what position they held in his organization, he knew their names, families, joys, and tragedies and personally attended many of their weddings, baptisms, and funerals. He genuinely enjoyed sharing a simple meal at their kitchen tables.

"He always seemed to know what was needed and never came empty-handed," longtime gardener Tim Baxter remembered, choking back his emotions. "Just yesterday, we talked about fishing. He knew I loved to fish. He said, 'Timmy, you should go. Life is short.' The shock is overwhelming. He seemed robust and healthy when I last saw him. Life is short—those were his final words to me. I guess you just never know. If anyone deserves to rest in peace, it's Mr. Dalton."

Andrew James Dalton is survived by Daniella's cousin, Isabelle Devereaux, and many friends. The Daltons were childless.

A memorial service will be held at the Holy Cross Chapel. He will be laid to rest in a private ceremony at the St. Joan of Arc Cemetery beside his beloved Daniella.

Effacé (eh-fa-SAY) Shaded. A direction of the shoulders indicating the torso's movement from the waist upward. The dancer brings one shoulder forward and the other back while the head turns or inclines toward the front. The angle of the dancer's body is aligned so that it is partly hidden from view.

Chapter Twenty-Seven

News of Brooke's incredible recovery spreads through L'Esprit like wildfire. C.C. and I design an enormous welcome back banner. It becomes a work in progress from the whole L'Esprit family. When finished, the colorfully decorated sign with over five hundred well wishes and crayoned drawings hangs proudly in the studio's reception area in anticipation of Brooke's return.

Just when we think things can't get any better, the reason behind Brooke's puzzling message regarding Miss Aimée reveals itself. Mr. Trent quietly announces their long-awaited engagement to our small group. Apparently, the same day we were busy snooping in the basement, Trent popped the question. Although Trent wanted to tell the world right away, after the couple learned of Brooke's condition, they decided to keep their good news temporarily under wraps. With Brooke's health on the mend, Miss Aimée shyly extends her ring finger for our admiration and gladly accepts our congratulatory hugs and kisses.

"Way to go, Mr. Trent! The least you can do is supply sunglasses so we're not blinded by the glare," teases C.C.

The diamond, truly spectacular, is rivaled only by the sparkle in Miss Aimée's eyes.

The excitement of the past few days has us confident that we can confess our blatant breech of the rules without punishment. We know Miss Aimée won't be pleased that we visited the basement without her permission, but we hope our discovery of L'Esprit's Whispering Statue will far outweigh her disapproval. Without a definite plan in mind, we enlist the help of Mr. Stan and Trent. Although skeptical at first, we convince them that we found the statue, and retrieving it will be the icing on the cake to an already extraordinary month.

While Miss Aimée works on choreography in one of the studios, the four of us head to the basement. I admit I'm not thrilled to be going again. In my opinion, the faster we can locate the statue and bring it up, the better. Mr. Stan holds the elevator gate open, but C.C. informs him that we prefer the stairs. Taking them two at a time, we arrive just as Mr. Stan and Trent step off the elevator.

"Libby, you look stressed. Are you okay?" Trent asks.

I hug the basement wall as he wheels a big red dolly into the narrow corridor.

"She's alright. It's just that the old elevator bothers her. She got physically sick the last time we rode it," C.C. says.

"Girls, I know this is where Daniella died, and you feel a special connection to her. But that was a long time ago. The elevator didn't kill her, the smoke from the fire did. I've been riding it for years. Trust me you two, it's safe enough." Mr. Stan gently puts his arm around my shoulders. "Libby, I know how you feel. I always think of her when I'm on it no matter how many years go by. But Daniella loved L'Esprit and would never want you to be afraid of anything here. Come on now. We'll make quick work of it. Let's load up that statue you say is down here, and we'll ride up together."

I know he means well, but Mr. Stan didn't feel his throat on fire or the rushing wind either. He didn't hear a disembodied voice in the dark whisper his name.

"Is the statue under a tarp somewhere in this hall?" Trent asks while clumsily maneuvering the dolly through the tight space.

"Yep," C.C. says, leading the way. "When we get to the light bulb that flickers, we'll find it."

We continue to walk in a single file line. Oddly, the lights cooperate.

"This is strange."

"What's that, Miss C.C.?"

"I honestly don't remember the statue being this far back. Do you, Libby?"

"No, but we were pretty scared."

"The mind is a funny thing. It can play tricks on you, especially when you're a bit frightened," Mr. Stan says.

"Look, C.C., isn't that the antique table and chairs where we found Daniella's trunk?"

"So where's the trunk now?" Trent asks.

"And why isn't this bulb flickering like before? Shouldn't the statue be right here?" C.C. points to the empty alcove. We search the area near the canvas tarps that lay on the dusty floor. Even Mr. Stan agrees they were recently used to cover something.

"It couldn't have walked out of here on its own, could it?" C.C. asks.

"I'm beginning to wonder," I say.

Baffled, Mr. Stan asks, "Girls, are you absolutely sure this is the spot?"

"Yes, we're positive!" C.C. insists.

"Stan, could someone from maintenance have moved it?"

"It's possible, Trent, but why would they take it and where?"

"Maybe they figured out how much it was worth. Mrs. Summers said it was made from a super expensive marble," C.C. says.

"That's true enough; it's a valuable piece. Maybe history is repeating itself. It was supposedly stolen once before," Mr. Stan says.

"Let's not jump to any conclusions. We haven't checked the storage room yet." Trent suggests we follow the hall to the end and keep looking.

As C.C. and I expected, its search yields nothing. Conceding defeat, we reluctantly turn back.

"I swear," C.C. says, "we honestly did see the statue. If Brooke were here, she'd back us up."

"And Daniella's trunk, too," I say.

"We know you're telling the truth. It's just an absolute shame they're not here now. I wanted to see that statue, and I'm sure it would have meant a great deal to Rose. She remembers it fondly," Mr. Stan says, his tone rife with disappointment.

"It would have meant the world to Aimée, too," Trent agrees.

On the return walk, our subdued group is lost in thought until startled by a peculiar hiss and flicker of lights.

"Maintenance is definitely getting a call. This wiring is old, and the Dalton House certainly doesn't need another fire," Mr. Stan grumbles.

"Hope they hold up at least until we can get out of here." Trent says, quickening his pace.

Just as Mr. Stan and Trent near the elevator, C.C. and I dart for the stairway. Had the lights not suddenly illuminated the basement ten times brighter than normal, we may have missed it.

Blocked and shaded by the open doors, a hand reaches

through the shadows. Approaching the darkened recess, the four of us gather around the magnificent artifact. Mr. Stan looks upon the statue's angelic face, sits with a thud, and rubs his eyes. When he realizes his seat is in fact Daniella's missing trunk, he bolts upward.

"How did we not see these? Who else has been down here? Where has this sculpture been hiding all these years?"

"Stan, our view must have been obscured when the girls came through the door. We must have walked right by it."

"Must have." Stan wrinkles his brow. "What other explanation can there be?"

"None that makes any sense right now," I answer. "Can we please get going before the lights do more tricks, and she vanishes again?"

Trent agrees and springs into action, asking C.C. and me to pull the trunk onto the elevator while he and Mr. Stan work at loading the life-size statue onto the dolly.

"No offense guys," I say. "I'll help, but I refuse to ride up with you."

Trent and Mr. Stan wrestle with the awkward cart. As C.C. pushes one end of the trunk, I drag the other. She slides off to catch the gate before it closes. When I try to sneak around to the other side, Mr. Stan accidentally obstructs my way while inching the cumbersome statue forward. The dolly hits a bump on the uneven floor, and the statue bounces from side to side, causing its heavy weight to shift precariously. I reach instinctively to protect myself. Before I can escape, the statue falls on an angle, pinning me in the corner, the elevator walls taking the brunt of the impact. Her face leans less than an inch from mine. With my hands solidly pressed against it, I hypnotically gaze into her marbled eyes. My body stiffens when the elevator door closes and frantic voices shout.

"Libby, can you hear us?"

"Are you okay in there?"

"Hold on! We'll get you out!"

Trent and Mr. Stan violently pound but cannot pry apart the stubborn gate. "She hates that thing! You have to get her out!" C.C. sobs.

Chicago, 1940

Isabelle's secrets are buried with Andrew James Dalton on a cold, sunless, February afternoon. In a rare spirit of cooperation, she and the equally bereaved Miss Winterset handle all of the final arrangements. If funerals could be grand, A.J.'s certainly was a sendoff fit for a king.

Isabelle, playing the part of the grieving widow, loves him to the end, preferring to pretend his bitter rejection had never occurred. She fools herself into believing that she could have been content with the tiniest crumb of his affection. "Til death do us part," she sighs.

L'Esprit will continue, she decides, but it won't be business as usual. Perhaps A.J. was right. She will remove herself from the classroom and hire another dance instructor. She can find no reason to continue her hateful teaching duties now that he's no longer there to impress. Daniella's portrait will be removed to the basement, and she will coax Maxwell Doll out of retirement to paint her likeness on a grander scale. The promise of a very handsome retainer might allow him to put aside his trepidations and return to L'Esprit, she schemes.

Isabelle then tends to one final piece of business. The statue—that miserable pile of stone that's mocked her from the very beginning—has to go. Desperate to be rid of it once and for all, she formulates an outrageous plan. If only she has the nerve to carry it out.

Arrière, en (ah na-RYEHR) Backward. A direction for the execution of a dancer's movement used to indicate that a given step is performed away from the audience. The dancer physically travels backwards.

Chapter Twenty-Eight

*T*he elevator that normally travels at an annoyingly slow crawl moves uncontrollably fast while blurry, multicolored lights whiz by at warp speed. I pinch my eyes closed, bracing against the statue, and feel the increasing warmth of its marble beneath my fingertips. Sharply the elevator stops, and the statue's dark eyes swirl to life with dancing wisps of incandescent light. A plume of mist-like vapor arises from within the solid marble. It encircles and guides me forward. *What's going on? Where is everybody?*

I wiggle around the statue and pull open the gate that ironically slides apart with ease. Trent, Mr. Stan, and C.C. are nowhere in sight. I follow the mysterious haze to an oddly familiar doorway. Just as Brooke described in her dream, I see her dancing next to a ghostly image of Daniella. As quickly as their image appears in front of me, they dissolve, and I'm left with a bewildered feeling of déjà vu. Other reflections of dancers dressed in costumes of the past come and go. The clock on the wall spins backwards before disappearing into the mist.

The interior of L'Esprit has changed dramatically. Thickly planked oak floors replace the carpet. Old-fashioned floral paper covers the walls, and the furniture is antique. The corridors are lively with children's laughter and piano music. Most surprising, Miss Aimée's office door is marked with Daniella's triple D insignia. In the L'Esprit that I love, but not the one I recognize, I move towards an unfamiliar voice. The woman at the massive front desk doesn't see me. She talks busily on a black, rotary telephone while her fingers fly over the keys of a clunky, metal adding machine. Her lapel pin reads, "Sarah Rose Summers." I swallow hard.

"Excuse me ma'am, can you please help me?" She doesn't react. I wave and speak louder. "Can you hear me? Can you even see me?"

She finishes her call and looks right through me. *Am I dead or just invisible?* The woman leaves her chair and hastily walks in my direction. I brace for the collision, but shockingly, only a subtle jolt of warm, liquid energy enters and exits my body. I hold my breath when she momentarily pauses to look over her shoulder as if somehow aware of my presence. When she continues, I weaken with disbelief.

With no other choice, I follow the vapory mist that serves as my guide. A small ramp I've never seen before leads into the dance studio. A young dancer scampers out. My confusion mounts as she, too, runs through me. Inside, a dance class is taught by the prima herself, the wheelchair-bound Daniella Devereaux Dalton. *How is this possible? Am I seeing ghosts, or am I the ghost?* I stand quietly. She's lovelier than her portrait as she rolls up and down the rows of dancers, politely correcting each student.

"Martha, honey, make sure your turn out comes from your hips and not your feet. You don't want to force or twist your

ankles or you'll end up harming your knees, and you know how
much I love your strong little legs. Helen, be sure not to squeeze
your shoulders or hide your face with your arms as you relevé.
Remember to keep your neck long and shoulders pressed down.
Port de bras should always be rounded. You don't want to hide
any part of your adorable face for even a second."

"Yes, Miss Daniella."

A striking, dark-haired gentleman walks in. *Could this be
A.J.?*

"Hello," one girl shyly says as she tugs his coat.

"Hi, Violet, how was class today?" He gently pats her head.

"It was wonderful, Mr. Dalton. I can't wait to come back
next week."

"We can't wait either. We miss you when you're not here."

"I know, but mama and papa miss me too. I promise," she
adds, skipping out the door, "you won't have to miss me for very
long."

As the small dancers leave, A.J. kneels and gently holds
Daniella's face in his hands. "How is my precious wife today?"
he says, stealing a passionate kiss.

Daniella's eyes sparkle. "Darling, my other dancers will be
arriving soon. We shouldn't let the children see us like this."

"Why? Don't you think a couple madly in love is a good
thing to see?"

"Of course it is," she says, hugging his neck.

Suddenly, I'm not alone. An attractive woman sweeps by like
a cold wind, and amazingly, I have newfound superpowers that
allow me to read her unspoken thoughts. *Damn that Daniella!
Even from her wheelchair she still manages to captivate him.*
"Excuse me, Dani, your next class is here. Shall I invite them in or
tell them you're too busy? And A.J., if you have a moment, there
is a pressing matter we need to discuss. I'll wait in my office," the

woman says, her voice dripping with jealousy and resentment. A.J. abruptly stands, and Daniella's glow vanishes.

The woman marches into her office, slamming the door in her wake. Remarkably, I slip through it as if stepping from one side of a cascading waterfall to the other. I feel dizzy when I read the name on the desk plate: "Miss Isabelle." The calendar on her wall indicates the year is 1923. Before I can mentally process the situation, she frantically touches up her hair and lipstick. With flawless skin, lustrous golden locks, and large blue eyes that are almost turquoise in color, she's a rare beauty. She douses herself in a heavy musk perfume, and once again I'm privy to what she's thinking as she stares into the mirror.

A.J., it's just a matter of time. Someday you'll be mine. I love Dani, too. Yes, she's my flesh and blood, and I'm grateful to her, really, I am. But God help me, I'm in love with you. Even though you're twenty years older, I'm not a child anymore. I'm the one you need. You told me just last week how much you appreciated me. You looked into my eyes and said that you and Dani both loved me. I know you meant to say you love me. Someday you'll realize that we're meant to be together. After all, Dani's the one who taught me that everything happens for a reason. She's the one who says there are no mistakes, only lessons to be learned— her accident couldn't have been a mistake, and my loving you can't be wrong either. It's all a part of God's plan. Dani would agree. Can't you see? She wants you to be happy! Us to be happy! I'm a patient woman. Eventually you'll be mine.

Dismayed by her obsessive thoughts, I listen, spellbound, reading Isabelle's private secrets like a book. Her red lips curve into a smug smile at the sound of his knock. A.J. has come to her as beckoned. Isabelle rushes to greet him, takes his hand, and holds it longer than appropriate. He gently extricates himself from her grasp and inquires, "What do you want of me, my dear, sweet Belle?" I find his term of endearment interesting, and I lean closer to listen.

Without warning, the clock on the fireplace mantel spins forward. Faces and images race furiously. The shadowy vapor tightens, and I'm reluctantly lured into the dreadful elevator. Trapped inside, I hug the statue as lights rapidly pulse from every corner. The floor vibrates violently, and I hold on with all my might.

Échappé (ay-sha-PAY) To escape. The feet of the dancer form a level opening that works from a closed to an open position. The step can be executed from the center of gravity to either the second or fourth position. From their original placement, the feet quickly travel an equal distance apart, creating an escape-like motion.

Chapter Twenty-Nine

*I*n *contrast to the allegro* speed of my first ride, this trip thankfully ends in a slow adagio that gently transports me to a spectacular celebration already underway. Party favors loudly intermingle with upbeat orchestra music as the door of the elevator slides open.

I arrive in the lobby of the Grand Dalton House on New Year's Eve, 1926. The glistening marble floors, magnificent crystal chandeliers, and red-carpeted staircase are far more spectacular than any photographs could ever reveal. Elegant couples glide smoothly around the room. Servants uniformed in pristine jackets and white gloves carry silver trays of hors d'oeuvres and champagne. Formally dressed gentlemen stand in affable circles smoking big cigars and telling even bigger stories. Good cheer and merry laughter resonate throughout the makeshift ballroom in anticipation of the midnight hour.

A.J. Dalton is clearly the most handsome man in the room. *But where's Daniella?* He breaks away from the revelers and approaches Isabelle. She's admittedly stunning in her low-cut, black evening gown with matching opera-length gloves. Her hair in a dramatic upsweep, she strokes a delicate heart-shaped locket that adorns her graceful ballerina neck. Isabelle's delight sours when A.J. whispers a private message in her ear. She responds with a casual shrug and a blank smile before turning away. He follows her with his eyes as she leaves the room. I alone witness her private fury. When Isabelle and I reach the top of the grand staircase, the laughter and music abruptly cease. Merriment turns to despair as hysterical cries ring out.

"Fire! Run! Save Yourselves!" The crowd scatters, rushing the exits. Taunting flames mercilessly lick the draperies and walls as black smoke billows out of control. I never knew a fire could travel so fast. Within minutes, the Dalton House becomes a raging inferno. Mysteriously protected, I cannot feel the searing heat that consumes the floor beneath my feet. Helpless, I'm mortified by my inability to change the deadly outcome.

A.J. pulls one person after another to safety, returning repeatedly to steer more partygoers from harm's way. Pitiful cries echo from every corner. Terrified guests line the railing of the smoke-filled balcony. In a final act of desperation, one man jumps. His body smashes into a large table twenty feet below. A.J. drags the limp figure away just seconds before an enormous chandelier falls, shattering into a million jagged pieces. Not his bloodied face from the sharp bits of glass, but A.J.'s absolute anguish, nearly kills me. Relentlessly he calls for Daniella and Isabelle. An elderly woman trips in his path with a badly twisted ankle. He sweeps her into his tireless arms and carries the woman into the loving embrace of her overwrought husband. This time when he returns, an onrush of firefighters demand that he leave.

"The Dalton House is mine. I'm responsible here. I can't leave. My wife and her cousin are still in there!" He breaks loose from their hold and storms through the blazing wreckage. "It's you! Thank God you're alive!"

Isabelle stumbles out of the blackened smoke, her gown badly torn. Soot-stained tears roll down her cheeks as she clutches A.J.'s arm. "We have to get out of here *now!*"

"I'm not leaving without her. Where is she? Did you do as I asked? Did you find her?" Isabelle chokes on the fumes. A large support beam breaks from the ceiling. It crashes just feet from where they stand.

"Oh please, A.J., let's go! I'm begging you!"

"Not without Dani!" He grabs her bare shoulders and screams above the roar of the chaos, "Just tell me, Isabelle! Did you find her? Answer me, damn it!" Scorching tendrils of fire nip at the hem of her dress.

"Yes . . . I mean, no. I can't think. A.J., stop shaking me! I don't know where she is. Don't you understand? I can't leave here without you."

"Don't you understand? I can't *live* without her!" A.J. moans with a gut-wrenching sob.

Isabelle nearly faints as two burly firefighters confront the arguing pair. A.J. curses, throwing wild punches. The determined firefighters physically haul him to the frigid street.

"You've done all you can, sir. There's nothing more any of us can do. The whole place is about to come down."

A.J., with the flames of hell reflecting in his eyes, repeatedly screams Daniella's name. Refusing Isabelle's comfort, he pushes her aside. In one quick movement, he slips into the mob, frantically searching their tormented faces for his beloved Daniella. Isabelle stands alone in the cold, starless night. She, like me, has become invisible.

Her hairdo in tangles and makeup badly smeared, she wipes her tears and strains to remove her singed and tattered gloves. Rubbing her wrist, she whimpers and anxiously searches the ground. Isabelle's expression dramatically changes from hopelessness to panic.

The mystic haze swirls counterclockwise; suddenly, I'm the eye within the storm. The macabre drama of the Dalton House collapse and the chilling screams of its victims thankfully fade. When the fog lifts, I find time has retreated to moments earlier. I'm greeted by an eerie silence.

Saut de l'ange (soh duh lahnzh) The step of angels. This soaring step is a springing jump in which the dancer's back is arched, forming a curve. Both legs bend in a backward attitude with the knees slightly apart. As the head tilts back, the arms lift en couronne (a raised fifth position in the shape of a crown). The dancer starts and lands in the same spot.

Chapter Thirty

C restfallen, I stand in the far corner of the sinister elevator, and this time I'm not alone. I'm saddened by the most dire scene of all.

Daniella sits in her wheelchair, banging on the metal gate. She pleads mournfully for help. I forget that I'm a mirage. Determined to set her free, I instinctively reach for the jammed door. I recoil when a stranger's hand reaches through the rapidly thickening smoke.

"Oh God, it's stuck! It won't budge!"

"Keep trying! Where's A.J.?"

"There's no one here but me!"

"Then you must find him!"

"There's no time! I won't give up, I'll get you out!"

Choking smoke penetrates the elevator. Daniella coughs and gasps, "It's too late, Isabelle. Please save yourself. You must let me go."

Isabelle's hands hold Daniella tightly. "No! No, I won't leave you!" she says as she furiously kicks at the unyielding barricade. Her eyes burn from the intense heat that sears her lungs.

"Tell A.J. how much I love him—how much I'll always love him. Promise me, Isabelle, that you'll keep the secret we share. He must never know the truth. The loss would kill him."

Able to read Isabelle's mind again, I listen to her wrestle with her conscience, each breath forcing her closer to an unthinkable choice. She grapples with this unexpected turn of fate as she continues to labor with the jammed door that imprisons her much-envied cousin. When her many attempts fail, she finally gives in and listens to the voice in her twisted mind. She convinces herself she's done everything within her power to save Dani. She decides to save the one life she loves most. The dark seed of opportunity firmly roots itself inside her cold heart.

"Trust me, I'll never speak of it."

"Go now! Tell him our dream must live on. L'Esprit must never die! Isabelle, you must survive. Watch over him for me!"

Daniella clutches her cousin's wrist. Isabelle abruptly pulls away, forcing Daniella to lose her balance and tumble from her wheelchair. She falls to the floor, holding Isabelle's broken bracelet in her open hand. Avoiding Daniella's eyes, Isabelle flees. Again, her selfish thoughts ring loud and clear.

A.J. will never know where she is! I must save him! Only this morning, I thought my chances were doomed. Tonight, the secret dies with her. He must never know of the miracle growing inside Daniella's womb, the secret she planned to reveal at the stroke of midnight. God knows this is terrible, but I know I'm right! Certainly A.J. would walk through this burning inferno to rescue her. Then what? Be lost to me forever?

Daniella lies motionless on the smoldering elevator floor. Blankly, she fondles the unfamiliar locket attached to Isabelle's bracelet. I kneel and hold her in my arms. Unlike everything else I've tried to touch while a stranger in this foreign land, I can actually feel her cool skin against mine. She turns and smiles softly, as if she recognizes me. She peacefully calls upon God to allow her message of love to reach her beloved A.J. Letting go, she places her soul into the hands of her Creator, grateful for her life's abundant blessings. Her last thoughts are of dancing— not on a stage, but reunited as a small child with her parents as they lift her gracefully into their arms, then with her husband as they waltz on their wedding day and stroll among the fragrant lilacs at Swan Lake. They dance tenderly past the windows of their cherished L'Esprit. She exhales a final prayer and hopes she's made a positive difference in the lives of others and that in some small way, she's been instrumental in serving God's plan.

Once again, I'm reminded of Brooke's dream by the appearance of a white light. Its brilliance melds with my vaporous guide. I see Daniella as she's gently embraced and lifted on angels' wings. Free from pain, she twirls circles of joy, cradling an infant girl in her arms. Leaping with the angels, she dances in front of the night's brightest star, and I hear her last wish, "Libby, my dancing angel—you have finally come to set us free."

Balancé (ba-lahn-SAY) Rocking. The dancer's balance switches from one foot to the other. The focus shifts with the transfer of weight from side to side and follows the direction traveled. The footwork may cross in front or behind. This is a seamlessly smooth alternating step.

Chapter Thirty-One

"*Libby, get up! Are you* okay? That statue must have knocked you off balance." Trent's voice pierces my consciousness. C.C.'s fingers lightly brush the hair from my face. She shudders at the sight of the black and blue welt forming on my forehead.

"Ouch! What's wrong with your head? Why are you on your knees? Weren't you pinned in the corner before the door closed a few minutes ago?"

I gather my bearings and discover I am indeed on the elevator's floor. No longer hugging Daniella but instead clinging to the statue of L'Esprit. Three very concerned faces study me as I struggle to reconstruct what just happened.

"Come on, honey, do you think you can stand up?" Mr. Stan reaches out his hands.

C.C. puts her arm around my waist. "Looks like you've got a major goose egg. Let's get you up to Miss Aimée's office right away. You don't look good. Should we call your parents? You might have a concussion. You don't feel nauseous, do you? Maybe you should go to the hospital." Her incessant line of questions makes my head ache even more. Dazed and disoriented, I can't answer a single one.

Leaving the trunk and sculpture behind, Trent carries me to Miss Aimée's office. C.C. follows closely. She jabbers nervously while Mr. Stan runs into the floral shop to inform Mrs. Summers of the incident. Resting on Miss Aimée's couch, I drift in and out. Trent tries to convince Miss Aimée of the statue's remarkable return. He assures her that at this very moment the sculpture stands wedged in the service elevator two floors below. When Mrs. Summers joins our group, we all confirm Trent's story. Roxy whines and licks my fingers, sensing everyone's concern. Mrs. Summers scowls harshly at Mr. Stan and Trent.

"I'm telling you, Rosie, it's like I said before, the statue has a mind of its own. It practically flew off the cart. We didn't mean for Libby to get hurt."

"Libby," Miss Aimée gently questions, "do you know where you are?" She lightly applies an ice pack to my throbbing head and continues consolingly, "I remember having a rough ride on that elevator myself once."

I take a sip of the water Mrs. Summers offers, and after a moment I'm strong enough to put their worried minds at ease. "I think I'll be okay." Opening my eyes, I'm surprised by the sight of Miss Aimée. She looks exactly like Daniella as she smiles at me. Their coloring is completely different, but for the first time I realize that their features are very similar. Still stunned and feeling queasy from the onset of a giant headache, my vision blurs. Miss Aimée's face transforms from flesh to marble. For a split second, I'm nose to nose with the legendary statue of L'Esprit again. Instantly I recall the exact details of what I witnessed and begin to cry uncontrollably.

"I remember! It was awful!" I say between sobs.

Miss Aimée immediately tells everyone to leave the room. Without hesitation, Mrs. Summers escorts the two men out with a wave of her disapproving finger. Roxy, ignoring the command, leaps onto the sofa and snuggles her head on my lap. C.C., who is reluctant to go, bends to give me a hug. She tenderly pats Roxy and orders her to take good care of me.

"I'm always here for you, Libby. I'm sorry about the statue and especially that you were stuck alone in that creepy elevator. It's over now. You'll be okay. You're looking better already. See, even Roxy's tail is wagging in agreement."

When left alone with Miss Aimée, she kneels close. With a mother's kind touch, she dries my tears with a tissue from her desk.

"Libby, you're safe with me. Can you tell me what happened?"

I whimper and groan. "You'll think I'm nuts."

"No, I could never think that. You don't know what I might believe. You saw something, didn't you? What was the statue showing you?"

"How could you possibly know I saw anything?"

Aimée sits on the floor with her back to me. I didn't understand it, but I heard her murmur, "Aunt Isabelle was wrong when she accused me of being a mixed-up teenager."

The event seemed unreal—too unreal to even describe. But upon her pleading, I try my best to explain. "I'm not certain what it all meant, Miss Aimée. The fire was pure hell! I wanted to help, honestly, I did. But there was nothing I could do!"

"I know, Libby. Now tell me everything."

I tell her every last detail. The descriptions of each scene rush like water bursting through a broken levee. When I finish, I wait for her to tell me I'm insane.

"You saw angels? A bracelet? Stars? I don't know anything about that. But God bless you. You're not alone, and finally after all these years, neither am I." A minute later, Miss Aimée says, "She never left this place, did she? I always knew she was still here. I just never knew why."

"How do you know she's here, Miss Aimée?"

She looks around nervously, "Twenty years ago I took that same brutal elevator ride but never traveled as far as you did."

"What?" I gasp. Our troubled emotions rock back and forth. The weight of my burden seamlessly transfers to Miss Aimée when her memories completely overlap my own.

Aimée glances at Daniella's portrait. "As a young student of L'Esprit, I went into the basement in search of one of Daniella's old ballet costumes, and I stumbled upon the famous marble statue that had been lost for decades. It stood next to this same picture of Daniella that for reasons unknown to me, had been exiled to the basement years earlier. Eager to surprise my great aunt and thinking she'd be thrilled by my discoveries, I enlisted the help of the building's janitor. Just like you, Libby, I became trapped with the statue in that hateful elevator and collapsed, hitting my head. Aunt Isabelle somehow found out about my excursion and managed to pry the door open; she dragged me out unconscious. When I awoke, she claimed I was delirious. I swear as God is my witness, I did see a part of the past. I saw Daniella begging for help and someone else reaching through the gate. But with the dark, spreading smoke, I never knew who it was." Miss Aimée fixes her tearful eyes on me. "Now I know why Aunt Isabelle stopped loving me that day."

Chicago, 1940

On a moonless night, Isabelle sets out alone for the seedier part of town. She knows it when she sees it. It's exactly what she's looking for. The bar is run-down and neglected, a place frequented by hard drinkers who don't care about ambiance or for that matter simple cleanliness—a place no respectable woman would ever enter, especially unescorted. Pulling the hood of her coat forward and hiding her face in its shadow, she enters and takes a seat at an empty table. It's dark, smoky, and loud— vulgar really. Determined, she has business to conduct, and the faster the better.

The wine that she feels obligated to order from the heavyset, garish barmaid is served in a glass that looks as if it has never been washed, its rim heavily smudged with old lipstick. She forces herself to press on and complete her mission. By now, several of the male patrons take notice of her. But tonight, she plays the part of the predator, and instinct tells her that the two muscular, hungry-looking men at the end of the bar are exactly what she needs. She instructs the barmaid to serve each of them a shot of something strong, and when they approach her table, she invites them to sit. Speaking slowly, so as not to be misunderstood, Isabelle spells out her plan. For a cash fee—more money than they've seen in a year—and a lifelong vow of silence, they're to feign a break-in at L'Esprit, and remove the statue. She wants it dumped in Lake Michigan—no questions asked. The deal is struck, and the plan is to be carried out that very night.

Alone at the Dalton House, Isabelle faces the statue for the last time. She's certain that its resemblance to Daniella is no mere coincidence. Unnerved by her lifelike eyes, Isabelle takes care to avoid them, especially now in the semi-darkness.

"Well, Dani, you've spoken to others. Have you nothing to say to me? I never intended for things to turn out this way. I just couldn't risk losing him. I didn't mean for you to die. You understand, don't you? I wanted him to love me, and now he's gone. Is he with you? Have you won again?"

Reaching to touch the statue, Isabelle draws back when a shock of current passes through her body. Her eyes register a range of emotions, anger and disbelief closely followed by defeat and resignation.

"Is that your answer, Dani? Then what's done is done. If my sin was loving A.J., so be it." Still shaken, Isabelle exits the Dalton House leaving, the back door slightly ajar.

In the dead of night, the two hired thugs stand in front of an empty pedestal. Maybe the broad's loony. Maybe this is a setup, although the cash filled envelope is exactly where she promised it would be. Overjoyed by their lucrative stroke of luck, they greedily divide its contents. Getting rid of invisible statues pays nicely, they agree. "If this is some kind of screwy joke, clearly we've got the last laugh."

Enchaînement (ahn-shen-MAHN) Bonded. A grouping of two or more dance steps set to work within a phrase of music. These series of separate yet related movements appear to be connected. The dancers' footwork is rhythmically linked.

Chapter Thirty-Two

itting upright on the couch, I squirm uncomfortably as Miss Aimée labors with her recollections. I listen intently as she reveals details of her troubled childhood. "Libby, when I tried to explain the unexplainable, Isabelle blamed my overactive imagination. She implied my story was nothing more than a pathetic ploy for attention. To her, the insinuation that Daniella didn't die alone was ludicrous. She insisted the statue no longer existed, demanding that I leave the past where it belonged. The janitor was immediately fired, and the history wall was stripped of practically every photo depicting the statue. I was placed in therapy and branded a liar! Isabelle threatened to have me committed, forbidding me to talk about the incident ever again. She said she was protecting the reputation of L'Esprit and insulted me further by saying my insane behavior was an embarrassment. The therapists must have been on her payroll because they never listened to my version of the truth. How could I blame them? It was an outlandish story. I was diagnosed delusional. After that, Aunt Isabelle grew extremely cold and distant. I never even turned to Mrs. Summers for comfort, ago-nizing over the fact that she might confront Isabelle. It seemed like my aunt banished anyone or anything she didn't like and made them conveniently disappear."

"You mean you've kept this secret to yourself all these years?"

"I had to pretend I made it up, otherwise Isabelle would have kept me in therapy and on those disgusting anti-depressant drugs. Eventually, she forced me to admit I never saw the statue. But I know I did see it, didn't I? And once I was alone with it inside the elevator, a portal to the past was revealed. After Isabelle finally went into the nursing home, I tried to return to that place in time, but without the statue it was useless. The doors to L'Esprit's history never opened again, at least not until today." Dejectedly, Miss Aimée drops her face to her knees. Roxy, sensing her emotional turmoil, affectionately licks her hand. "I thought Isabelle loved Daniella. I thought she loved me, but I was wrong."

When Daniella's portrait suddenly glows with a soft lumi-nescent light, I'm covered from head to toe with uncontrolled chills. My mind opens to the angelic prima's presence, and I'm filled with a heightened awareness. I willingly pour out my newfound understanding to Miss Aimée.

"Isabelle did love you; she just didn't love herself anymore. She never wanted her secrets uncovered. She's lived with horrendous guilt ever since the fire. Sad and embittered, she's too afraid to die. Don't you see? Like the statue, you symbolize everyone's undying love for Daniella. Isabelle once shared a deep affection for her cousin, but she grew dark and envious because she coveted Daniella's talent, fame, and worst of all, her husband. She convinced herself that in order to save the life of the man she loved, she had to let Daniella die."

"Let her die? Man she loved? Libby, what are you saying?"

"Isabelle hated the fact that Daniella was admired through-out her lifetime. Even after the accident when Isabelle thought she'd finally be recognized as a premier ballerina or at least the best teacher, it was Daniella who was most loved and adored." Miss Aimée diverts her eyes, finding it hard to listen to the vile truth.

"Miss Aimée, Isabelle knew that she had neither won the favor of the public as a dancer nor as a teacher at L'Esprit. And she never gained the love of the one man she most desired. No one knew it, but she was hopelessly in love with A.J. After the accident, she flaunted her affection, but he was so blinded by his love for Daniella that he barely noticed her. He cared for Isabelle but only in a brotherly way."

"Please don't tell me that my Aunt Isabelle started the fire."

"No! She didn't. She tried to save Daniella at first, but she feared for her own life. In a split second, Isabelle committed a single desperate act that was both an attempt to win A.J.'s love and permanently remove Daniella from the picture. It's possible that her silence killed Daniella and saved A.J."

"Wait a minute; you think my great aunt was in love with A.J.?"

"It's true, Miss Aimée. I think she might have gone crazy with jealousy after Daniella told her of her plan to tell A.J. she was with child at the stroke of midnight."

"Daniella was pregnant? How can that be? Why didn't anyone know?"

"I wouldn't be surprised if your aunt paid off Daniella's physician to keep him quiet, convinced that the deception would spare A.J. additional suffering. Maybe someday she hoped to be the mother of his children."

"Libby, if what you're saying is true, Daniella and A.J. are not at peace. Is that why they haunt L'Esprit? Do they want revenge? Because at this very moment, I know I do!"

"No, I don't think so. Daniella's been trying to expose the truth all these years to give Isabelle the one thing she cannot give herself."

"What's that?"

"Forgiveness. They're here to help her, and I think Daniella helped Brooke, too."

"What do you mean? What does Brooke have to do with any of this?"

"While Brooke was in her coma, she dreamt of Daniella. She said Daniella told her that Isabelle deserves to die. I think what she was trying to say is that Isabelle deserves to die in peace."

After a long pause, Miss Aimée sighs, "Oh Libby, you don't know Isabelle like I do. I'm not sure what she deserves. She's created her own miserable existence by keeping so many dark secrets buried."

"I know Isabelle never showed you the love you deserved, but look at the caring and giving person you've become. And in some ironic way, Isabelle was instrumental in saving this place."

"How? By practically destroying me?"

"Daniella couldn't be saved, and Isabelle knew A.J. would never leave Daniella. If they had both perished that night, The Grand Dalton House and L'Esprit would no longer exist, and none of us would be together today."

Miss Aimée sniffles and dabs her eyes. "I didn't think of it that way. I suppose we're not meant to know if the greater glory comes in our living or dying. It's funny how our actions can affect others and impact the world long after we're gone. I'd like to think I'm capable of choosing the highest good as Daniella did, but I'm not so sure. For twenty years I've wondered, never fully understanding. Libby, you don't know what hell that woman has put me through." Her eyes narrow; her anger grows intense.

"Her silence may have killed Daniella, but her cruel words killed a part of me, too."

"I'm truly sorry, Miss Aimée."

"Don't be. Thanks to you, I'm no longer ensnared in Isabelle's web of deceit. I know what I must do!"

The tone in her voice frightens me.

Present Day

Nurse Maggie distributes medication on the third floor of the Oak Hills Nursing Home and hears Isabelle moaning in her sleep. Her words unclear, only Daniella understands Isabelle's tormented dream.

I'm trying, but the door won't budge! Don't you see? I can't save you! I'll lose him! I love you both, but I must save him! The horrid scene replays over and over as the flames of her guilt consume her. She lies drenched in sweat, doomed to spend another agonizing night alone in her wretched, self-inflicted state of hell.

Thirty miles away, Aimée spends a restless night battling demons of her own. Visions of Isabelle smothered with a pillow or choked to death are two of her compelling options.

Tour de force (toor duh fawrss) An impressive and crucial movement. A dancer attains a triumphant level of technical skill when performing a series of brilliant combinations such as pirouettes or any dazzling jumps or beats. A central and vital step.

Chapter Thirty-Three

The courtyard of the Oak Hills Nursing Home is particularly sunny and peaceful this morning. Patients sit in wheelchairs and chat with family members, enjoying the welcome warmth of the day. The large, leafy maples appear greener than usual, contrasting with the bright blue hues of the cloudless sky. Aimée approaches the entrance and smiles at the elderly gentleman she's come to know from her many visits. Alone, he slowly glides back and forth on a wooden swing made for two. Tiny sparrows gather at his feet and peck at the scattered breadcrumbs he lazily drops.

"You look different today, Aimée. Did you finally give up on the crotchety old bat and come to see me instead?" He gives the empty space next to him an inviting pat.

"Oh Charlie, your offer is tempting, but it's imperative I see Aunt Isabelle right away."

"You mean she can't wait five minutes?" he says with a pout.

"No, this matter has waited decades too long already." Aimée bends to kiss his cheek.

"That's okay, mission accomplished," he says with a cheerful smirk. "Here comes the real love of my life." As Aimée walks away, she turns to see his adorable granddaughter wrap her arms around his neck. The blissful look on his face puts her at ease for having refused him.

She enters the building feeling inexplicably calm. Ready to even the score, she gives her pocket an affirming squeeze. Isabelle's door stands slightly ajar. Lying in bed, she stares vacantly out her window. Her bony, arthritic hand clutches the collar of her high-necked nightgown. At nearly one hundred, her aged body has withered—her innocence and beauty long since faded. Although desperate for the relief a forgetful moment might bring, her calculating mind remains razor sharp.

Everlastingly cantankerous, Isabelle greets each day with contempt. Preferring solitude, she dines alone. Shunning the compassionate care of the nursing staff, she refuses to participate in any of the home's social events. Dubbed "the ice queen" by fellow residents, she pompously lives up to her royal reputation.

Before Aimée enters the room, she double-checks her pocket's condemning contents and draws a long, deep breath.

"Good morning, Auntie. I trust you're well and the nurses are taking good care of you." Isabelle merely glances and tightly grips the top of her gown. She nods begrudgingly.

Privately, she welcomes Aimée's visits. But seeing her life as unredeemable, she feels she does not deserve the joy others are granted in their golden years. Alone and unloved, only the demons of darkness keep her company. The purpose of her days is the constant manipulation of her circumstances, and today is no different. She barks her command, "Sit down, Aimée! I don't need you hovering over me."

Aimée defiantly stands.

"Are you deaf, child? Didn't you understand me?"

"No, I think for first time in our relationship, I finally do understand you."

Isabelle clenches her fist tighter. The bluish-green veins in the top of her hand pulse as though they might burst through her emaciated skin. With an evil glare that weeks earlier would have sent shivers through Aimée's spine, Isabelle fires back, "And what exactly is that supposed to mean?"

"Let's face it. You've always given me the impression you'd rather I didn't come. You never wanted to reminisce about L'Esprit or take pleasure in memories. 'The past is ancient history; let's leave it there!' you'd say. For years I've wondered what I did so infinitely wrong. But it's not what I did, is it, Aunt Isabelle? It's what you did."

Isabelle doesn't speak nor does she blink.

"You let me think I was crazy, but I wasn't, was I? I did witness something on that elevator twenty years ago. Something you never wanted anyone to know. Because of you, I was never able to take the full journey as intended. But yesterday someone else took that trip, and she was shown everything."

Isabelle covers her ears. Aimée forces her arms apart and pins them to the bed, none too gently.

"You *will* listen! You need to hear this. Daniella's message was meant for *you*."

Isabelle thrashes her head from side to side. "Damn it, girl! You don't know anything."

"That's where you're wrong!" In stark detail, Aimée retells what Libby witnessed. She slowly extracts the cold metal from her pocket and boldly dangles it in front of Isabelle's face. "You held her hand through the gated door! You left her to die without telling anyone! But she wasn't alone, was she? She was carrying their unborn child. Admit it! You were blinded by your obsession with A.J.! This belongs to you, not Daniella!"

Isabelle snatches the bracelet from Aimée's trembling hand. She cowers when Aimée reaches for her throat, grabbing the top of her gown uncovering the heart-shaped locket that's hidden beneath. "This necklace matches your bracelet, doesn't it? You even had the audacity to have it painted into your portrait. You pretended they were his lavish gifts, but he never gave them to you. You're the one who's delusional, not me!"

Isabelle's mouth quivers as Aimée relentlessly continues, "We'll never know for certain who should have lived or died that night, but it wasn't your choice to make. You knew Daniella was never at rest, didn't you? You felt her presence just as strongly as Libby and I do today."

Isabelle looks away mournfully.

"You've wasted your life thinking Daniella was haunting L'Esprit seeking revenge, but she wasn't. Don't you get it, Aunt Isabelle? She forgave you the instant you left her alone to die. You might have spared A.J.'s life that night when you prevented him from attempting to save Daniella, but he could never love you. Because of your bitterness, you foolishly rejected any chance at knowing love, even mine. In spite of everything you've done, you didn't end Daniella's happiness, and you won't ruin mine either. L'Esprit's legacy will live on. You, I'm sad to say, will someday be forgotten. I pity you, Aunt Isabelle, and I'm trying very hard to forgive you."

Only Isabelle knows the truth involving her final confrontation with A.J. Although her silence may have killed Daniella, certainly her wicked words were equally deadly. Aimée senses Isabelle's torment and softens, "It's never too late to heal. I hope you can make peace with yourself but most importantly with God."

Before Aimée leaves, she searches Isabelle's eyes for the tiniest hint of remorse or kindness. Seeing none, she says, "I'll always remember the love and compassion you once showed me, and I'll always be grateful you entrusted me with L'Esprit. Goodbye, Aunt Isabelle."

Divertissement (dee-vehr-teess-M$\overline{\text{AHN}}$) Diversion. A series of short dances designed to showcase the talents of individuals or groups. These numbers enhance the enjoyment of the overall production.

Chapter Thirty-Four

The details of my elevator ride through time fascinate C.C. and Brooke, but out of respect for Miss Aimée's privacy, we form a pact of secrecy. Preparations for nationals are well underway with an extreme schedule of rehearsals that keep us occupied from morning until night. In the Grand Dalton House lobby, the flurry of activity around the water fountain finally ceases. The sculpture that is hidden behind draped scaffolding awaits its highly anticipated unveiling. Tonight, a special event will honor Brooke's phenomenal recovery and the return of L'Esprit's long-lost statue.

Everyone is in high spirits. The performance troupe will showcase the routines that successfully pre-qualified at regionals. Our annual program serves the dual purpose of a final dress rehearsal and fundraiser for L'Esprit's New York-bound dancers. And we're certain that the announcement of Brooke's solo performance will fill the Dalton House's fifteen hundred seats to capacity. Intrigued spectators, including students from other studios and members of Brooke's hospital team, promise to attend.

"We know your doctors won't clear you to compete at nationals, but at least you can dance your solo tonight in the show." I hug Brooke's shoulders from the backseat of C.C.'s car; my goofy ear-to-ear smile reflects in the rearview mirror.

"L'Esprit hasn't seen this much activity since the days of Daniella and A.J.," C.C. says. "Do you two think Miss Aimée has any idea about the engagement party we've planned?"

"Nope. I'm sure she's in the dark, but with the complete studio involved, it will be another miracle if she doesn't catch on. She thinks everyone's staying to see the presentation of the statue," Brooke informs us.

"Don't go crazy—I'm not supposed to tell anyone. According to my mom, Shelby Windham plans to attend tonight and has tickets in the front row. She's supposedly doing a follow-up segment on the return of the statue and my grandpa Bailey's funding of the fountain's restoration."

"Are you serious? Don't tease us, C.C.!"

"Have I ever lied to you before? You'll just have to wait and see."

"If that's true, everything has to be just right!"

"It will be, Brooke," I assure her. "Mrs. Summers and Mr. Stan have everything under control. The caterers, the music, and the decorations—it's all set! It'll be the best celebration The Dalton House has seen in years."

"What more could we possibly cram into one evening?" C.C. says as she turns into the studio's parking lot.

We unpack her overstuffed car and carry our load of costumes, dance bags, and makeup kits through the theatre's dimly lit backstage area. The butterflies in my stomach flutter again at the thought of dancing in this historical landmark. Its Greek, Roman, and Byzantine architecture features dramatically high ceilings embossed in gold. Massive chandeliers softly light the cavernous room, exposing the priceless murals, mosaics, and sculptures that line the walls. The heavy, red velvet curtain trimmed with scalloped fringe matches the plush upholstery of its multileveled seating.

Miss Aimée and Trent, busy consulting with the crew on sound and lights, give us a wave as we head to our dressing room. Trent shouts, "One hour 'til show time! Break a leg, girls."

I'm reminded of Miss Dana who first explained to me how the popular expression originated during the Shakespearian era. After a particularly good performance, the cast would take a curtain call and bow. If they were fortunate enough to get another call, they'd bow again. If the audience continued giving them a standing ovation, they'd finally bend their knee, thus breaking their bodyline. I loved learning that of all the theatrical superstitions, "break a leg" is the most commonly known and means good luck—the exact opposite of what it implies.

We stake out our corner of the dressing room and arrange our costumes in the order of the fast changes we'll soon be making. Brooke, who's had several private fittings with L'Esprit's personal seamstress, secretly keeps hers undercover.

Troupe dancers hurry around delivering flowers and small notes of encouragement for each other. One of the last girls to arrive shouts, "Hey you guys, the ticket booth is mobbed. The line stretches out the door. Looks like every spot in the house will be sold—even the standing room!"

Parents volunteering as ushers lead arriving audience members to their seats. In the wings, Miss Aimée reverently presses her hand on a piece of charred floorboard salvaged from the original stage. The relic hangs in an open, wall-mounted case. L'Esprit's beloved prima once danced on this very wood. Before every performance, she traditionally touches it and asks for Daniella's blessing.

Mr. Trent's voice comes over the dressing room speaker, "Fifteen minutes to show time. Your highly nervous director requests your immediate presence on stage. V*ite, s´il vous plaît.* For you non-French speaking divas, that means get your tutus in gear if you please."

As we file backstage for final directions, we each follow Miss Aimée's lead and pat the precious wooden heirloom. Our troupe, nearly unrecognizable in full costume and flawless makeup, holds hands, our focus glued to our teacher. "This is it, kids," she says. "This is the big night we've all been waiting for. Next stop, nationals." It excites me to know I'll soon be dancing my routines on a New York City stage.

"So much has transpired this year. It's been a remarkable journey," she says. "You've worked extremely hard, and I know you're ready. You're going to be spectacular. Remember, it's not the color of the ribbon or the size of any trophy you might win that matters; it's the joy you feel when you perform that makes this experience worthwhile. I know many of you aspire to dance professionally or even dream of being famous, but those moments can be fleeting. Real greatness isn't about how others view you but rather how you see yourself. Know that dance will forever be a part of your treasured childhood memories. Let's all do our best to make them beautiful."

Miss Aimée looks at the three of us. "The true gift of Daniella Devereaux Dalton's life was how her goodness and love of dance transcended time and ultimately triumphed over tragedy. Leave your mark on someone's heart tonight as she once did. I'm already proud of you, and I know your families are, too. When you perform, I want you to strive for excellence, not perfection. This is your time to sparkle in the spotlight like stars in heaven."

She pulls Brooke into her arms, her voice barely above a whisper, "Brooke is living proof that miracles do happen.

Although it's not customary to have dancers crowding the wings—as if you wouldn't have snuck in anyway—tonight I'm making an exception. When Brooke performs before intermission, you're all invited backstage to watch." With that announcement, an enormous cheer erupts, and we scatter to our spots and freeze in our opening poses.

"Have a wonderful show, kids! We love you!" Aimée and Trent shout from stage right, giving each other a quick hug and kiss. As they slip on their headsets and cue music and lights, the red velvet wall slowly parts to a spontaneous explosion of applause.

Pas suel (pah s<u>uhl</u>) Solo dance.

Chapter Thirty-Five

O ur nervous jitters soon forgotten, we race from one costume change to another, glowing in Miss Aimée's praise. We're proud to present her small group lyrical piece dedicated to Brooke, and we can tell it moves them both. Before we know it, Brooke's solo is next. A rhinestone-studded white tutu with a strapless sweetheart bodice exquisitely enhances her graceful neck, shoulders, arms, and tiny waist. The ribbons of her pink, satin pointe shoes are neatly squared and tucked. Not a single strand of hair strays from her low chignon. Her jewel-adorned tiara looks like a halo upon her pretty blonde head. Radiant, she literally glistens from the inside out. In a dark corner of the backstage, she stretches her dainty, yet powerful ballerina legs. Her bright blue eyes sparkle with anticipation.

I don't remember drawing the slightest breath during her entire routine. Brooke's piece, inspired by her dream of Daniella, completely mesmerizes the audience. She floats as if magically partnering with the great prima. Her impeccable footwork is only outshined by her compelling and passionate performance that leaves the audience spellbound. C.C. jokes that we could have financed our trip to nationals with the sale of tissues. Brooke bravely holds her final pose until the music fades and the theatre falls into a moment of absolute silence before it erupts into wave after wave of thunderous applause. She never loses her composure, even as she slowly steps out of the dimming spotlight into our waiting arms. We laugh, hug, and fight back our tears in a useless attempt to preserve our many layers of painstakingly applied makeup. With the audience still on its feet, the ovation shows no signs of stopping. Before Brooke can object, Miss Aimée and Trent push her on stage for a final curtain call. Her cheeks turn bright red when her two brothers approach. She bites her trembling lip at the sight of their wet faces and huge smiles as they hand her an enormous bouquet of red roses, a sign they've accepted the truth of her miraculous healing. After one last curtsey, she gracefully exits the spotlight and stage.

Some dancers cry quietly while others openly sob in the wings. Miss Aimée, temporarily helpless, buries her face in Trent's chest. The terrible reality of almost losing Brooke mixes with our uninhibited joy. Mr. Trent and Miss Aimée hold Brooke tightly. C.C. and I join the embrace and are soon surrounded by the rest of the cast. The impromptu group hug empowers us to release our suppressed emotions once and for all. C.C. lightens the mood. "Brooke, don't let this go to your head. You know we're just trying to get closer to Trent."

"Keep your distance, girls," Miss Aimée says, "he's all mine, and I'm not sharing."

"Fifteen minutes until the second act," Trent announces with a cute wink. "And right now, dancers, your faces look like a Picasso painting—and I don't mean that in a good way."

We squeal with laughter and make a mad dash to the dressing rooms.

"Won't that be a fun act to follow?"

"Yeah, thanks a lot, Brooke." I pretend to agree with C.C. "We might as well put on our cover-ups and go home!"

"You guys can't be serious. I was just the warm-up act. I think they're ready for some real dancing now."

The energy in the theatre from Brooke's inspirational solo elevates the rest of our routines to a new level. During the finale, we dance our hearts out, and again Jarrell's hip-hop production brings down the house. We're ready for NYC, and we know it!

After a quick sweep of the dressing rooms, Mr. Trent, Miss Aimée, and I join the members of the cast already assembling in the lobby of the Grand Dalton House. We walk through the vacant wings, and I'm entranced by a small, white light hovering over center stage. It hangs midair, casting a tiny light into the blackness of the theatre. It shines like a lonely star in the midnight sky. I have the distinct impression that it's moving across the stage. Miss Aimée senses my uneasiness and takes my hand.

"Libby, that's the theatre's ghost light. Haven't you ever seen one before?"

"Ghost light? No, I haven't."

"It's nothing more than a light bulb atop a black pole. From a distance, it gives the illusion that it's floating. According to theatre lore, it protects the stage between performances and serves to ward off dark energy. It's considered bad luck to ever let a stage go black. No theatre wants their ghosts to feel abandoned."

My thoughts instantly fly to Daniella. "I like it, Miss Aimée. No one should feel alone in death or in life."

"If you're referring to Daniella, then I wholeheartedly agree!"

~Behind the closed doors of the silent theatre, the soft, shimmering orb of light dances away. Later, the stage manager notes the darkened stage and plugs in the ghost light while quietly cursing the young crewmember for shirking his responsibility.

Manège, en (a͞hn ma-NEZH) Roundabout. While executing a sequence of connected steps or turns, the choreography moves completely around the stage in a circular fashion. The dancers travel full circle.

Chapter Thirty-Six

The festive crowd that greets our arrival once again breaks into spontaneous clapping and cheering. Miss Aimée gives a grateful wave. C.C. and Brooke, who are still dancing on cloud nine, scoop me away. "What took you so long?" Brooke impatiently asks. "We thought you'd never get here!"

"We checked it out. Everything's ready. Mrs. Summers and Mr. Stan took care of every detail," C.C. adds.

The foyer looks elegant enough for a wedding reception. Dozens of crystal vases overflow with colorful flowers that reflect in the candlelight. Bright smiles decorate every inch of the glistening lobby. "This is amazing! How'd they get this done so fast? I saw them in the audience during the show."

"Most of the parents helped at intermission. Mrs. Summers could probably manage a small country. Honestly, we've never seen anyone more organized," Brooke says.

We weave our way through the spectators who have gathered around the draped fountain and take our place in the front row. Miss Aimée, poised and confident, places her hands on the edge of the raised podium. Looking on proudly, Trent positions himself next to us and the rest of L'Esprit's staff.

"Good evening, ladies and gentlemen. I'm Aimée Harris. On behalf of the staff of L'Esprit, I would like to thank you for attending this evening's national preview show and for helping to make it such a tremendous success. These young dancers have worked extremely hard, and we couldn't be more pleased with their accomplishments. We also know we couldn't do it without your constant support and appreciation for the performing arts. We look forward to our national competition in New York." Leading another round of cheering, she continues, "They certainly look ready. Don't you agree?"

Everyone concurs with robust applause. C.C. turns and blocks Brooke and me from view. She pretends to bask in the adoration of her admiring public. Brooke stifles a laugh. "Dream on, girlfriend! I think their eyes are meant only for Trent."

Embarrassed, we chuckle when we realize Trent overheard Brooke's remark, but good-naturedly he plays along. "Yes girls, it's all about me, and it never gets old."

When the applause dwindles, Miss Aimée goes on. "Although our focus is on the future, the time has come to honor L'Esprit's past. Speculation and mystery have always surrounded our beloved statue, but tonight we put the rumors to rest. It does exist, and now thanks to Mr. Preston Bailey and his generous donation, it's safely home where it belongs. The statue originally stood in this foyer over three quarters of a century ago as a symbol of A.J. Dalton's undying love for his wife. After Daniella Devereaux died and A.J. lost his will to live, the finding of this statue motivated him to rebuild their dream and keep her legacy alive. This evening, we honor their triumphant spirits. I sincerely hope that this exquisite sculpture will remain a source of inspiration for generations to come."

She gently pulls a gold-braided cord. "At this time, it is my privilege to present to you in loving memory of A.J. and Daniella Devereaux Dalton, the legendary statue of L'Esprit." As the white satin drape softly falls to the marble floor, Mr. Stan precisely on cue, hits a switch throwing the room into semi-darkness. The newly configured fountain instantly illuminates with a soft aura while water trickles down its three sparkling tiers. All eyes lift to its top where the angelic figure stands majestically. Truly a magnificent sight to behold, she seems to float above the dancing pool as she once did in A.J.'s vision at Swan Lake. The marble base encasing her legs shines with sparkling droplets like highly polished diamonds. One hand of the sculpture touches her heart, while the other reaches out. Her eyes gaze into the sky. Mrs. Summers studies the statue quizzically.

"Is something wrong, Rosie?"

"No, Stan, she's as beautiful as ever—just a little different than the way I remember." The old black and white photos confirm her observation. In previous pictures the statue's right arm, chin, and eyes searched straight ahead. Tonight, her smile is more defined, her new focus unquestionably heavenward.

A quiet rumbling of voices rolls across the lobby as fascinated onlookers exchange remarks regarding the statue's incredible return. Our inner circle—those who'd experienced the mysteries and powers behind the piece firsthand—share a private smile.

Mr. Stan, handsomely dressed in a pinstripe suit and red tie, approaches the podium. As he takes the microphone from a surprised Miss Aimée's hand, he grins and calls Trent forward. "Speaking of legacies of love, we have another love story unfolding in our very own Dalton House tonight. They've kept it a secret, but it's time they share their joyful news with the rest of us." Trent accepts the microphone while sweeping Miss Aimée into his arms.

"After years of pleading, Aimée has finally agreed to accept my proposal of marriage and will now make me the happiest man alive. Ladies and gentlemen, I give you the woman I plan to grow old with, the true love of my life—the future Mrs. Michaels. Like A.J. and Daniella, may our love be eternal."

Mom's camera clicks rapidly as multicolored confetti and streamers cover the blissful, kissing couple. The party is in full swing when Trent leads a blushing Miss Aimée to the dance floor. On Mrs. Summers' signal, the hired staff begins serving crystal-stemmed glasses of chilled champagne to the adults. Piano music, played this time by earthly hands, accompanies the newly engaged couple. The screams of L'Esprit's dancers mingle with the congratulatory shouts of the excited guests.

Others join the couple on the dance floor, encircling the honored pair. For a surreal moment, I stand on the marble staircase envisioning A.J. and Daniella. When Miss Aimée floats into Trent's arms, I'm thankful for L'Esprit's continuing circle of love.

Early the next morning, Aimée receives a phone call from the nursing home informing her that Isabelle passed away during the night. A few days later, a small package arrives at L'Esprit. Among its contents are Isabelle's bracelet and necklace. The hinged locket, the one she held close for so many years, falls open into Miss Aimée's shaky hands. It contains three badly worn, tiny pictures; one of A.J., another of Daniella, and the last, a childhood photo of Aimée. A carefully penned, tattered, and heavily creased piece of paper drops onto her desk.

Aimée ponders the words long and hard amid a flood of mixed emotions,

Forgive me.

Present Day

Isabelle Agnès Devereaux is laid to rest on a fresh July morning, her thirty-minute graveside service sparsely attended. She had far outlived her contemporaries, leaving few to mourn her passing. Given her surly nature, those who survived her—with the exception of Aimée—find it difficult to genuinely grieve.

Myself, along with Aimée, Trent, Mrs. Summers, Mr. Stan, C.C., Brooke, a handful of caregivers from the Oak Hills Nursing Home, and a few of its more mobile residents including Charlie, sit respectfully on white folding chairs, each deep in our own thoughts and recollections.

The nursing home's gray-haired chaplain recites the age-old prayers for the dead. He invokes God's mercy on her while suppressing memories of his many rebuffed attempts to help Isabelle fill her spiritual void. As the service concludes, the gathering sings a final hymn; its last lines float upward in the sweet summer air.

'Let God's love surround you with His peace and might,
Let God's love surround you with His love and light.'

Aimée, the last to approach, places a single, long-stem red rose and a fragrant sprig of lilacs upon Isabelle's unadorned casket. Tied with Daniella's signature purple ribbon, her small note simply reads:

Forgiven.

Enlèvement (ahn-lev-MAHN) Carrying off. In a final elevated motion, the danseur lifts his partner in a raised pose. With the ballerina suspended in air, the couple grandly exits the stage.

Chapter Thirty-Seven

We say goodbye to Mrs. Summers and Mr. Stan at the airport's security check, promising to do our best at nationals, have fun, and not get lost in the big city.

"I'll die of curiosity if you don't call daily with competition results," Mrs. Summers threatens.

"And rest assured, Aimée, we'll take good care of L'Esprit while you're gone," Mr. Stan says.

The sudden beeping of a metal detector alerts us there's a problem.

"Oh, have mercy! It's B-BOP Studios and Whitney Ruthers," C.C. says.

"Looks like Whitney's stuck at security. She's probably wearing every dance medal she's ever won," Jarrell laughs.

"Do you suppose they'll frisk her?" I ask.

"That's probably what she's hoping for," C.C. says.

"Where's her pal, Tia?" Brooke asks, looking around.

"No one's seen her since the last day of school. Maybe she finally figured out that she can't dance and isn't competing," Jarrell says.

"Maybe her parents decided to stop supporting her lackluster dance career," C.C. says.

"Mrs. Ruthers should wise up and do the same," I say.

Sensing another unpleasant Whitney Ruthers scene, we hurry to our gate. The last sound we hear before boarding the plane is Mrs. Ruthers' unmistakable rant. "This is absurd! Does my daughter look like a terrorist?"

Her words resonate throughout the concourse until they're overpowered by the security guard's authoritative command. "Ma'am, step aside immediately!"

Buckled securely into my window seat, I listen intently as our pilot's announcement fills the plane. "Good evening, ladies and gentlemen. This is your captain speaking. Welcome aboard flight 1112 with nonstop service to New York City."

He goes on speaking, but I never hear another word. The reality of attending nationals consumes my jumbled thoughts. So much has happened since I became a part of the L'Esprit family. It has, without a doubt, been a life-altering year of new friendships and wild adventure. I know the events were real, but I sometimes worry that in the years to come my encounters with Daniella will diminish into nothing more than a fantastical dream.

Although we booked our tickets together online, I end up separated from my L'Esprit friends. From several rows behind, I wave at Jarrell and Brooke, who is lazily paging through the latest issue of her dance magazine. C.C.'s red curls bounce when she turns to scope out every cute guy sidling down the narrow aisle. But when a greasy haired stranger dressed in a dark, rumpled overcoat—the same man that I thought I saw studying C.C. earlier at our gate—slowly makes his way through the cabin, she gives him a bold, questioning look. He diverts his eyes while tucking what appears to be a small photograph inside his breast pocket. I don't like the shifty look on his face, and my gut tells me he's bad news. But C.C.'s enthusiastic thumbs-up on the next handsome guy makes me forget my worries, and I laugh out loud. Her smile at Miss Bea leading a parade of B-Bop dancers turns into a scowl when Miss Bea's oversized carry-on slaps her in the back of the head. "Where's Whitney?" C.C. mouths while smoothing her hair. I shrug and point to the two empty seats a couple rows away.

In the rear of the plane, Miss Aimée and Trent hold hands while visiting with the other L'Esprit teachers. Our parents animatedly discuss the Broadway tickets my dad scored, compliments of the *Trib's* theatre critic. I look out my window and am relieved to see our luggage tied in lavender ribbons, and I count our costume bags as they roll up the conveyer belt, satisfied they've made it safely on board. We're thrilled that Trent will be on staff at nationals and that he's chosen C.C. and me to work as his assistants. Brooke, who is still not cleared by her doctors to compete, will run his music. But somehow C.C. and I know she'll master every step before we do.

The celebration that filled the Grand Dalton House weeks before has quietly faded into a cherished memory. It has become a twinkling in time encapsulated in the hearts of those who were fortunate enough to attend. Soon, my dad's article and my mom's pictures commemorating the event will be framed and added to the wall of L'Esprit's colorful history. Although Mom took dozens of formally posed photographs, I like the candid shots best. Trent and Aimée staring deeply into each other's eyes, their foreheads tenderly pressed together. Miss Aimée's hands gently resting upon Trent's cheeks, her engagement ring softly reflecting the camera's flash. Mr. Stan beaming with a boyish grin while he dramatically dips a startled Mrs. Summers in his arms on the dance floor, and another picture reveals their stolen kiss. Brooke, C.C., and I favor one of the three of us with bouquet-laden arms loosely wrapped about each others' shoulders. I especially love that A.J. and Daniella's statue can be seen high above in the background. These will be the new images that L'Esprit's future young dancers might someday study as I once did, searching for their own connection to this legendary place.

To me, the statue is more than an exquisite piece of marble, and I know the rumors about it will never completely cease. Some will claim to hear her voice whisper above the trickling fountain while others will say supernatural forces still lurk in L'Esprit's darkest corners. Regardless of the suspicions of a few, Miss Aimée and I know the statue's purpose is fulfilled. No longer needed as a conduit between heaven and Earth, it remains stationary, cold to the human touch. Its beauty continues to stretch far beyond the physical realm, the nameless sculptor having divinely captured the true essence of the human spirit.

I may never fully understand why Daniella and I share our particular view of the world in choreographed motion. And I'll always wonder if I chose L'Esprit or if L'Esprit chose me. We're linked through dance, but yet it's so much more. Living life as Daniella did is an art in itself; truly she knew no bounds. Her life was laced with tragedy. Yet she chose to see it as whole and grace-filled, forever kind and forgiving; her passion was its catalyst. She danced as she lived, a reflection of God's love.

Lost in my thoughts, I'm barely aware of C.C.'s dream guy as he settles into the seat next to mine. Her green eyes flash when he smiles at me. I can't help noticing a small tattoo on the underside of his forearm. It pokes from beneath the rolled-up sleeve of his white button-down shirt. His accent piques my interest when he says hello. Nervously, I keep the conversation going and ignore the tiny voice in my head telling me to be quiet.

He listens politely even after the plane lifts off the runway. As we rapidly ascend, I scan the terrain below. Spotting L'Esprit, I take it as a good omen and crane my neck, keeping it in sight as long as possible.

Before I can return to my handsome seat partner, my eyes lock on two brilliant crisscrossing stars on the horizon.

"Did you see them?" I ask, roughly grabbing his muscular arm.

"Oui, I did. Maybe it was a satellite or another plane. It could have been a couple of shooting stars, but I've never seen any do that before."

"Me neither," I say. Together we watch the streaking light until it fades from view. Still holding his sleeve, I'm embarrassed for having tugged so boldly. "Sorry!" I say letting go.

"No problem. I consider spontaneity a good thing," he says with a playful grin.

His fully exposed tattoo begs my attention. Its unique pattern oddly resembles a many-edged shooting star with a trailing blue comet-like tail. Foreign words are scripted inside, *Ayez la foi.*

"What does it mean?" I ask, hoping *I think you're hot* isn't stamped on my forehead.

"My mother's an artist; she designed this for me after we moved to L.A. from France. It simply means *have faith.* By the way, I'm Daniel. My friends call me Danny." I close my eyes and smile, hoping he can't hear the pounding of my heart. Since the first time he sat down, I'm speechless. With heaven's message delivered in this unexpected way, I vow to always have faith. With A.J. and Daniella's legacy of love and message of forgiveness fully revealed, I believe they joyously withdrew in peace. She's heaven's prima now—dancing forevermore in God's divine light.

Danny's voice brings my head out of the clouds. "I'm competing at the Stairway to the Stars Dance Convention this week."

"You're kidding. So am I! Looks like we'll be spending the week together in the same hotel room—I mean ballroom." I turn five shades of red. *This guy is so good-looking, I don't even know what I'm saying.*

He laughs and gently squeezes my hand. When C.C.'s mysterious stranger stands, balls up his coat, and stuffs it into the overhead compartment, my mood changes. "What's up with that guy?" Danny asks.

"I don't know. But he keeps checking out my friend."

"Who? The redhead? Don't worry. Maybe he thinks she's pretty—like you."

"Thanks, you're sweet. I bet the L.A. girls you dance with all look like movie stars. Where's the rest of your studio anyway? Are you traveling alone?"

"No," he winks. "I'm with you now."

We lean back, sharing the small seat divider with our arms comfortably snuggled against each other. I savor the mind-numbing warmth of his touch and resist the impulse to pull apart or nestle closer. Nothing has ever felt more right. But when the flight attendant announces that we're headed for stormy weather and the captain turns on the "fasten your seatbelt" sign, my body chills. Goose bumps never lie. Suddenly, I'm certain the ominous message is less about our bumpy flight than whatever drama awaits us at nationals.

I want to totally trust Danny, to tell him everything. That the shooting stars were A.J. and Daniella's Grand Enlèvement. And that I fear my friend has a stalker onboard.

The intensity in his eyes says—if given the chance—he'd understand.

Acknowledgements

~Our dancing hearts wish to thank GOD above all for setting us on this path and the promise to always finish what He starts.

~Our FAMILIES for their unending love and support.

~Our EDITORS: Dave Smith, Marcela Landres, Jill Lindberg, and April Swick for their wisdom and guidance.

~Our EDITORS, SECOND EDITION: The outstanding TEN16PRESS team: Jenna Zerbel (Editor), Kaeley Dunteman (Art Director), Lauren Blue (Interior Designer), and Shannon Ishizaki (Owner of Orange Hat Publishing, who artfully keeps all the balls in the air). The word "no" does not exist in their vocabulary. Thank you for all the "Yeses!"

~Our EARLY READERS: Jenny Clarkson, Lesley Connor, Dee Dee Huehnerfuss, Julia Jacobs, Cindy Kilkenny, Jill Lindberg, Annie Polack, Sue Polack, Anne Schimmel, Mary Shandley, June Swick, and Rachael Tenuta for their invaluable insights.

~The CLOSE KNITTERS: Judy Chu, Lee Pansch, and Sue Polack for the gift of laughter and true friendship.

~Our talented WEBSITE DESIGNER, Cindy Kilkenny, for establishing and maintaining our site www.DancersatHeart.com.

~WISCONSIN AUTHORS: Lesley Kagen, Sandra Kring, Tim

Van Wagoner, Rochelle Pennington, and W.D. Gagliani for generously sharing their expertise and encouragement.

~The many STUDIOS, TEACHERS, DANCERS and their families for your love and inspiration, especially Mary Cummings and Kellie Plath in honor of the past. May you remain passionate dancers at heart.

~Our FUTURE READERS for your patience and enthusiasm.

And last but not least, ROXY, the furry little angel at our side wagging her tail throughout our journey to publication.

We thank you all!
Ayez la foi

Glossary

Adage, Adagio (French: ah-DAHZH) In dance it has two meanings: (1) a series of exercises following the center practice, consisting of a succession of slow and graceful movements which may be simple or of the most complex character, performed with fluidity and apparent ease. These exercises develop a sustaining power, sense of line, balance, and the beautiful poise which enables the dancer to perform with majesty and grace. (2) The opening section of the classical pas de deux, in which the ballerina, assisted by her male partner, performs the slow movements and énlèvements in which the danseur lifts, supports, or carries the danseuse. The danseuse (ballerina) thus supported exhibits her grace, line, and perfect balance and achieves combinations of steps and poses which would be impossible without the aid of her partner.

Allégro (ah-lay-GROH) Brisk, lively. A term applied to all quick, bright, and brisk movements. The most important qualities to aim at in an alle'gro are lightness, smoothness, and ballon (springiness).

Allongé (ah-lawn-ZHAY) Extended. The dancer's bodylines are long and reaching. Whether through the length of the leg and foot or in the delicate placement of the fingertips, the dancer's extension is at its fullest.

Arabesque (ah-ra-BESK) A basic ballet pose having many variations. The position of the body is supported on one leg which can be straight or demi-plie' (bent) with the other leg extended behind and at right angles to it. The arms are held in various harmonious positions, creating the longest line possible from the fingertips to the toes.

Arrière, en (ah na-RYEHR) Backward. A direction for the execution of a dancer's movement used to indicate that a given step is performed away from the audience. The dancer physically travels backwards.

Assemblé (ah-sahn-BLAY) Assembled. Joined together. A dance step in which the working foot sweeps along the floor before being lifted into the air. The dancer pushes off the ground with the supporting leg and lands in fifth position demi-plié. A dancer starts with one foot and ends on two.

Attitude (ah-tee-TEWD) It is a position on one leg with the other lifted back, the knee bent at an angle of ninety degrees and well turned out so that the knee is higher than the foot. The supporting foot may be a'terre (flat) or sur la pointe or sur la demi-pointe (raised on toe or half toe). This position has many variations.

Balancé (ba-lahn-SAY) Rocking. The dancer's balance switches from one foot to the other. The focus shifts with the transfer of weight from side to side and follows the direction traveled. The footwork may cross in front or behind. This is a seamlessly smooth alternating step.

Ballon (ba-LAWN) Bounce. A light, elastic jump in which the dancer bounds upward, pauses momentarily in the air, then descends before rebounding like the smooth bounce of a ball.

Barre (bahr) Typically, a cylindrical piece of wood fastened horizontally to the walls of the practice room used by the dancer for support when performing practice exercises essential for developing the muscles correctly, turning the legs out from the hips and gaining control and flexibility of the joints and muscles.

Bourée (boo-RAY) Changing steps. A progression of quick little steps en pointe or demi-pointe executed in a great variety of directions or in place.

Brisé (bree-ZAY) Breaking. A dance step that travels in any direction with a small, broken movement of the feet. A brisé is an assemblé, beaten and traveled before landing in demi-plié in fifth position.

Cabriole [ka-bree-AWL]. Caper. A step of elevation in which the extended legs are beaten in the air. May be done in all directions, including turning or with a double beat for greater brilliance.

Changement, grand (grahn shahnzh-MAHN) Big Change. The dancer's feet literally change position in relationship to each other while in the air. This movement begins in a deep demi-plié and requires a strong push off the floor in order to lift the dancer higher. The goal is to remain grounded the shortest length of time, while suspended in midair as long as possible.

Chaînés (sheh-NAY) Linked together. An abbreviated form of the term "tours chaînés déboulés." These small, quick turns are executed in rapid succession, beginning either with a piqué or tombé, and may be done on pointe or demi-pointe. Usually performed in a linear or circular motion, these connected turns are chain-like.

Chassé (sha-SAY) Chased. A step in which one foot replaces another, literally chasing the first foot out of its original position. A chassé is executed forwards, backwards, side-to-side, or turning in the air (usually at a fast tempo). A dancer's feet move quickly as if being pursued.

Coda (koh-DUH) The last part of the pas de deux.

Croisé (krwah-ZAY) Crossed. One of the directions of the shoulders. The crossing of the legs with the body placed at an oblique angle to the audience. The disengaged leg may be crossed in the front or the back.

Danseur (dahn-SUHR) Male dancer.

Danseuse (dahn-SUHZ) Female dancer.

Déboulé (day-boo-LAY) Rolling. The dancer executes a series of quick turns that spin, traveling forward in a single direction. The step rolls like a ball.

Demi (duh-MEE) A halfway position.

Derrière (dey-RYEHR) Behind, back. Any movement, step, or placing of a limb in back of the body. The addition of derrière to a particular step implies that the working foot is closed at the back.

Devant (duh-VAHN) In front. This term may refer to a step movement or the placing of a limb in the front of the body. The addition of devant implies that the working foot is closed in the front.

Divertissement (dee-vehr-teess-MAHN) Diversion. A series of short dances designed to showcase the talents of individuals or groups. These numbers enhance the enjoyment of the overall production.

Doublé (Doo-BLAY) Doubled. A step such as a turn is doubled.

Écarté (ay-kar-tay) Separated. One of the nine positions of ballet in which a dancer's legs are open in the second position with the working foot held in tendu and the body placed diagonally. A dancer's position is thrown wide apart.

Échappé (ay-sha-PAY) To escape. The feet of the dancer form a level opening that works from a closed to an open position. The step can be executed from the center of gravity to either the second or fourth position. From their original placement, the feet quickly travel an equal distance apart, creating an escape-like motion.

Effacé (eh-fa-SAY) Shaded. A direction of the shoulders indicating the torso's movement from the waist upward. The dancer brings one shoulder forward and the other back while the head turns or inclines toward the front. The angle of the dancer's body is aligned so that it is partly hidden from view.

Emboîté (ahn-bwah-TAY) Fitted together. The dancer springs lightly into the air from a fifth position demi-plié alternating from one leg to another, landing with a bent knee that must move beyond the supporting leg during each exchange. The step moves forwards, backwards, or turns. The tightly connected footwork fits like a lid upon a box.

Enchaînement (ahn-shen-MAHN) Bonded. A grouping of two or more dance steps set to work within a phrase of music. These series of separate yet related movements appear to be connected. The dancers' footwork is rhythmically linked.

Enlèvement (ahn-lev-MAHN) Carrying off. In a final elevated motion, the danseur lifts his partner in a raised pose. With the ballerina suspended in air, the couple grandly exits the stage.

Entrechat (ahn-truh-SHAH) Interwoven. A movement in which the dancer jumps into the air, beating her feet while rapidly crossing her legs in front and back of each other. The dancer's motions are braided together and connected with quickness and strength.

Entrée (ahn-TRAY) The entrance.

Étoile (ay-Twahl) Star. A title reserved for the leading female or male dancer of the Paris Opera.

Failli (fa-YEE) Giving Way. A fleeting movement done in one count. From fifth position, the dancer springs into the air, turns slightly, and lands in demi-plié on one foot. Brushing the back leg first through fourth position croisé, she finishes in demi-plié with her body inclined.

Fondu (fawn-DEW) Sinking. A dancer's position is lowered by bending the knee of the supporting leg. Whereas a plié is done on both legs, a fondu is executed on one. The dancer's body appears to melt.

Fouetté (fweh-TAY) Whipped. A movement of great variety of styles in which the raised foot whips rapidly in front of or behind the supporting foot, or the sharp whipping around of the body from one direction to another.

Glissade (glee-SAD) Glide. The dancer's working foot slides along the floor, lifting to a strong point slightly off the ground. The opposite foot pushes away from the floor so that both knees are straight and both feet are pointed for a moment before landing in a closed demi-plié fifth position. The dancer's step floats on air.

Gran, Grand (grahn) Big or large movement.

Jeté (zhuh-TAY) Thrown. A jump from one leg to the other in which the working leg is brushed in the air and appears to be thrown. There is a wide variety of jetés, and they may be done in all directions.

L'Esprit (le-Spree) French. The spirit.

Manège, en (ahn ma-NEZH) Roundabout. While executing a sequence of connected steps or turns, the choreography moves completely around the stage in a circular fashion. The dancers travel full circle.

Pas de bourrée (pah duh boo-RAY) Bourre'e step. A progression on the pointes of demi-pointe by a series of small, even steps with the feet close together. It may be done in all directions and turning.

Pas de chat (pah duh shah) A cat's step. From fifth position, the dancer's toe raises behind the side of the opposite knee that is bent in demi-plié. The supporting leg then springs upward to the side to mirror the other, and for a brief moment both legs pass each other in the air. The dancer's feet land almost simultaneously in demi-plié fifth. This movement is named because of its similarity to the leap of a cat.

Pas de deux, grand (grahn pah duh duh) Two dancing together. Differing from a simple pas de deux, this dance is created in five parts: the entrée, adage, a variation for the danseuse, danseur, and the coda. The grand dance of two would not be attainable for the ballerina without the aid of her partner; the dancers work together as one.

Pas de valse (pah duh valss) Waltz step. A graceful movement in which the body sways with various arm positions. This step may be executed facing or en tournant (turning.) It is similar to a balancé, except the dancer's feet do not cross.

Pas suel (pah s<u>uhl</u>) Solo dance.

Penché (pahn-SHAY) Leaning, inclining. A movement in which the body leans forward, the head being low and the foot of the raised leg the highest point.

Piqué (pee-KAY) Pricked. Executed by stepping directly on the pointe or demi-pointe of the working foot in any desired direction or position with the other foot raised in the air.

Place, sur (s<u>ewr</u>-plahss) On place. A term used to indicate that the execution of a step does not move. The position is fixed, remaining in one spot. The dancer does not travel in any direction.

Plié (plee-AY) To bend. A subtle lowering of a dancer's position through the bending of the knees that may be done *grand*, full bending, or *demi*, half bending. This exercise helps the joints and muscles become soft and pliable and the tendons flexible and elastic, while improving the dancer's sense of balance. Pliés enable the dancer to spring upward on jumps and leaps and protectively cushion her landing.

Pointe, en (ahn-pwent) On the points. The raising of the body on the tips of the toes.

Porté (pawr-TAY) Carried. This ballet movement travels a dancer's step in the air from one spot to another.

Port de bras (pawr duh brah). Carriage of the arms. Any graceful movement of the arms.

Relevé (ruhl-VAY) Raised. A position of the supporting foot in which the heel is raised from the floor, and the dancer is balanced on the ball of the foot or toes, if on pointe. A dancer's lowered position lifts.

Renversé (rahn-vehr-SAY) Upset. The upper torso is forcefully bent during a turn in which the normal balance of the dancer is disturbed yet the equilibrium is maintained. The body bends from the waist to the right, left, or back with the head following the movement.

Sauté (soh-TAY) Jumped, jumping. A spring into the air with the toes first to reach the ground and then the sole of the foot followed by the heel. In the rising from the ground, the foot moves in reverse order.

Saut de l'ange (soh duh lahnzh) The step of angels. This soaring step is a springing jump in which the dancer's back is arched, forming a curve. Both legs bend in a backward attitude with the knees slightly apart. As the head tilts back, the arms lift en couronne (a raised fifth position in the shape of a crown.) The dancer starts and lands in the same spot.

Sickled Awkwardly curved. An incorrect position of the foot in relationship to the ankle. The toes are twisted inward while the heal protrudes out and back. A complete misalignment of the foot—not the proper placement.

Sissonne (see-SAWN) A jump of many variations done in the air, taking off on two feet and landing or finishing on one.

Studio Rat ('st(y)üd-ē-ō 'rat) A term applied to any dance student who considers the dance studio his or her second home. Every spare moment is spent training, rehearsing, and perfecting their art. Though extremely competitive, studio rats always support each other. They aspire to become assistant teachers, national champions, and dance professionals.

Terre, à (ah tehr) Grounded. The dancer's foot is completely pressed to the floor. Even in a typically raised dance position such as an attitude or arabesque, the foot remains firmly planted.

Tendu (tahn-D̄EW) Stretched.

Tombé (tāwn-BAY) Falling. The dance movement appears to fall forward or backward onto the working leg, finishing in a demi-plié. A dancer falls.

Tour de force (toor duh fawrss) An impressive and crucial movement. A dancer attains a triumphant level of technical skill when performing a series of brilliant combinations such as pirouettes or any dazzling jumps or beats. A central and vital step.